G000043578

THE AUTHOR

MICHAEL SIMMONS was educated at St Paul's School and Emmanuel College, Cambridge. He is a retired lawyer who practised in Central London and the City for over 50 years. He also had a part-time career as a legal journalist, lecturer, writer and consultant in professional services management and marketing. He has written a number of books, including *The Lawyer Who Couldn't Sit Still*, an account of his long law career, which was published by The Book Guild Ltd in 2011.

BY THE SAME AUTHOR

The Lawyer Who Couldn't Sit Still

Anatomy Of Professional Practice

Successful Mergers: Strategy, Planning and Execution.

LOW LIFE LAWYER

IN THE FOOTSTEPS OF BECHET

MICHAEL SIMMONS

The Book Guild Ltd

First published in Great Britain in 2016 by
The Book Guild Ltd
9 Priory Business Park
Wistow Road, Kibworth
Leicestershire, LE8 0RX
Freephone: 0800 999 2982
www.bookguild.co.uk
Email: info@bookguild.co.uk
Twitter: @bookguild

Copyright © 2016 Michael Simmons

The right of Michael Simmons to be identified as the author of this
work has been asserted by him in accordance with the
Copyright, Design and Patents Act 1988.

All rights reserved. No part of this publication may be
reproduced, transmitted, or stored in a retrieval system, in any form or by any means,
without permission in writing from the publisher, nor be otherwise circulated in
any form of binding or cover other than that in which it is published and without
a similar condition being imposed on the subsequent purchaser.

This work is entirely fictitious and bears no resemblance to any persons living or dead.

Typeset in Garamond

Printed and bound by
CPI Group (UK) Ltd, Croydon, CR0 4YY

ISBN 978 1 91087 847 7

British Library Cataloguing in Publication Data.
A catalogue record for this book is available from the British Library.

For Oliver
(1965 – 2015)

AUTHOR'S NOTE

When a lawyer who has been in practice for fifty years or so purports to write a novel, the critical reader searches for traces of autobiography or true events concerning his clients and colleagues. I am sorry to have to disappoint you in that regard. This book is the product of my fertile and febrile imagination only. I certainly make no appearance in it nor do any of my clients, colleagues or friends. It is all pure fiction. You cannot imagine how liberating it is to make it all up after so many years spent professionally in search of the truth. I should have started writing fiction earlier in my life. Fantasy can be a far more comfortable place than reality at times.

ACKNOWLEDGMENTS

After many years of comparatively successful legal journalism, I was arrogant enough to think that I knew how to write a novel. My first attempt resulted in a shipwreck. I was rescued from drowning by my old school friend, Mark Lovell, who took infinite pains to act as my muse and get me afloat once again. My wife, Samantha, was a constant source of encouragement and a skilful editor. My son, Edward, came to my aid when my computer decided to rebel and fixed it after experts from all quarters had failed. I have always relied on my secretary of more than fifty years, Joyce Reeves-Russell, to put me right and she cheerfully obliged here yet again.

CHAPTER ONE

NOBODY WANTS YOU,
WHEN YOU'RE DOWN AND OUT

Richard Gregory sat alone in a corner of the smoky saloon bar feeling sorry for himself. A well-built man in his early forties with an olive complexion but looking much older with the obvious evidence of long term dissipation already blurring his strong features, he was dressed conservatively in a dark suit, white shirt and club tie all of which looked in need of some careful valeting. His crippled leg ached as usual and the painkillers prescribed by the doctor were increasingly ineffective. He had placed his stick by his side as unobtrusively as possible as he was still vain enough not to want people to know how much he depended on it. He was less reluctant to admit how much he depended on alcohol to deaden the pain not only of his damaged leg but also of his blighted career.

He was sitting near enough to the bar to hear the conversation of the group of burly, leather jacketed drinkers gathered there. They looked like the standard mix of second-hand car dealers, market traders and taxi drivers that you find going through the turnstiles at Highbury or White Hart Lane on a Saturday afternoon to occupy the more expensive seats. He heard a newcomer to the group, Bob, questioning the others, following the usual vapid and inconclusive arguments on the respective merits of Arsenal and Tottenham Hotspur.

'Who's the toff sitting on his own over there that you guys buy drinks for?'

'Oh him, he used to be a hot-shot lawyer but he got into some sort of difficulty. Now he does bits and pieces of legal work for us and keeps us out of trouble for the price of a few drinks. Come on, buy him a pint and I'll take you over and introduce you. You never know when you might need him and he still does a decent job.'

Bob hesitated. 'He seems a bit familiar. I used to spend a lot of time in the jazz clubs and he looks like a clarinet player I used to follow. Dick Gregory was his name.'

'That's him. He used to do that too.'

'Fuck me, he hasn't aged well!'

And so Richard met his first new client of the evening.

He was not to be the last. Richard had indeed enjoyed a stellar career as a lawyer. Laid low once, he had reinvented himself but after failing again he had not yet managed a further professional reincarnation. He still had a grubby piece of paper which certified him as a solicitor of the Supreme Court of England and Wales but anyone bothering to check his bona fides with the Law Society would find that he was not a paid up member and that there were numerous blots on his record. Nevertheless, he could still manage to draft the simple contracts that his current clients needed and give them advice to keep them out of jail.

In fact, he thought to himself, he was not done yet. He would yet show them all what he was made of. Bill Noakes, one of the loudest of the group at the bar, had asked him to review the lease of some premises in Holloway Road near Highbury Magistrates Court which Bill was planning to use for the sale of second-hand cars. Above the showroom, there was an office for which Bill had no use. Richard was planning to ask him to let him have it cheaply so that he could establish a new practice as a criminal defence lawyer serving the local court. Nobody could accuse him of a lack of versatility in his career, he thought to himself somewhat ruefully.

Bill was in full flow with a long and complicated story so now was not the time to approach him with his scheme. Anyway, it was about time that he started drinking less and the best way to begin was to tell this motley crew of clients that he expected in future to be paid in cash for his work for them rather than in beer.

It was an unpleasant and shabby pub, somewhere off Camden

High Street. Even if you wanted to, the lighting was far too sickly dim to be able to read by. The hardwood floor had not been swept for ages and every time the door in the corner leading to the lavatory opened a nauseating smell of stale urine and strong disinfectant combined wafted into the room which in turn mingled with the aroma of cheap tobacco and male sweat. The barmaid was totally in keeping with her surroundings, trying desperately to keep her straggly, dyed blonde hair out of the watery pints of beer that she was constantly pulling. A smile might have helped but she looked just as depressed as her surroundings.

London in the late 1960s was still a rather down at heel place with far too much bomb damage from the war apparent and that end of the High Street was the shabbiest of all. He could have joined the group but he did not enjoy their conversation. For their part, they viewed him as coming from a superior breed but they could take considerable pleasure in the fact that he had fallen so low, far lower than them, at least for the moment. He philosophised inwardly, always a stupid thing to do when you have had too much to drink and realised that his current life was the stuff of Greek tragedy or on a more homely level the subject matter for the type of story that filled the pages of the more lurid Sunday newspapers.

A Dixieland jazz band shambled onto the stage and tentatively started playing. He keenly assessed the blowing of the clarinet player. He could do far better than that or at least he could have done in the past. From leading the university jazz band in his first year at Cambridge to playing professionally in London and with the best in New Orleans, he had enjoyed a stellar musical career. For one mad moment he thought to stride up to the bandstand and seize the clarinet from the unfortunate player's lips until he remembered that he could only hobble and that he had not touched an instrument for more than a year. Whatever they tell you, it is necessary to practise constantly to keep playing well or at all. New Year was long past but he saw no reason why he should not make a resolution, forgetting that he had made the same resolution a few minutes before. Tomorrow he would drink less and use the money saved to buy a second-hand clarinet. After a few weeks of concentrated practice he reckoned he could begin looking for a few gigs. He could start by replacing the stumbling incompetent who at that moment was butchering the clarinet solo in *Weary Blues*.

He was ready for another drink. This time his client bearing gifts was also accompanied by an enormous American dressed from head to foot as a cowboy. They were introduced to each other and the American's story was that he was a naturalised British subject who urgently needed a new passport. He produced the photos and completed forms. All that he required was a signature by a person of status confirming that he had been known to him for a reasonably long period of time. In those insalubrious surroundings, Richard qualified as such a person. Without hesitation, he countersigned the form to the effect that he had known him for two years when in fact he had known him for less than ten minutes. He added his current address, a sordid bedsitter off Holloway Road and his designation as a solicitor. He gratefully accepted his fee, another pint, and thought nothing more about the transaction.

The band had packed up and his clients had departed for the night. There was nothing to keep him in that place any longer so he slowly limped and weaved his way home. As on so many nights, he could not even bother to undress but fell onto the unmade bed. Usually he was unconscious almost before his head hit the pillow but on this occasion something was worrying him. In his befuddled state, he could not think what it was. Had he left his keys in the front door lock as he had done a number of times before? No, there they were on the cluttered bedside table. It had to be something else which left him with this sense of impending doom. As he could not solve the conundrum, he shrugged it off and drifted into a comatose sleep.

It was not to be a night free of dreams. Richard found himself in some sort of vestibule where beautiful angels relieved him of his shabby, crumpled clothes, bathed him in sweet smelling water and then dressed him in shining white robes. Double doors were flung open and he was in an enormous celestial concert hall. The anticipated odour of incense was replaced with the pungent aroma of marijuana. There on the bandstand, similarly robed, was the unmistakeable figure of Sidney Bechet, holding out a clarinet in one hand and a soprano saxophone in the other. With a beaming smile on his broad and craggy face he welcomed Richard.

'Come on up, Dick Gregory, you crazy English cat, and join our swinging scene. You gave your life to jazz and now you get your reward.'

Bechet offered him the choice of instruments. With no limits on time, the two of them played endlessly, swopping sublime solos as well as instruments, driven on as they were by a rhythm section of a power and swing like none that Richard had ever experienced before. They played the whole Bechet repertoire including many numbers that Richard had never tried. It did not matter: every sound emanating from their horns sounded equally sublime. He was Mezz Mezzrow reincarnated but playing at a level that Mezzrow never even hoped to reach. For the first time in ages he felt truly happy.

CHAPTER TWO

ON THE SUNNY SIDE OF THE STREET

THE HEADMASTER. I never liked Richard Gregory. As his headmaster, I was supposed to view him with the same aloof and impartial detachment as I treated the other boys in the school but it was difficult. In many respects, our relationship was far too close. After a busy war, I had returned to lead the school where I had been a pupil. This was not a particularly unusual story as I had spent my life as a schoolmaster after Oxford until the war intervened, during which I held various staff appointments in North Africa and Italy. Matthew Gregory was my contemporary at school but I saw less of him as he went to Cambridge and then followed a career in the Indian Civil Service. He had always been a sickly child and I was not at all surprised to hear through mutual friends that he had been invalided out and returned to England.

I was surprised though to receive a visit from a pallid Matthew accompanied by his somewhat dark-skinned wife. Belinda came from one of those long serving colonial families who had spent many generations in India. There had obviously been some intermarriage and Belinda's beauty and regular features were remarkable. She dominated the conversation and it seemed to me that Matthew was not long for this world. Their young son, Richard, was a very clever boy, she told me, and she wanted him to follow in the father's footsteps at our school. The problem was the classic one of funding. As Matthew's service had been cut short, his pension had been correspondingly reduced and they would be relying largely on the generosity of the school's trustees to subsidise Richard's education.

Perhaps mistakenly, I accepted an invitation to visit them

in Shropshire in the school holidays. They had bought a rather run down and sprawling former rectory near Bridgnorth which Belinda was trying to turn into a paying bed and breakfast establishment. Matthew looked worse than when I had last seen him and I was fascinated and at the same time repelled by their ten-year-old son, Richard. He had inherited a good deal of his mother's beauty which did not seem out of place in him as a boy. Unlike his mother, a generation on ensured that no questions would ever be asked about his non-European origins. The Indian blood in him was sufficiently diluted. His impenetrable dark eyes gazed at me in a way that made me feel uncomfortable in spite of my daily experience with dealing with boys of all shapes and sizes.

'I just do not know what is going on in your head,' I thought to myself. That impression remained with me throughout our long relationship. As I was there in their home, I carried out an informal interview and was able to agree with the parents' assessment that Richard was indeed a very clever and talented boy, though I was left with many reservations. There seemed to be a dark side to him and he was only revealing to me the minimum about himself which he felt I needed to know.

I duly twisted the trustees' arms and a bursary was made available out of the school's slender resources to allow Richard to join us at age eleven. Matthew did not live to see this and I attended a rather sad funeral in a not very attractive church where Belinda, as the new widow, did and said all the right things. As a bachelor I found her extremely attractive but my tentative advances were ignored. I did not take it personally and my timing was hardly ideal. I felt she had a coldness to men generally. I was proved right in as much as she never remarried and there seemed to be no successor to Matthew in any form in her life. All her love was concentrated on Richard.

I watched Richard's progress carefully through the school. I took pains to show him no favours in spite of our links. In so many ways he disappointed me. He was hugely talented but almost perversely he refrained from exercising those talents as much as possible, being careful to do the very minimum academically to get by. Even though our Empire was crumbling away almost on a daily basis, our school was programmed to turn out colonial administrators and we endeavoured to inculcate boys with the sets of values and sense of duty that the career required. Richard clearly was not receptive to the benevolent form of propaganda that we were offering. While undoubtedly the cleverest boy in the school, he did only sufficient work to scrape into the top five. He was an excellent footballer and controlled the team from inside forward. There was no objection to him being captain of football but once again the sports masters took the view that he could have done so much more to convert an average school team into a great one. While he had little need to practise, such was the extent of his talents, the other members of the team certainly did, while Richard often failed to turn up. Then on match days he slotted into the team naturally and rarely failed to give a commanding performance. He brought out the best from the other players with the accuracy and variety of his passes.

He was particularly gifted in music and was lead clarinet in the school orchestra. Once again, he seemed to reach the high standards required with the minimum of practice time which caused a certain amount of resentment with the other members of the orchestra. One area of music where to the disapproval of certain members of staff he exerted himself was in the foundation and running of the school jazz band. Even I found his improvisations on clarinet thrilling but it was typical of him that he should show such an interest in a form of music which had so many associations with the dark side. He had somehow made friends with the proprietor of the only music store in the town who was also fanatical about jazz and lent Richard a constant supply of classic jazz records and also the latest releases. This was one area where he was seen to apply himself. He virtually monopolised one of the practice rooms in the music school which was equipped with a gramophone. He repeatedly played the clarinet parts and solos in his newly acquired tunes until he had mastered them to perfection. I could not fail to notice the contrast between his relaxed attitude to life generally as compared to his dedication to perfecting his jazz playing.

He was captain of his House and popular in a distant sort of way with the other boys. His last year at school was approaching and I was wrestling over whether or not to appoint him head boy.

***

RICHARD. My mother worked hard to send me to board at a minor English public school. My father had been in the Indian Civil Service. He had been sent home sick with an inadequate pension. They bought a small guesthouse near Bridgnorth in Shropshire but he never readjusted to the English climate and he soon died, leaving my mother with an even smaller widow's pension. I was an only child and did what I could to help her with the lodgers. By the age of fourteen I was a very proficient breakfast chef. She and I were in constant conflict. She always expected so much of me while all I wanted as a lonely only child was time and space to think so I could work out who I was and where I wanted to be in life. Nevertheless we loved each other dearly and our rows always ended in a warm embrace and complete forgiveness.

***

BELINDA. Of course I worried about Richard, Here we were in a strange land. My family always talked about England as home but none of them had ever visited the place. Home for me was the sultry heat and teeming streets of Calcutta and also initially for Richard, although I was intent on seeing that he adapted to his new land and became the English gentleman that his dear father would have wished him to be. I was thick skinned enough to put up with the social slights of the Shropshire pseudo gentry who quickly realised that I was a person of mixed race and hence to be socially shunned, although I was determined that the stigma would not extend to my son who fortunately inherited the looks and colouring of his father. I believe that I succeeded and he was not even aware of the problem. At least, he seemed so unconcerned that he could not possibly be. At times I wanted to shake him to make him work harder until I realised that I was trying to inflict upon him the insecurity of my own background. Being a perfect mother was not easy.

I did not feel that his prep school was doing enough to make him ready for the move up to public school. Richard was far too relaxed about these important matters and we had constant battles over the extra tuition that I was determined to give him. He had a lot of catching up to do as the Indian educational system had completely lacked rigour. I was often exhausted by his difficult attitude but I knew that one day he would thank me.

***

RICHARD. At school I was lazy but successful. I was in the top five in the classical sixth, destined all being well for an open scholarship to Cambridge. If I had worked half as hard as some of my companions, I would have been even higher in the rankings. I was a tricky inside forward and captained the school soccer team. I played lead clarinet in the orchestra and founded and led the school jazz band. This was an activity largely disapproved of by many members of the staff. The fact that I spent so much time practising my jazz playing made it even worse. It was as though I was celebrating the Black Mass as far as the masters were concerned. As a senior boy, I was allowed into town on Wednesday afternoons. There was one rather run-down music shop and I started hanging around there. Initially, it was the big band sound that fascinated me: Billy May, Glen Miller, Count Basie and Duke Ellington. Maurice, the rather seedy proprietor of the shop, took a bit of a shine to me, probably for the wrong reasons, though he never gave me positive proof that he was homosexual. He started playing me records of the jazz played by the small groups. I was completely knocked out by Louis Armstrong, Bix Beiderbecke, Jelly Roll Morton and Sidney Bechet especially. On my strict promise to keep them in good condition, he would lend me records from his stock and I would return them and exchange them for new delights the following Wednesday. In the week, I would commandeer one of the music rooms that had a gramophone. I would play the records again and again, accompanying on my clarinet until I was satisfied that I had it right. I started by slavishly copying what was on the records but soon learned to improvise and weave my own story around the main theme.

I was captain of my house and in my view at least had done more than enough to qualify me on the face of it to be head boy of the school. But making a great show of how hard I was working and sweating in public to achieve anything for all to see was not my style. Jazz playing apart, you could never count on me as a model of constant application. Still I was confident when the summons came to visit the headmaster in his study that the job was mine. It was time for him to appoint the head boy for next year.

The meeting did not get off to a good start.

'Don't sit down, Gregory.'

This did not sound like the beginning of a close relationship in running the school together in the future.

'I need not list your achievements. They are well known to both of us. I would have no objection to your gliding through your school career like a swan if only I thought that your little feet were paddling furiously under the water, but I know from my observations that is not the case. You are extremely talented but unbelievably lazy. You could achieve so much more if only you were prepared to make the effort. I only hope that at some later time in your life events will conspire to galvanise you to employ your talents to the full. As things are, you are a bad example to the other boys and I will not allow it to contaminate them by elevating you to the position which your abilities deserve and you clearly desire. I propose to appoint Arbuthnot as head boy. He does not have one half of your qualifications but he is always seen to try his hardest and he is a team player. This is the example that I wish the rest of the school to follow. I expect you to serve him loyally as his deputy. Good day.'

I left the room spitting blood. The thought of assisting that plodder, Arbuthnot, for the final year of my school career was totally repugnant. I had always run rings round him on the football field and elsewhere. I was not inspired to change my ways by this reverse. My school leaving report contained the immortal words from the headmaster: 'the leopard has not changed his spots'.

I was awarded the expected minor scholarship but before I could go up to Cambridge I had to do two years' national service. My mother used some obscure family connection to get me a commission in a rather prestigious cavalry regiment despite my fear of horses. I was assured at my interview that my involvement would be with armoured cars only and the horses were reserved for ceremonial occasions in which I, as a mere national service officer, would not be participating. I enjoyed the Officer Cadet Training Unit and passed out high enough with my usual minimum effort. I was posted to Malaya to wage war in the steaming jungle against the Chinese. There was not an armoured car in sight. I was put in charge of a troop of absolute ruffians. We survived by watching each other's backs. Despite the difference in our educational backgrounds, I found that I had much in common with them. We also managed to kill a considerable number of Chinese and I was mentioned in dispatches.

To go on leave was to enter another world. I was able to get myself regularly to Singapore or even more desirably to Bangkok. I did not know which was better: to put behind me that constant fear and anxiety of life and possibly death in the jungle or the pleasurable sensation of a hot bath and the luxury of wearing freshly laundered clothes. Like most cloistered public schoolboys, I was obsessed with sex, the thought of it rather than the act itself. We were completely deprived of the company of women during term time and my status as an only child had not helped me in the holidays. The massage parlours, bars and brothels were now readily available to me. Unlike most of my officer companions, I was not merely interested in my own sexual satisfaction. Perhaps it was the fact that I was the only child of a widowed mother whose aim in life was to please her but I got almost more satisfaction out of giving pleasure to my women than I obtained from my own climaxes. I suspect that a Freudian analyst would have enjoyed having me on his couch. At first, I thought that the answer was in delaying my own orgasm. After the initial and overwhelming shocks of pleasurable surprise at making love to a woman and feeling her warm flesh close to mine, I found that I developed considerable stamina and could continue sexual intercourse for a long time but that was not the answer. I often succeeded only in making the woman sore, especially if she was insufficiently lubricated. I was not shy so I talked to the women whose time I had purchased to find out what gave them pleasure. They were only too happy to enlighten me.

From then on, I entered into a delightful world of discovery. It was so easy to give pleasure but I seemed to be one of a very small number of men who were prepared to make the effort. I became increasingly popular with the women whose time I purchased and there were even a few who refused payment. We had to find the opportunity for our lovemaking when they were not busy with other clients. There were occasions where they asked me to stop giving them pleasure as they found it too exhausting when they needed their energy subsequently to simulate sufficient ardour to satisfy their paying customers. I realised how much play acting was involved in commercial sex. The woman had to pretend arousal while employing the minimum energy on that particular trick. It was all about management of the available resources. I was determined to break that pattern and by and large I succeeded.

I felt that I was receiving my doctorate even before I had entered university as an undergraduate. My study of women showed how different they were from each other. Furthermore, what gave pleasure to one on Monday could be merely a source of irritation on Tuesday. I sailed home from Malaya with a variety of new techniques and tricks, none of which frankly were particularly complicated but required application and on some occasions almost limitless endeavour.

***

The Cambridge that I had seen when I went up to take my scholarship and that was described to me in meticulous detail by old boys from my school had much changed. In addition to the hardened veterans like myself there were an equal number of boys who had come up straight from school. Initially the boys found the transition to the new life far easier. The veterans had to resume academic work after two years away as well as banishing the memories of those corpses of friends and enemies alike buried in the ghastly jungle. I signed up for the university soccer trials and following a series of freak injuries to better players found myself in the Cambridge team destined to play at Wembley against Oxford. That was a strange experience. I was overawed by the size of the huge concrete bowl and did not play very well. The stadium was only a quarter full and many of those were private schoolboys admitted cheaply whose treble shrieks sounded like a demented flock of starlings. Cambridge won but it hardly mattered. I gave up soccer immediately after that game. I had had my moment of glory and was shrewd enough to realise that last year's star in my position would be returning from injury to reclaim his place in the team for the coming year. I was bored with the training that I was expected to do. At school I had got by with the minimum but here we were expected to put in hours on the pitch and in the gym every day. I had far better ways to spend my time. As it was, I was able to swan around Cambridge swathed in my voluminous light blue scarf and enjoyed the admiration of all who saw me.

I took my clarinet along to auditions for the university jazz band. I was far and away the best on my instrument and in fact the natural leader of the band. We were kept busy with engagements at least twice a week throughout the academic year but rising to a crescendo in the weeks after the exams, especially in May Week. Playing had its disadvantages in that the other men could rush to select the available women while I as a musician was unable to compete, blowing my lungs out on the bandstand. In my first year, I very much enjoyed the notoriety that my sporting and musical endeavours gave me but they were gained at a price as there were so many other pleasurable pursuits in Cambridge that I could have been following, not least the pursuit of women.

The female undergraduates were as young and inexperienced as the boys who had not done national service. They were of no interest to me. As they were selected for their academic ability, good looks, charm and poise were often in short supply. Those few who broke the mould were ridiculously spoiled and pampered to the point that many found it difficult later to cope with normal life. They were invited everywhere and there was so much happening all the time in Cambridge that this could mean the choice of a ball or two parties almost every night. Not for nothing was it said that Cambridge life was all balls. I observed this with detached curiosity but I had no ambition to become one of the many worker bees swarming around the very few queens.

I needed my sexual satisfaction and the university seemed unlikely to provide it. I was used to experienced women. I found the answer on Saturday nights at the Dorothy, a rather upmarket dance hall which was frequented by some students but mainly by people of the town. Reg Cottage and his orchestra played strict tempo music for ballroom dancing. I took a few lessons and added that to my list of accomplishments. Fiona was in her mid-thirties and had a responsible position in a local bank. She was divorced and lived on the outskirts of town with her two small children. At the weekends, the children went to stay with their father. We spent our first evening dancing and talking. I cycled her home and was happy to accept her invitation to come in for a drink. The drink developed into a kiss and we both quickly realised how hungry we were after our long abstinence. Breakfast in bed with the Sunday papers was a bonus. Spending the weekend with each other became something to look forward to. If I had a gig on Saturday night I was always the first in the band to pack up and leave as a warm bed at Fiona's was waiting for me.

***

FIONA. When Richard first came over and asked me to dance, I was expecting nothing more. He was obviously much younger than me and I found undergraduates on the whole boring and far too full of themselves. I was finding life difficult on my own with a full-time job and two school-age children to bring up. It was good that Denis took them off my hands at weekends so that I could have a bit of life of my own. I have always loved dancing and I missed that more than anything with Denis gone. Not having sex was less of a problem. It had never been much good with Denis although he gave me two lovely children. We were both far too young and inexperienced when we met. I had taken a couple of men home from the Dorothy before but it was no better and I had not wished to repeat the experience. We had gone to bed but I felt nothing much with them. We were only going through the motions and doing what was expected of us.

It was totally different with Richard from the very start. From the moment we started talking I felt his interest and concentration on me alone. As I thought, he was much younger than me, but he had packed a lot into his life so far and I felt that he would go a long way. Ours was not the usual dance hall chat and I felt that I wanted to know more about him. I was excited when we first kissed and I felt like a block of ice which was at last being thawed. I had made love to a few men before Denis but they all seemed intent on getting their own satisfaction and I was always left unsatisfied, asking myself the same question every time. 'Is that all there is?' Frankly I could give myself more pleasure and I usually did when I was on my own again.

Richard by contrast concentrated entirely on giving me satisfaction. Unlike the other men, he seemed to have no worries about his erection and achieving his climax. He seemed to have a sixth sense about what I liked to do and have done to me, even though I often did not know myself. If he was not completely sure he was not afraid to ask me either by words or gestures. For the first time in my life, I felt completely free and uninhibited. I certainly wanted a lot more of what Richard had to give me and knew that this was going to be not just another rather embarrassing one night stand. I realised that for the first time in my thirty-five years I felt like a complete and very satisfied woman.

***

RICHARD. So far as I was concerned academic work at Cambridge was a complete irrelevance. The standard of classics teaching in the college was abysmal. By the end of my second year I had nearly regained the knowledge imparted to me in my last year at school. The university lectures were a joke, given by academics who had no skill in passing on their no doubt extensive knowledge to mere undergraduates. Their main interest was in their writing and research. I had the impression that most of them viewed their teaching duties as an irritating distraction. To find out what they were trying to tell the students, the answer was to read the books which they had written. I did not bother to do that. It seemed me that the lectures existed so that the callow undergraduates of both sexes could eye each other up and perhaps go as far as to make tentative assignations. With a minor scholarship, I should have gained a first or at least an upper second. In the examinations at the end of the first year I settled for a third. It could have been worse. I had come to the conclusion already that any Cambridge degree irrespective of the class achieved would be the passport to a good job.

***

BELINDA. I was so looking forward to Richard's return in the summer holidays. At Christmas and Easter he had arrived in a flurry of dirty laundry and we hardly had time for a serious conversation before he was gone again. This time he would be home for at least two months. He had secured a menial job as a porter in the local hospital and I was planning to cook him some nourishing meals as I felt he was not looking after himself sufficiently in Cambridge.

My view was confirmed when I saw how thin he was.

17

When he told me his exam results we had our first row. I knew he could do so much better than that and I expressed my deep disappointment. When he told me that he had invited some woman from Cambridge called Fiona to stay with us for the weekend I was not happy. When she arrived, I was shocked to find how much older she obviously was than my Richard. I feared that he was throwing his life away on someone unworthy. Despite my thoughts, I showed her to the nice room that I had prepared for her. When I took Richard his cup of coffee on Sunday morning as was my usual habit, I omitted to knock first on his bedroom door. We always had a leisurely chat to start the day. I was very upset to find this Fiona woman in bed with him. We had not been churchgoers since I felt the social disapproval and prejudice of the vicar and his congregation but I had done my best to bring Richard up with strict moral standards. What he did in Cambridge was his business but to do that under my roof was insufferable. I slammed the door on them as I left his room in tears.

We never discussed the matter for the rest of the holidays and I mourned the fact that our previous closeness seemed to be gone forever. It was almost a relief when I packed his bags with clean clothes and saw him off at the station for the start of his second year.

***

RICHARD. I went back to Cambridge for my second year determined to make considerable changes in my style of life. I had already given up playing football and I subsequently resigned from the university jazz band. While my scholarship and full state grant combined were adequate for my living expenses I wanted to enjoy a more expansive lifestyle. I knew that I could get paid work with the many bands playing in the town in pubs, clubs and at special events. I had the advantage of being able to sight-read and had already had various approaches to join other outfits. The relationship with Fiona was becoming rather boring and predictable. I needed more women in my life.

I first met Colin in his father's menswear shop when I was trying to persuade the local traders to donate gifts for the college tombola on Poppy Day, Cambridge's rag day. I was touring the back streets with a college porter's trolley which was steadily becoming piled high with a variety of items. We immediately became friends and quickly found that we had a shared interest in pleasuring older women. I was sick of the minor public school snobberies and assumptions which governed life in college. The high walls which surrounded it truly cut its occupants off from the realities of life. Colin was refreshingly down to earth and different. We very much hunted as a pair. I was happy to pass on to him the benefit of my Asian experience and in return to receive an education as to what went on in the world outside the cloistered claustrophobia of university existence. I changed my style of dress from the stock in Colin's shop so that I no longer looked like a student but could pass as one of the young men of the town who congregated on the street corners on Saturday night. In other words, I dressed like a Teddy Boy with my hair slicked back with grease in a style known as the duck's arse or DA, with a quiff at the front. The outfit included a long jacket rather like a Victorian frock coat, extremely tight trousers, a string bow tie hanging down and very uncomfortably narrow winkle-picker shoes. Elvis Presley would have approved. Such was the liberal and open nature of university society that my extraordinary appearance created no adverse comment.

***

COLIN. We didn't see much of the university in Burleigh Street. We could have been in another town altogether. If I had not been so idle at school I could have been a Cambridge student myself. I was good enough, or so the teachers told me, but I failed my School Certificate. So I left school at sixteen and my father gave me the menswear shop to manage while he looked after ladies' fashions around the corner in Fitzroy Street. I had been doing this now for a few years and was getting a bit bored. I always had an eye for women and they it seemed for me. I had got to the stage where I was fed up with the younger girls who did not know what they wanted. 'Stop it' might mean what it said or perhaps not. If I tried again it might be OK to carry on or I might get another 'stop it'. Should I carry on and see if she said 'stop it' again? I never got the hang of the rules, if indeed there were any rules. If I went too far even if she gave every sign of enjoying it at the time I might get a threatening visit from her dad and big brother in the shop the next day or even taken out round the back and beaten up, so I decided that older women who knew their own minds were a safer bet. At the time I was going out with Minnie, an Irish nursing sister at Addenbrooke's Hospital. She was no beauty but she was teaching me a lot and at the same time was grateful for all the energy and attention I was giving her.

Richard was far from my idea of an undergraduate. He was not posh and he was not a snob. I loaded up his trolley for his tombola with old stock and he said he would be back the next day for a chat. I wasn't so certain but there he was, sure enough. He was interested in my life and we found we both had a liking for older women, having got bored with young girls who did not know what they wanted. He told me about his adventures in the brothels of Thailand and I passed on to him the lessons that I had learned from Minnie and those before her. I asked Minnie to bring one of her friends along for a double date, another sister at the hospital. We got very drunk and ended up in the stock room behind the shop making love to our respective partners on piles of clothes in the pitch dark. It was a crazy evening. The following week it was Richard's turn. He arrived just as I was closing the shop with two schoolteachers from out of town who he had picked up at the tea dance at the Dorothy. We ended up again in the stock room and I was beginning to worry how I would tell my father that so much new stock had been soiled and was now unsaleable.

Under my influence, Richard changed his style of dress. I kitted him out from stuff in the shop like a real Teddy boy. I often wondered what the people in his college thought but he didn't seem to care. When we went out hunting together in the evenings, I used to dress the same way. We made a right pair. He talked to me as an equal and he used to invite me along to hear him play jazz so that I got to feel that I was having all the advantages of a university education without having to work for it.

***

RICHARD. The year ended with another scraped third in classics. I was hauled before the senior tutor who strongly expressed his displeasure. I surprised him by telling him that I wanted to switch to law. This required compressing two years' work into one and coming up to Cambridge in July and August for an extra term known as the 'Long Vac' term. Cambridge always looks its best in high summer and the hordes of attractive female foreign students coupled with the lack of undergraduates completed a very enticing picture. I allowed myself to be persuaded to take up the post of outdoor activities' organiser of an organisation called the Long Vac Club, an entity the stated objective of which was to promote intercourse between university and foreign students. Such a mission inspired me. My greatest achievement was to organise a punt party to Grantchester and back for 500 people. I spent my time racing up and down the river in a canoe, fishing exotic foreign girls out of the water. They found that exposure to the water rendered their tight shirts transparent and hence displayed their lovely breasts to better effect.

I made an exception to my rule only to pursue older women. There was a breathtakingly beautiful young French student dressed invariably in tight-fitting purple. She had long, dark red hair cut in a deep fringe. With her snub nose and sparkling eyes she was a cross between Brigitte Bardot and a Renoir model. The male undergraduates surrounded her with their tongues hanging out but none of them made a move. I did and was shocked to find that she was only seventeen. She already had some sexual experience but was delighted by the tricks I taught her. She came from a very good family and was destined to marry well. I would have liked to have been a fly on the ceiling on her wedding night when her husband discovered what a hot and skilled little package he had married as no doubt he thought that he had abstained until that solemn occasion to preserve her virginity.

My final year passed in much the same manner as the last one. I had little or no time for work. I had overlooked the fact that I had had a good basic grounding in classics while law was a completely unknown quantity. About six weeks before the final exams, I looked at some specimen examination questions and answers. I panicked completely. Not only did I not know the answers but the questions themselves meant nothing to me. They were as impenetrable as Sanskrit. For the next six weeks, I lived in the university library every day from opening to closing time. I acquired enough knowledge to be awarded my habitual third. I now approached the Appointments Board to find articles of clerkship for me with a suitable firm of solicitors in the City of London – or three years indentured slavery as it was sometimes described.

CHAPTER THREE

KEEPING OUT OF MISCHIEF NOW

BELINDA. I was so disappointed at Richard's exam results and the way he was turning out generally. I hated his style of dress and was almost thankful that Matthew was not alive to see it. I approached a local firm of solicitors, the best in the town, who were willing to give Richard articles for no premium as I felt that if only I could get him home and once again under my influence things would undoubtedly improve but he would have none of it. I had been helpful before Richard went to Cambridge by speaking to Matthew's cousin, Alec, who was a major in a socially prominent cavalry regiment and that introduction had led to Richard being accepted as an ensign in the regiment for his national service. However, I felt that we had now grown so far apart that even if I could get him entry into one of the best firms of solicitors in the City of London he would not accept it from me. It was all very hurtful.

***

Richard had originally fancied a career at the Bar. It had been portrayed as so much more desirable and glamorous. Nearly all the law tutors at Cambridge were barristers and they very obviously described their own branch of the profession as the one for which to aim while the life of a solicitor was derided as definitely second best and rather menial. He examined this myth carefully and discovered another side to the story. If you had done brilliantly in law at Cambridge there were scholarships to help you through your training at the Bar but none of them were open to him with his poor third. Once you had passed the Bar exams, you had to find a pupillage. Here connections, brilliance, luck and money came into play. Connections would readily secure one for you and unless you were totally useless a decently lucrative career at the Bar would follow. Brilliance transcended most obstacles and should lead to a similar result. The possession of a private income bought time to succeed, without which poverty – perhaps but not necessarily short term – was a likely outcome. The benefits of luck were self-evident. A combination of all four elements was ideal. The fewer of the elements available decreased one's chances. He had nothing in his favour. His mother hardly had enough to keep herself and he did not fancy a precarious existence relying on his prowess with the clarinet and the proceeds of nightly lectures on law in far-flung polytechnics. He had already seen a few examples of failures at the Bar at old boys' gatherings of his school and he had no desire to join that particular band of seedy wraiths.

The solicitors' branch of the profession was not without its problems for him. Not only was there little or no pay during the three years of articles but he was likely to be asked to stump up a premium at the outset together with substantial stamp duty on the deed of articles. However, once he was qualified he would at least earn a reasonable salary and there were good prospects of advancement. He also noticed that law firms were becoming more interested in taking on graduates, particularly from Oxbridge, and were prepared to offer incentives to recruit them.

The Appointments Board supplied him with a list of firms in the City of London which were looking for a Cambridge law graduate to take on as an articled clerk. He identified those that offered travel and especially accommodation expenses. By judicious hitch-hiking, he could make a profit from the outset. If he crammed a number of interviews into each trip he could do even better by claiming travel expenses from each firm. On the accommodation front, he had a standing invitation to sleep on the living room couch of a friend's flat in Belsize Park so it was quite a lucrative operation for him as he claimed overnight hotel expenses as well for each interview. He smiled to himself as he completed the first 'creative' application form. Here he was embarking on a career in the law dedicated to honesty and upholding the rights of man. Before he even started he was instinctively fiddling his expenses. Was he ashamed? Not one jot. Was he a lone wolf or one of the flock in his petty criminality? He neither knew nor cared. All that he did know was that it helped his bank balance. There was the added spice that his mother certainly would not approve.

He always remembered to pack his clarinet. The Hundred Club in Oxford Street and Cy Laurie's in Great Windmill Street were his night-time destinations. The former was housed in a cavernous and ill-ventilated basement in Oxford Street while Cy's was in the premises of the old Panama Club opposite the Windmill Theatre, the home of decorous striptease and blue comedians, near Piccadilly Circus. By standing close to the bandstand with his clarinet prominently displayed, he almost always got an invitation to sit in. The Hundred Club was the more daunting as he was not yet in the same class on his instrument as Wally Fawkes, Ian Christie or Bruce Turner, but Humphrey Lyttleton was very kind to him. Perhaps it was his public school accent that helped. Cy Laurie's was a much rougher and wilder place but more to his taste. Cy was a slavish adherent of Johnny Dodds while Richard favoured the more florid clarinet sound of Sidney Bechet. They played some good duets together and it was a pity that none of them were recorded for posterity.

On his first visit to Cy's, there was a big crowd of groupies around the stage, including some attractive girls most of whom seemed to be of the art school type and of no great interest to him. It was difficult to make out details, dazzled as he was by the lights beamed on the stage as well as the thick swirls of tobacco smoke which filled the low-ceilinged room. He did however manage to lock eyes with an older woman dressed in tight, shiny black leather who was standing on her own and concentrating on what the band was playing. In the interval he made a beeline for her and over drinks in the bar discovered that she was American and had developed her love for jazz in the clubs of New Orleans. Diana was married to a Texan oilman who was off working on a rig somewhere. At the end of the evening he gladly accepted her invitation to go back to her flat in Bayswater for a drink. The drink was quickly forgotten as they tore hungrily into each other. Richard propelled her through the open door of the bedroom onto the large double bed. They both found it difficult to strip the skin-tight leather from her sweaty body. In bed the tricks he had learned were very much to her liking and he now knew that he could in future swap the lumpiness of the couch in Belsize Park for the pneumatic comfort of Diana's bed and supple body.

***

DIANA. Marriage to Carl was not easy. He gave me a good life as a senior oilman but he drank far too much. When he was home we always ended up snarling at each other and it was a relief when the news came through that he was off on an assignment on some far away rig. Paradoxically, I was always glad to see him back. We had decided not to have children while we continued this style of life and his heavy drinking meant that our sex life was nearly non-existent. I was building up a head of steam of sexual frustration and the occasional one night stand did nothing to help. I was turning into the original cat on a hot tin roof. When Carl was away, I was free to indulge my passion for jazz. I could lose myself in the music and the atmosphere of the clubs.

I knew there was something special about Richard as soon as Cy Laurie invited him up onto the bandstand. There was a relaxed intensity about him. He was shy while at the same time confident. His playing mirrored these contrasting qualities. I felt myself becoming wet at the thought of him inside me. I realised with delight that he was watching me as closely as I was gazing at him. I have always thought of the clarinet as the most phallic of instruments and now his was pointing it at me as though it wished to penetrate my inmost depths, as if 'hey, have I got something for you!'

He sought me out in the interval and bought me a drink at the bar. He was even younger than I had thought but he had a lot more to talk about than the average jazz musician. He spoke of the frustrations of life at Cambridge. The contrasts he perceived between the protected existence of the college kids which was so different from the hard reality of the outside world, especially for people like himself destined to struggle to make a living. In that regard he was torn between his need to have a respectable career as an attorney as against his desire to exist in the twilight world of a jazz musician. I for my part told him about the frustrations of my own life surrounded emptily on the one hand by creature comforts and losing myself in constant reading but wishing to break out and do so much more.

He found it hard to tear himself away from me when the break was over to return to playing but he left me with the feeling that my search for satisfaction might be over. We met again as soon as the band packed up for the night and after another drink at the bar he accepted my invitation to come back to my flat for a nightcap. As soon as we were in the apartment, we fell into a deep and passionate embrace. I was wishing that I had not worn my black leather catsuit which I had bought on a trip to Israel with Carl as it was so difficult to get off, bathed in perspiration as I was, partly from the heat of the Panama Club but more from the depths of my desire.

I was so ready for him that I felt that our lovemaking would be over far too quickly but I was delightfully surprised at how Richard intuitively assessed the situation and slowed me down with hard hands to gain the maximum satisfaction for both of us from our mutual desire. There was a part of me in my head that was looking down at us and assessing the situation, realising that he had been superbly taught in the school of sex by some woman or women to become a straight-A student, but of course he had to be given the credit for his willingness to learn. His concentration was all on me and my satisfaction. Unlike most men with whom I have made love, he subordinated his desires completely to mine. All the months if not years of sexual dissatisfaction dissolved as I came again and again under the skilful yet tender ministrations of his fingers, tongue and penis, separately or in combination. Eventually, when it was time to give him his satisfaction, I was so consumed with gratitude that I made sure I gave him the orgasm of his life. We slept like exhausted children.

***

Not surprisingly, he was hardly at his best at the next day's interview but it didn't matter as he didn't like the firm anyway. The Cambridge term was over and so was his official involvement with the college and university. However, nobody seemed to object to his staying. He had the double delight of many gigs and a variety of women in Cambridge in Colin's company, then listening to and playing top quality jazz coupled with the excitement and sophistication of Diana in London. He knew it could not last indefinitely as he would have to find a suitable law firm and put the pleasures of Cambridge firmly behind him.

His eventual choice of a firm was almost perverse and born out of desperation. The problem was that all the firms seemed so stuffy and alien to him. He was drawn to the bohemian lifestyle of a jazz musician but he was sufficiently hard-headed to know that he had to capitalise on his Cambridge law degree and acquire a professional qualification which would be a licence to print money – or so he hoped. The problem was that he was running out of options. He had visited and rejected or been rejected by almost all the firms on the Appointments Board list.

The night before the fateful interview he slept fitfully, unlike Diana, who was snoring softly beside him with the smile of a woman sublimely satisfied imprinted on her face. He was lost in a vivid dream. He was in a smoke-filled cellar in an alley off the Boulevard St Michel on the Left Bank in Paris. The place was low-ceilinged, small and crowded. At the end of the room on the stage was the unmistakeable figure of Sidney Bechet surrounded by a group of young and earnest white jazz musicians. Sidney saw and recognised Richard. He beckoned him forward.

'Give Dick your clarinet,' he said to Claude Luter, standing with the band beside him. 'He's only young but he already plays so much better than you.'

Before they could start playing, Sidney turned his large Creole face towards Richard.

'I have something important to say to you. You can be up there with the all-time jazz greats. Why do you want to waste your life as a weasel lawyer? I have been in courts with plenty of that breed. They do no good to anyone except themselves, believe me.' Before Richard could recover from his astonishment and respond, Sidney raised his gleaming soprano sax to his lips with the opening chorus of *Really The Blues*. Richard had no alternative but to join in and weave his notes around Sidney's lead. He awoke to the sound of the music in his head. Diana was still gently snoring. Had Bechet helped to resolve his confusion? No. But his mind was now made up. From now on, playing jazz would be an enjoyable hobby if he had the time but financial independence only came with a career in the law and that was what he needed most of all.

***

He was led by a harassed and washed-out looking secretary into the senior partner's office, a large, gloomy room filled with far too much oversized mahogany furniture. Behind the desk sat no less than three partners with the same look of expectancy on their faces, although Richard had no idea what they were expecting. Age differences apart they all looked cast out of the same mould. If this was a fairground booth, Richard fantasised, they were ducks in a row and he would take pot shots at them to win a prize. There was an air of pretension about the lawyers sitting opposite him, as if they were striving to appear more exalted socially than they really were. The aim seemed to be to replicate the atmosphere of the officers' mess of one of the regiments of the Brigade of Guards. Each wore a stiff white collar on a coloured striped shirt and a black suit. The bowler hat and tightly rolled umbrella could not be far away. Their ties were all of the same unrecognisable minor public school. He learned later that all the partners lived within a five mile radius of Guilford station. 'Welcome to Bleak House,' was his unspoken thought.

Their questioning of him was pathetic. It was almost as if they were overwhelmed by the academic aura that they thought he exuded. 'What games do you play?' He resisted the temptation to answer: 'None that you would have the cojones and stamina to join in,' but responded weakly by referring to his former prowess at Cambridge as a footballer while inventing a regular date as a tennis doubles player. He had in fact indulged in an interesting bout of mixed doubles only last week on the floor of Colin's stock room in Cambridge and this time they had been bold enough to swap partners at half time with very pleasurable and contrasting results. Variety was truly the spice of life.

Richard found it far more difficult to answer the next question tactfully: 'Why do you want to join our firm?' He uttered insincere words about its reputation and standing in the profession, the variety and importance of its clients and the work done for them coupled with the hope that he would fit in well enough to have a long-term career with the firm. The truthful answer would have been that he had exhausted his options. He disliked equally all the firms that he had seen. This one seemed in most ways indistinguishable from the others, certainly no better and probably not much worse, coupled with the fact that he was now desperate to find a place to launch his career.

They seemed far more eager to have him than he was to join them. He was dreading the mention of the premium that he would have to pay but was assured by the senior partner that he would not be expected to pay anything as they were so happy to have their first Cambridge man on board. That clinched it for him even though he could expect no salary in return for his labour.

He now had to equip himself with the appropriate gear. The umbrella was easy: he helped himself to a fine specimen at a gentlemen's club in Cambridge where he was playing a gig and all those present were far too drunk to notice. Colin produced from his extensive stock what he called his 'funeral director's suit' and Richard picked up the bowler in a seedy second-hand shop much frequented by college porters. His ties were all his own, ranging from old school, to regiment, to college, to university, to soccer blue. Richard stood in front of the mirror in his new gear and a feeling of profound depression washed over him. Unworthy though the feelings were, he inwardly cursed his parents for not being rich enough to endow him with the funds to enjoy the life that he felt he deserved. So many of his contemporaries were in that position who did not have one half of his musical talent and drive to enjoy a good life. He had sold out for security and for a moment he did not like the face looking back at him from the mirror; but the feeling swiftly passed.

He was expecting a culture shock but his first day was still a surprise. He had forgotten to ask the starting time. He breezed along at 9.30 am to find a large, gloomy room with gnarled old managing clerks, busy at their high, wooden desks, along one side and spotty faced, young articled clerks, no doubt paying a heavy premium for their five years of servitude, down the other, with the space in the middle filled by elderly, female secretaries and copy-typists in their shapeless, woollen cardigans. There was a pervasive odour of unwashed bodies and clothes which was not to his liking but he knew he would have to put up with it.

Not a partner was to be seen. The first sighting was at about 11.30 am. The partner arriving was immediately surrounded by fawning clerks and secretaries. Other partners soon entered and were similarly greeted. Richard now expected to see the law in action. He was wrong. As soon as the wheezing grandfather clock in the corner struck twelve they were off to their clubs in Pall Mall in a squadron of taxis previously booked for them by their secretaries. That was all the office saw of them until about 4.15 pm when they returned in a haze of cigar smoke and brandy fumes in order to sign those letters considered too personal to allow their managing clerks to replicate their signatures as they usually did.

At 5 pm on the dot, like a troop of penguins the partners again made for the door to their patiently waiting taxis for the journey to Waterloo and then home to their wives and children. In three years of articles Richard never saw a partner do a stroke of work. It was all done by the managing clerks, most of whom had left school at fifteen at the latest and who made up with practical experience what they lacked in academic and intellectual qualities, with just a little help from the five-year articled clerks. He thought it was a somewhat odd way to run a practice. The partners' role was confined to bringing in the clients, massaging their relationships with them and spending the profits. Their marketing activities consisted of extensive socialising. The firm paid out a fortune in club subscriptions for everything from Surrey County Cricket Club to the Oddfellows. One's golf handicap was far more important than legal knowledge. The formula seemed to work as the firm and its partners gave off all the signs of prosperity. From talking to his friends who also worked in the City, not only in the law but in other professions, he discovered that this was the general pattern of City life.

His own position in the firm was somewhat anomalous and ambivalent. As a Cambridge law graduate with only three years of articles to serve, he could be of considerable use to the firm. He tended to find on his desk those cases that experience alone could not solve and by good luck rather than judgement he gained useful and practical experience of the law while earning substantial fees for the firm from the work assigned to him. The managing clerks did not call him 'sonny', but they did not call him 'sir' either. Somehow, news of his exploits in Malaya had reached the other articled clerks so that they were completely in awe of him and tended to leave him alone.

At first, life was economically very tough. He received no salary of course and while living with Diana he was fed and clothed. However, she resented him going off to play gigs unless she accompanied him. There was an almighty row when he announced that he was deputising for Ian Christie with Mick Mulligan's band for a gig in Birmingham and staying overnight. They were going up by car and with all the instruments and gear to be transported there was no room for Diana. The reputation of the Mulligan band as reprobates and ravers made the argument worse. They did not speak to each other for several days after his return. In fact, after the gig he had got very drunk and spent a celibate night in a seedy hotel.

The situation eased when the partners resolved to pay him a salary which partly reflected his worth to the firm while providing him with a tiny office which might have done previous service as a broom cupboard. At that moment, Diana announced that her husband was returning home from his oil rig and Richard would have to move out. He was sure that the husband would be happy to find such a sexually satisfied wife who had some interesting new tricks to show him in bed.

Richard needed quickly to find somewhere new and cheap to live and the answer was to exchange the comfort and luxury of Diana's Bayswater flat for a very run down and depressing, but affordable, room in Bloomsbury. He felt that he now needed his independence as living with Diana had become rather stifling.

***

DIANA. The problem was that I had fallen completely in love with Richard. I was a slave to the wonders of his lovemaking. I was completely hooked. I despised myself for what had become an addiction. I hated to let him out of my sight. I was insanely jealous of other women, whether real or imaginary did not matter. I watched him and them like a hawk. I made ridiculous scenes if he would not or could not take me with him when he was playing. I have always looked down on whining and clinging women and now I had become one. However much of himself he gave me, I still wanted more.

We spent a lot of time in bed just talking, something I had missed with Carl. Richard in many ways was a strange mixture. He felt a great debt to his mother for the sacrifices she had made for him and wanted to succeed in life as his way of repaying her. However, he knew that he had to distance himself from her to combat the suffocating aura of her all-embracing love. He actively despised those in life who had had it easy and it seemed that he had been surrounded at school, university and elsewhere by these types. At the same time, he envied their ease and relaxation in life which contrasted so much with his constant need to strive and achieve. His seeming lack of an underlying morality worried me. I felt that he was prepared to turn his hand to almost anything if it would help him achieve his ends, whether legal or not. His abundant charm concealed a cold, hard and calculating inner core. I loved him but that was not to say that I liked him. I knew increasingly that he was using me and that there could be no long-term future in our relationship. I was just a convenient stepping stone on his ever upwardly mobile professional and social path.

Carl had just announced that he was coming home. Half of me wanted him back in the comfort of our limited life together, while the other half wanted to consume and be consumed by Richard. I knew that life with Richard was a dream only. He was not prepared to give himself to me in life the way he gave himself totally to me in bed. I knew that I would never penetrate that deep coldness within. Just as part of me was outside watching us together so part of him also was a detached observer but it was a far bigger part than mine. I wrestled with myself and I am ashamed to admit that the material comforts that Carl provided weighed heavily in the balance. I told Richard that Carl was coming home and that he would have to move out. I was kicking my addiction.

***

The house where he was to lodge was a damp and decaying Victorian monstrosity in Little Russell Street behind the British Museum. Each room was let separately and the lodgers were all self-conscious characters who saw themselves as refugees from the Bloomsbury Group. A few were on the way up but most were definitely on the way down. Sunday morning was Richard's dedicated bath time. The only bathroom in the house was situated in the basement, separated by a thin plywood partition from the landlady's kitchen. Lighting the geyser to heat the water was a hazardous activity. After the initial explosion, scalding water gushed out to be mixed with rust-tinged cold. Once the mix was right, he lay soaking while the landlady's eggs and bacon fried on the gas stove no more than six inches from his head. Smells generally good or bad played an important part in life in Little Russell Street. There was only one lavatory with wash basin on each floor and he quickly learned to distinguish by smell which of his fellow lodgers had used the facilities before him.

After one unsatisfactory encounter in his somewhat lumpy single bed, Diana made it plain that slumming in Bloomsbury was not for her.

***

DIANA. We met on a wet and windy evening outside Tottenham Court tube station. I had just had my hair done and I was not pleased by the havoc that the elements were creating with it. Richard had told me that his place was just round the corner from the subway so I had not taken my usual precautions to cover up. Also, when I left home the sun had been brilliantly shining and for once I forgot just how changeable London weather could be. 'Damn,' I thought, 'there goes my investment!'

The shock when he opened the front door of his new lodgings was profound. I was greeted by a mixed aroma of stale cabbage soup, bad drains and rising damp. He had made an attempt to tidy his room but I was feeling less amorous by the minute. The Victorian washstand with china jug and bowl might have fetched a few shillings in some flea market but was of little practical use. The spluttering gas fire with its broken porcelain elements hardly heated the room at all. I let Richard undress me but the lumpy single bed with its twanging springs and clammy sheets to which he led me did nothing to improve my mood. Even Richard's lovemaking skills could not conjure up a response from me. For the first time ever, our lovemaking was a complete failure. The disgusting shared toilet and washbasin where I was supposed to put myself together afterwards made me realise if there was previously any doubt that our relationship was over.

RICHARD therefore turned to haunting the galleries of the British Museum for his sexual satisfaction. He was surprisingly successful. Perhaps it was the erotically arousing nature of some of the exhibits but it was rare for him not to fall easily into conversation with some lonely female culture seeker and from there to persuade her to come back for a drink to his nearby bohemian lodgings. From that point surrender seemed the easy option and he had some rapturous and abandoned couplings which seemed to be enhanced by the relative anonymity of the situation.

***

SHARON. I was not enjoying my term's placement in my sophomore year studying fine arts at the Slade School. Michigan University was much bigger but far more friendly. Being stuck in digs in Cockfosters at the end of the Piccadilly Line did not help. I had nobody to talk to. I was used at Michigan to a teeming faculty hall where the problem was lack of privacy and time on my own. Here, I had far too much of both. The lack of sex did not bother me. I had lost my virginity quickly in the back of some jock's car before I left high school. Sex on my dates at college had been equally unsatisfactory.

Spending another Saturday afternoon reading in my room suddenly became too much for me and on impulse I used my season ticket to take me to Holborn and the British Museum. I soon became lost in the amazing contents of the Egyptian Galleries but I could not miss the fact that I was being followed and that the person following me was a good-looking man. I was wondering when he was going to start talking to me and I have to say that I was looking forward to the prospect.

'Do you think in two thousand years' time people will be looking at our relics?' was his not too original opening gambit. I answered that I thought it quite likely provided that the atom bomb had not destroyed all traces of our civilisation. We then continued companionably around the galleries until the sudden announcement of closing time.

We had exchanged by then a lot of information but surprisingly not our names. I assumed this omission was some kind of quaint British convention. He asked me if I would like to come back to his place for a drink: it was just round the corner. Frankly, I relished the possibility of danger. This was not what well brought up girls from Sperryville Virginia were supposed to do but I was a long way from home. His room was more sordid but less suburban than mine and I gulped down the wine that he offered me. I was ready for his embrace when he lunged at me and I think he was surprised at the passion of my response. We competed in the speed we could undress each other and I expected it to be all over as quickly as it had been before but I was wrong.

He knew how to take his time and concentrate on pleasing me. Up to now, I had got far more pleasure from the little gadget which I christened 'my pocket rocket' and which I kept in my bedside drawer than I had from any man. This was different and I was feeling the type, depth and number of sensations that I had only dreamed about.

By the time I left his room I could hardly walk from so much concentrated pleasure. It was only when I reached Holborn Station that I realised that I did not know his name nor he mine. What's more I had forgotten my earrings. I did not go back for them.

***

At work, he surprised himself by how much he enjoyed practical problem solving for real people. Many of the cases given to him by the firm were stimulating and interesting. He took over an enormous file relating to a boundary dispute between two neighbours which had been going on for years. Learned counsel and six court hearings had done nothing to resolve it. Richard read the papers and applied some lateral thinking. The parties had become blinded over time by their mutual hatred. There was an easy solution by each party giving up a little of the elements in dispute while at the same time exchanging other pieces of land which at a stroke vastly increased the value of their respective holdings. The firm found itself with a grateful client and Richard received a written commendation. On another occasion, one of the managing clerks had failed to obtain a court order before acquiring a large and valuable building in the City from a charity. The textbooks indicated that the transaction was void and there would be huge problems and costs involved in rectifying the situation with a big risk of losing a large and important new client. Richard used his charm to move mountains and secured a backdated order from the court with the connivance of the Charity Commission, something that on the face of it could not be done. The client never even knew there was a difficulty.

He supplemented his scanty knowledge of law from Cambridge by learning the art of research in the libraries. By the time he left the office to enrol in the crammers where law graduates were allowed to study, he was streets ahead in legal knowledge and application in comparison with his fellows who seemed to have spent most of their time rolling and re-rolling their umbrellas. As a result, he was able to take it fairly easy and still play jazz in the evenings, managing to get a reasonably respectable pass in the final exams. He was now qualified as a solicitor but how was he to make the best of his brand new qualification? Should he take active steps to find a job or should he just wait and see what came along?

CHAPTER FOUR

UNDECIDED

RICHARD. Surprisingly, I felt a sense of post-examination anti-climax. I had put more into the learning process than I had realised at the time. An unexpected letter from Diana provided the ideal short-term solution. Despite the unsatisfactory nature of our last encounter, she had relented. She had been looking after her elderly, sick mother in Florida and now desperately needed a break. She knew my exams were over and guessed that I might be at a loose end. The enclosed airline return ticket to Miami clinched it. As suggested, I remembered to pack my clarinet.

The jungles of Malaya had acclimatised me to the brightness of the light and the sticky heat of southern Florida. Diana was deeply tanned and welcomed me ecstatically at the airport. We immediately checked into an Art Deco hotel on South Beach and after a quick shower I realised that I was there to satisfy her long pent-up need which happily corresponded with my own.

We awoke in the early evening ravenously hungry and set out to explore the nightlife. I saw a poster announcing that the Bunk Johnson New Orleans Jazz Band was in town and appearing that night in a local tavern. I went back for my clarinet and, after fresh lobster in a beach shack washed down with a couple of ice-cold lagers each, we joined the queue for the concert. We were early and managed to get seats near the front. I had several of Bunk Johnson's records so I knew the style but I was shocked to see how old and decrepit all the musicians were. In the first interval, I went up to George Lewis, the clarinet player, who was tiny beside me. I offered to buy him a drink and asked if I could sit in during the second set. He replied that he needed a break and I could take his place in the first two numbers. I was a little overwhelmed but I could not back out now. Fortunately I knew both tunes well, *The Old Grey Mare* and *Beale Street Blues*. I was introduced as Dick Gregory, the famous clarinet player from London. Despite the hyperbole or perhaps because of it, I did not do too badly. George Lewis then came back and we played dual clarinets on 'High Society', taking alternate choruses with Alphonse Picou's classic solo and driving the audience into a frenzy of applause.

Diana was delighted at my happiness and this set the tone for the following two weeks. We drove around the State as the mood took us. This was well before Florida became the tourist trap that it now is and we enjoyed simple accommodation with through draughts and mosquito nets in place of the soon to become ubiquitous air conditioning. Fresh seafood was everywhere and people seemed genuinely pleased to see us. We staggered lazily from lovemaking to sleep to sunbathing to sightseeing and back again and we both rejoiced in that complete lack of responsibility to people and events outside our own little cocoon. We managed to wreck one hotel room with our takeout stone crabs and mustard sauce. I used the hammer supplied far too vigorously and fragments of shell and crabmeat flew all over the room and were even embedded in the ceiling. Away from the stresses and strains of London we were completely compatible in our interests.

The Keys and Key West in particular suited our relaxed mood. The lifestyle of the people became our own. We eventually tore ourselves away to explore the Everglades with their sinuously sinister alligators and the Orange Belt, an all-black area, where shabby little town after town had a chapel facing a bar on every street corner. Tarpon Springs was a pleasant surprise with its Greek lettering on all the shop fronts and its restaurants and bars serving a community of sponge divers transplanted totally from their Mediterranean island. We took long walks along the beach at Captiva Island trying, guide book in hand, to name the vast variety of seabirds. The rough sand abrasive on the soles of our bare feet contrasted with the strangeness if not insanity of the huge collection of Salvador Dali paintings in their gallery in St Petersburg. Coming across beautifully sculpted but long neglected memorials of the Civil War with long lists of names, often the same family name, made us realise that this was more than just a tropical paradise. There were reminders for me of the equivalent memorials in my own country: of the many who lost their lives, especially in the First World War. It was a sobering thought among so much sybaritic enjoyment. In later life when I heard people sounding off about the boring nature of Florida I always smiled sweetly and said nothing. I felt that if I failed as a lawyer I could always become a travel writer as I was fascinated by the experience of new places.

So much pleasure becomes too much. As our time together was coming to an end, we each began to retreat into our protective shells and became more distant from each other. Diana was thinking about having to return to look after her mother and I about the uncertain future that lay before me in London. When we said our farewells to each other at the departure gate at Miami Airport, there was an air of inevitability that neither of us would ever recapture that mood of near paradise in our lives again. My inner thought was that a wonderful chapter in my life had just ended. I was very grateful to Diana but I could not see her playing a positive role in my future life. She was much older than me and I did not fancy being the co-respondent in her messy divorce. I said nothing but I doubted whether our paths would cross again.

***

DIANA. If only Richard knew how torn I was. Throughout our trip, I had deliberately masked how deeply I felt for him. When I was with him, I came alive. It wasn't just the sex. Sure, that was magnificent and all-consuming. I was touched to my core by his youthful uncertainty combined with a natural cunning and worldly wisdom which created an atmosphere of constant enquiry and excitement. This was such a contrast to my dull existence with Carl, surrounded as I was by all the luxuries that he generously provided for me. It was like living in Texas! Then again, there was the time I had to spend with my mother who was becoming an increasingly querulous invalid and who was satisfied by nothing that I did for her.

I saw Richard off at his gate for London, then sat in the car and cried my eyes out. I was tempted then and often afterwards on impulse to buy a ticket to follow him but I knew that he was destined for a different life in which I would play no part. The difference in our ages alone was too much and I knew that behind that student-like, insouciant façade there was a coldness and calculation which I did not wish to face. I had to settle for the life that I had and there was to be no more escape.

***

RICHARD. I would have hated to face the usual cold of the northern climate but luckily London was experiencing a heatwave, though it was nothing compared to what Florida had to offer. My mood of uncertainty was not greatly helped by finding a note from the firm at Little Russell Street inviting me to sherry with the partners in the boardroom followed by lunch to celebrate my qualifying as a solicitor. Was this hello or goodbye? I presented myself at the office the next day sleekly suntanned but horribly jetlagged. The attitude of the managing clerks was noticeably more respectful. The butterfly was emerging from its chrysalis.

At 11.45 am precisely I was summoned by the senior partner's secretary to the boardroom, a place which I had rarely visited before though I had had the occasional fantasy of having sex with the least unattractive secretary in the firm on its long, highly polished mahogany table. I banished those improper thoughts to be handed a glass of the kind of sweet sherry which is served in so many suburban drawing rooms and which I hate. There was no choice. All eight partners, most of whom resembled Tweedledum or Tweedledee, shook my hand by way of congratulation and the senior partner announced that he hoped I would be joining them in the partnership. This news came as a pleasant shock to me as I was dreading having to put myself about on the job market.

I then joined him and his second in command in a taxi to

enjoy a passable lunch at the Carlton Club washed down with an excellent claret, and the proposal was laid out in full. They had been impressed by the extra dimension in terms of the type and quality of work that I had done for the firm and they felt that there was more to come now that I was qualified. In addition I would be able to tap my contacts to introduce influential and lucrative new clients to the firm. Accordingly, they wished to offer me an immediate salaried partnership, a first for the firm, at a salary which I knew to be at the bottom of the market scale, coupled with a commission of ten per cent of fees paid to the firm by clients introduced by me. I felt that I should play a little hard to get and not reply immediately though I was inclined to jump for joy and loudly shout 'yes'.

I asked for time to consider their kind offer and whether I could have a copy of the firm's accounts to peruse meanwhile. This latter request seemed equivalent to impugning their wives' chastity and I was told that it was inappropriate for a mere salaried partner to seek or receive such information. That terminated the business of the day and I now listened to a long account of their respective rounds of golf over the weekend which interested me not one iota. I was asked whether I was planning to marry in the near future and replied that my recent studies had left me little time for social life, which was unfortunately true, but that I was keen to put the world of a student behind me, which was partly true. I went on to say that I was eager to become established in their community, which was not true at all. Would I be buying a house in the Guilford area was the next question, but I answered to the effect that a flat in town was more suitable for my continuing bachelor status. Did I see a gleam of envy in the eye of the younger of the two? 'Which golf club was I planning to join?' This question threw me completely. I felt that to answer with the question 'What golf clubs are there?' would be letting myself down. My knowledge of London clubs at the time was restricted to 100 Oxford Street, Cy Laurie's and other jazz clubs. I thought it best to play for time while at the same time appearing judicious.

'Naturally, I would wish to take your advice while at the same time conducting a comparative survey of those within easy travelling time of my future home.'

Needless to say, I never did join a golf club.

At this point, having retired some time ago to another room for coffee, brandy and cigars I noted a general unrest in the room. At first I thought that there might be a fire but I soon realised that everybody was preparing for the mass migration back to their offices in the City for the ritual of signing the post. I by contrast went back to a pile of long unanswered letters and other paperwork which I valiantly tried to wade through in my brandy-befuddled state. It was an impossible task and I gave it up with an expletive, took a refreshing walk home, had a long nap and resolved in future to get all my important work done before midday if I was invited to repeat this ritual of a long and liquid lunch.

CHAPTER FIVE

YOU TOOK ADVANTAGE OF ME

First things first: Richard needed a home. Little Russell Street was no longer suitable for his new status. He scanned the to let columns in the *Evening Standard*, looked at a few inadequate flats and eventually found what he wanted in Lexham Gardens in Kensington. It was a first floor flat with high ceilings and very suitable for the type of entertaining with which he planned to ensnare his future clients. There was a spare bedroom and he resolved to let it to a female university student who would cook and clean for him in lieu of paying rent. The selection process was long as it was difficult to combine the qualities that he sought with the will to do the job. He eventually settled on Mei Ling, a Malayan Chinese postgraduate student at the London School of Economics.

The salary he was to receive was not generous but he reckoned that he could supplement it substantially with the commission he could earn. He knew how the partners in the firm attracted their clients and he resolved to do the opposite. Their kind of club life was not for him. He had a ready-made catchment area in his school and his regiment together with his college and Cambridge generally. He had also through his jazz playing acquired a potential following, though he would have to be careful how he handled the more sinister element as clients. He had left far behind nearly all those who had studied law with him and who were taking on lowly jobs in law firms or in industry. In fact, some of them could turn out to be potential clients or sources of introductions.

The first day back at work with his new status was very different from his initial tentative arrival as an articled clerk. His broom cupboard had been enlarged to twice its original size and he was introduced to his new secretary, Dorothy, a young and pretty girl up from the country. No longer would he need to seek favours to have his work done by the overloaded beasts of burden who served the managing clerks. It was tacitly understood that he was there to work so he would be adopting the hours of the managing clerks rather than the partners unless they condescended to invite him again to lunch.

***

DOROTHY. I was shaking with nerves when I first met my new boss, Richard Gregory. After grammar school and secretarial college in Margate, I had worked for not much pay in the typing pool of a local insurance company. The work was dull and the bosses even duller. I was ambitious so I decided to seek a job in London as a legal secretary, even though the additional salary was largely spent on the cost of my season ticket and the hours of travelling were brutal. Initially, my status in the firm's typing pool and the nature of the work were little better than my local job but I had been chosen to work for Mr Gregory who was talked about in the office as the coming man. He was said to be very handsome and dashing, particularly in contrast to the other partners who I thought were a bunch of fuddy-duddy suet puddings. He had been away studying at law school when I joined the firm so this was our first meeting.

He was certainly good looking but not my type: too flash and conscious of the impression that he made. However, he put me at my ease immediately and made me feel that he would be good to work for. He drove himself ruthlessly hard and expected the same from me. When I made mistakes, his charm slipped and his remarks could be very cutting. On a bad day, I would have to retire to the ladies' room several times to have a good cry but he always noticed eventually that he had upset me and would be very contrite and anxious to make up. If I took home a bunch of flowers on the train in the evening, it meant that I had had a very bad day and made lots of mistakes but we had both got over it. He had a brilliant brain which I had to admire. It was most of the time a pleasure to help him. Ours was a good working relationship and I hoped it would go on for a long time.

***

The next two years passed very swiftly. He was given all the firm's work that was beyond the capacity of the managing clerks to handle. Before his time the file of a difficult case would be wrapped in a large sheet of white paper and secured tightly with pink tape just as in the time of Dickens. It would be inscribed 'herewith case to counsel to advise' which was about as intellectually demanding as the sender could manage and it was despatched to one of our learned friends to deal with, the barristers in the Temple or Lincoln's or Gray's Inn. Richard viewed it as a point of pride to cut off the supply to them as much as possible and solve these problems himself. Educationally and socially there was a huge gulf between the forelock-touching managing clerks who were from humble backgrounds and had not attended a public school and the young graduates at the Bar, largely recruited from Oxford and Cambridge. While the managing clerks called them 'sir', he found it difficult to show respect for people with whom he had not only studied shoulder to shoulder but often got blind drunk at the same sleazy student parties.

His own clientele was coming on nicely. He had some discreet visiting cards printed with both his and the firm's addresses. He had to be careful not to be caught offending the professional rules against advertising. These seemed designed solely to preserve the status quo so that no newcomer could break into the cosy professional monopoly long established probably by equally nefarious means. 'Pull up the ladder, Jack, I'm alright' could well have been the motto of this entrenched profession.

Mei proved an accomplished cook in western as well as oriental styles. As a result, invitations to his dinner table were prized and while he did not always convert his guests into immediate clients he established an atmosphere of warmth and goodwill which could later bring good results professionally. He also gave cocktail parties in the flat every few months which were very useful at bringing his existing clients and new contacts together. Mei would recruit other Asian students to act as waitresses and he let her redecorate the somewhat shabby flat to enhance the oriental theme, particularly with wallpaper from Sandersons covered with swirling dragons and porcelain lamps from Liberty's made from antique Chinese ginger jars.

His invitations produced a great amount of reciprocity so his social life was very much more of the same and largely male dominated. He was working very hard as well. He was truly burning the candle at both ends. Gradually, he was taking over the resources of the firm exclusively to service the needs of his clients. By the end of the first year, he had complete call on the services of two of the managing clerks. He then had his big breakthrough. Larry Gage was the friend of an Oxford acquaintance who brought him to one of Richard's cocktail parties. The Gage family controlled a defunct Malayan tin mining company which had previously been quoted on the London Stock Exchange. Its assets had been expropriated by the local state government which had recently paid massive compensation. The company was now sitting on a vast sum of cash in the bank. The choices were to return it to the shareholders or convert the company itself into a bank and use the cash for the business of lending.

'Do you know how to convert the company into a bank?' asked Larry. Needless to say Richard did not have a clue but he masked his ignorance and resolved to find out.

'Of course, Larry, I will let you have a business plan and timetable for your board to approve.'

A visit to a library and a few enquiries at the Bank of England and elsewhere proved that the answer was not so difficult to find. He then asked for help from a stockbroker and accountant, both of whom specialised in that area. Making use of their experience and his newfound knowledge, he wrapped his solution in professional mystery which he then presented to Larry who authorised him on behalf of the family to go ahead. He duly performed his magic and presented his first five-figure bill which was paid gratefully by return, but this was only the start. The Gages proved incredibly loyal clients and he received all their subsequent legal work. This mainly involved the preparation and completion of security documentation, as the money was lent out to builders and property developers charged on their land and buildings or homeowners who wished to borrow more against their increasing equity. He was soon exclusively employing two thirds of the firm's managing clerks on his work.

He was making his professional reputation on the basis that he could achieve what his clients wanted. This contrasted with most of his professional brethren who made a living by putting obstacles in their clients' path and always saying no rather than yes. If the client's method to achieve his objective was faulty, he would seek an alternative and on the face of it legitimate way of accomplishing the required ends. This course of action did not seem to appeal to his rivals who appeared to have a less secure grasp of the relevant law and were terrified of getting it wrong. They acted as if they were frightened of their own shadows.

There was a downside to Richard's strategy. The City rumour mill as ever was remarkably effective and certain shady operators got to hear that there was a lawyer in practice who was prepared to show a remarkable degree of flexibility in structuring their nefarious transactions. It was all something of an intellectual exercise to Richard and he rarely paused to consider the underlying morality and legality of the deals that he was seeking to cloak with a covering of outward legitimacy. Richard himself was naturally drawn to people operating in the shadows. He hesitated, often indulging in continuous internal dialogue purely in the interests of self- preservation: 'should he accept or reject certain seedy clients and their dubious types of business?'

The fact that the firm's name and reputation for fusty respectability gave him considerable cover was something of a double-edged sword. If his transgressions were discovered, he would have some protection against the outside world as only one of a number of members in a well-known partnership with a good reputation but if his guilt was established, he risked being thrown out on his ear by his colleagues with his professional career wrecked irreparably.

The partners might have little idea of what was going on in their firm but the managing clerks were not fools and read their Sunday papers avidly. The fact that their staple diet was the *News of the World* meant that they recognised the best known crooks and swindlers and on more than one occasion Richard had to dump a potential client when shown a lurid article relating to the prospect in question who had been recognised as he sat in the waiting room.

His social life outside work time and client-gathering activities was sadly neglected. Mei had succumbed to his charms after one particularly successful dinner which she had hosted as well as cooking for him. She normally slept in her own room unless they had need of each other and theirs was clearly not a progressive relationship. They were merely temporarily fulfilling each other's sexual requirements.

***

MEI LING. When I answered Richard's advertisement in the *Evening Standard* I was very much on my guard. Before I left Malaya to study in London, my parents had drummed into me details of the dangers that I would experience, including being sold, as they quaintly put it, into white slavery. In view of my Asian origin, 'white' hardly seemed the appropriate colour but my parents' ideas of London were gained from an excessive reading of Dickens and other authors of the period. I sensed in Richard a deep coldness at his core which he masked with many layers of carefully acquired charm. I did not like him but the job he offered suited me as it provided me with a home and the duties Richard outlined to me did not seem too onerous and would give me plenty of time to work on my thesis. Unlike most of the Malayan students in London, I did not come from a rich family and I had to make my meagre savings last for the two years of my course. My studies were far too intense for me to take a normal job, even part time.

Working for Richard was not difficult and increasingly was becoming a pleasure. I rationalised that I was lonely but I was becoming more and more drawn to him. He was a fascinating mixture of the coldness, which I have referred to already, and vulnerability. I liked his brainpower and we were fast becoming friends. I had abandoned a fiancé at home to take up my scholarship in London and I did rather miss our previous sex life. I suppose that it was inevitable that Richard and I would eventually become lovers. He had also been working very hard and had not been involved with any other women for some time so far as I knew. I had cooked, prepared and hosted a very successful dinner party for some important clients and prospects and we had both had a lot to drink. He helped me with the washing up and somehow as a result of his gratitude and euphoria I ended up in his bed. He was a very sympathetic and considerate lover and he skilfully relieved me of the months of sexual frustration that I had been far too busy to acknowledge. I did feel that his lovemaking was a little too contrived and accomplished. I wondered where he had acquired his polished technique.

In spite of these reservations, the problem was that I was falling gradually but deeply in love with him. Sadly, this was not reciprocated. Richard was completely honest with me. We were good friends and indeed business partners who came together on some nights when we both needed sexual satisfaction but otherwise slept in our own rooms. Ours was a temporary arrangement only until something better came along. I pretended to accept his terms and the boundaries on our relationship while inwardly hoping that in time they would change and he would start loving me as much as I loved him. I felt passionately that we were ideally suited for a long life together and he would never meet another woman who matched and understood him so well and could do so much for him. I knew that my parents would be unhappy if I married a man who was not from my own community but I felt that they would ultimately accept him. Frankly, if they did not, my love for Richard was so strong that I did not care all that much.

BELINDA. While he was studying, Richard never asked me up to London to see him. His visits home were also very infrequent, which I understood as he was so short of money. Now that he was qualified and with a good job in the City, I was very pleased to be invited to visit him. His flat, which was beautifully decorated, was too small to accommodate me so he put me up in a nice hotel round the corner on Cromwell Road.

However, I took an instant dislike to his servant, Mei Ling, who obviously had already wormed her way into Richard's bed. Having a small amount of native blood in our family I did not wish to have grandchildren whose fine Anglo Saxon features would be adulterated by a further Asian strain. I raised the issue with Richard which I felt was necessary. This resulted in a blazing row so I packed my bags and went home. Clearly, I now had no influence on my son whatever.

***

His salary had risen considerably but he relied largely on his commission to fund his lifestyle. He had been too busy to open the subject of a change of status before with the partners but after two years he felt the time was right. He had been working ridiculously hard and had concentrated on developing his own clients to such an extent that he had hardly been aware of what had been going on in the firm unless it impinged on him directly in relation to servicing his work. He knew that the firm had followed their success with him by recruiting a couple more articled clerks from Oxbridge, but they seemed to have not chosen so well with the new entrants who so far had made little impact and seemed more interested in their social lives than in acquiring the skills to become good lawyers.

The Carlton Club lunch was restaged with the same *dramatis personae*. His approach seemed to be treated favourably. He could advance to the equity with a capital payment of only half the norm in view of his work contribution over the last two years. The figure mentioned was still large enough to make his eyes water. He was assured that his bank would lend it to him if by chance he did not have the money readily available which indeed he did not. He would be able to draw monthly a sum about twenty per cent on average more than the current amount he was taking home. He was not overwhelmed by the generosity of the offer and asked to see the firm's accounts, an offer which this time could not be refused.

He took them home that night and compared them with the amount of fees from clients introduced by him as well as the fees for work personally done by him for the firm's clients. In the last year, his introductions represented some thirty per cent of the firm's turnover and he personally billed and collected about twenty per cent of that figure. He did another simple calculation which showed that without his contribution the firm was hopelessly insolvent and the partners enjoyed their comfortable Surrey existence entirely thanks to him. They needed him far more than he needed them. Even if they doubled their offer he still would be getting nothing like a true reflection of his worth to the business. Surely it was time for this particular rat to leave their sinking ship.

CHAPTER SIX

SOPHISTICATED LADY

MEI LING. It had been a particularly good evening. Richard rarely thought to take me out but he had wanted to discuss the problems about his future with me in different surroundings where I was not putting dinner on the table as well. I appreciated his sensitivity and also the old world, French luxury of Boulestin with its classic food and ancient waiters. Afterwards Richard had made love to me beautifully with complete concentration on my desires. We lay bathed in satisfaction and perspiration in a heap of tangled limbs but I could feel that Richard was worried and mentally miles away.

'Do you want to talk about the firm's offer?' I prompted. Over dinner he had shown me the firm's accounts and told me the details of their offer to him.

'Yes, very much. You know how I value your opinion. I feel that it would be cowardly to accept their offer or even to go back and try to improve it but frankly the alternatives scare me.'

I agreed with him that their offer was not worth serious consideration. It looked to me that, as soon as Richard had become a salaried partner, the others had relaxed and just let him shoulder the burden of bringing in and doing the work.

'What about joining another firm?' I continued. 'You would be a valuable addition almost anywhere.'

'I know,' he replied, 'but far too many law firms are run on the same basis as mine and I risk going from bad to worse, from the frying pan into the fire in fact. Those few top firms that are properly run will not need my clients or my ability to attract new ones. They already have enough so they won't pay me my true worth.'

I already knew this and I was trying to draw Richard to the

inevitable conclusion that he had to start his own firm. I was excited at the prospect as I knew how much I could help him and that working together in the new environment would bring us closer.

'I could start my own practice but the prospect really frightens me. I may be a good practical lawyer and able to attract clients who come back for more but I have zero experience of running a business. We have already seen where a badly run firm ends up.'

I did my best to reassure him and give him confidence. I told him that, as I had just submitted my thesis and had time on my hands, I was happy to work full time on the project as his business manager. 'I am not just an academic economist,' I assured him. 'Understand that centuries of Chinese shopkeepers are in my blood.'

The decision was made there and then to go ahead. Richard's confidence in my advice and future help aroused me again and I stroked him into life once more to enter me for a second but gentle bout of lovemaking before we collapsed into an exhausted and peaceful sleep.

***

RICHARD. That night in bed I discussed the problem with Mei Ling. She was not merely an academic economist but clearly had a good business brain. We agreed that I could not accept the offer and that I should get out of that atmosphere of failure as quickly as possible. But what should I do? The obvious answer was to join another law firm. However, both in my interviews for articles and in my subsequent professional dealings I had come to the view that most were run on similar old fashioned lines with the same lack of attention to profitability and I had not much chance of improving my position. There were a few great firms, household names, which acted for leading clients. I could have a good job with one of them which would give me a secure career and in all probability genuine prospects of advancement over a prescribed and probably lengthy period of time. In other words, if I kept my nose clean I would eventually make partner, but I fancied the life of the hare rather than the tortoise. The problem was that they would have no interest initially in one of my great strengths which I had already shown I possessed, the ability to bring in and develop clients. I reckoned that this was one of my best attributes and the type of firm in question would not reward me with money for it, at least in the short term until I became a partner and there was no guarantee that I would ever achieve that status. We were faced with a dilemma.

I needed to give serious consideration to the risky alternative. I could go it alone. I would need time to set up my office and Mei offered all her help. She made it obvious that this was the path that she wanted me to follow and did her best to downplay the risks. She had so much confidence in my ability to succeed. I wished that I shared it. The fact that at that moment she was particularly happy and relaxed having just experienced a shattering orgasm may have helped her decision. I realised that at this stage of my career she would be invaluable to me. Her worth long term was another matter altogether but we could sort that out when we came to it. Characteristically, the firm had not provided me with a contract so we agreed that giving three months' notice was quite enough. The five managing clerks engaged exclusively on my work should shift with me. If they stayed, there was no work for them to do so it was in the firm's interest as well as my own. I believed that all my clients would jump ship and join me. I had made a point of remaining close to all of them even if I did not do their work personally.

Apart from helping my mother with the books relating to her bed and breakfast, I had no experience of business as a legal training prepares you for nothing other than giving legal advice and doing legal work. Frankly, I was scared of the unknown path I was about to tread. Mei was extremely helpful. I felt that centuries of Chinese business acumen were being made available to me.

The first requirement was to find the right premises. They had to be in the City in order to reassure my existing clients, but they needed to be inexpensive enough not to bankrupt me in my first year. Ideally, there would be room for expansion if I was successful and required more staff. We saw any number of unsuitable offices and I was beginning to get depressed as time was ticking away. The partners had accepted my notice without any display of emotion. Perhaps they were too stupid to realise that they were facing economic disaster. Just when I was beginning to think that we would never find anything satisfactory, we looked at the former firemen's living accommodation above the defunct fire station in Moorgate which had been on the market for office use for several years. The rooms were in a terrible condition but there were a lot of them. The landlord was desperate and the rent was cheap. He was prepared to let me lease what space I wanted initially and add to it if the need arose.

I was alarmed at the likely cost of making the place fit for occupation. While I did not need marble halls to retain and attract suitable clients, I wanted something that looked like respectable solicitors' offices. It was Mei who came up with the answer.

'You need my Eastern magic here. If you can pay up front for the materials, I can mobilise the labour from my Malayan Chinese community. I know the skilled tradesmen you need and the basic labour will be provided by my fellow students.'

The work would be done out of normal business hours and everyone would be paid in cash.

My savings were limited so I made an appointment with some apprehension to see my bank manager. I had never needed to borrow before and I had no idea how my application would be received. I need not have worried. Just as I was setting off for my meeting, Mei produced a brilliant business plan for me to show him, accompanied by the classic words 'You may find this useful.' As a work of fiction it was masterly. He was falling over himself to lend me more than I wanted. There was no question of any security being offered. I had none anyway. Somehow, the fact that I was opening a new solicitor's practice seemed to be the key that unlocked the vault.

***

THE BANK MANAGER. Richard Gregory was not at all what I expected. When he made his appointment to see me, I asked the clerk in charge of his account as I always did for what information he had that would be of interest to me. There was nothing. It was just a normal, well-run current account which had never overstepped the line and gone into overdraft. I was used to city solicitors and frankly I found them a pretty unsavoury breed. After grammar school, I had joined the bank and slowly worked my way up by dint of hard work to manage an important branch. I had married far too young and burdened myself with a wife who found the social side of my work, entertaining and being entertained by customers, very difficult. She could be an embarrassment to me sometimes but there was no question of my divorcing her and starting again. The bank would not tolerate it. By contrast, the solicitors were all ex-public school men who behaved as if the world owed them a living and they were rarely disappointed.

Richard was different. I knew that his credentials were impeccable. He was public school but he had gone to Cambridge which showed me that he had a brain which he was prepared to use. He had all the superficial charm of his class but I felt that it marked a deep uncertainty and insecurity. He was asking for a modest and unsecured overdraft to open and develop his own practice. This of itself was unusual as his type characteristically cling together in large firms with long-standing, respectable reputations and take no risks. By contrast Richard clearly was prepared to take a chance. The question was whether I was prepared to back him. He produced a written business plan which had obviously been prepared for him by some clever economics graduate. I gave the appearance of perusing it carefully but I knew that if I lent money here I would be backing the man and not the plan. I thought quickly and decided to go ahead. That very morning I had received a circular from head office telling me that we needed more growth in our lending.

'OK,' I thought to myself, 'you asked for it and now you're getting it.'

***

RICHARD. Having the premises organised, everything else fell into place. The clients were more than happy to come with me

58

as were the managing clerks and their secretaries. The partners at first seemed unhappy that I was taking on a majority of their staff but harsh reality prevailed. I was actually reducing their salary bill for personnel for whom they had no work. I could not help laughing inwardly at the paradox that they had showed no emotion whatsoever at the announcement of my departure which was going to hit their pockets extremely adversely, while objecting vehemently to my news that I was following up by relieving them of the consequent burden of salaries for redundant personnel. No wonder that they were in such a financial mess.

A visit to the new office late at night was a revelation. It resembled a Cantonese shipyard. There were men up ladders and scaffolding. There were more men painting the walls and sanding the floors. There were electrical wires trailing everywhere. As work progressed on the offices, we bought second-hand furniture and office equipment at rock-bottom prices. Mei was a very tough negotiator. The same crew then set to work sanding, painting and polishing it.

We were ready to open for business three days before the anticipated completion date. I could not have done any of it without Mei. She asked for no reward but I noticed that she had moved permanently out of her room, which had become her study, into my bed. For the time being it was a very satisfactory arrangement but I knew it could not be long term. Did she? I tried to analyse why I felt our personal relationship could not last as her qualities in so many ways made her suitable to be my wife. I rejected the disgusting arguments put up by mother but I still felt nevertheless that I should eventually marry into my own class and culture. Mei was very westernised and I had used her touches of the exotic East a little shamelessly to ensnare my clients but I felt that deep down there was a gulf between us. I sensed it very much when one of her aunts came to visit us. To please Mei, I agreed to spend an evening with them. It was not the talk of family and friends unknown to me that put me off. I expected that, but it was more the unspoken assumptions drawing me into their close family circle and the aunt's disingenuous remarks about the children that she assumed Mei and I were about to have. I found myself developing an acute case of claustrophobia which was not helped by my feeling that Mei secretly was thinking along the same lines as her aunt and was gradually taking over my life.

The changeover from the old to the new firm was as nearly seamless as possible. Morale was high among the staff and the clients seemed delighted to have their work done by the new firm in its sparkling, fresh offices. Favourable comments were made about the oriental style and lightness of the décor. Mei Ling's influence was apparent everywhere. In fact, new work was coming in at an ever faster pace. Mei had submitted her thesis for consideration and consequently had time on her hands. I appointed her office manager and found her a room as her own private office. It was the best appointment short term that I ever made.

During the last three months I had neglected my client-gathering activities as I had been far too busy setting up the new firm. I now redoubled them. We added a small kitchen beside the new boardroom which was created by knocking together two of the former firemen's bedrooms. We also recruited part time a cordon bleu chef to cook lunches for potential new clients and those who might introduce them. I was not sleeping well as the enormity of what I had undertaken was now sinking in. Thanks to Mei's projections, I knew how much cash I needed to take in every month to keep the ship afloat. It was all set out in a schedule, the details of which were burned into my brain in figures of fire. I had the managing clerks to process some of the work but I was still doing a disproportionate amount myself. Moreover, I was responsible for bringing it all in. I felt like the stoker on the steam train desperately shovelling more and more coal into the mouth of the furnace to keep the train running. What I needed was time to myself to think about the strategic direction of the firm but there was no time.

The Gages were responsible for a dangerously large percentage of our turnover. They had proved wonderful clients but I worried about them leaving me or going out of business. This situation suddenly became even better or worse, depending on your point of view. One day, Larry came to see me to announce that he had decided to seek a re-quotation on the Stock Exchange and simultaneously raise a lot more capital to increase the size of the business. He assumed that I would handle the work and I did not tell him that it was well beyond my experience and capacity. Fortunately, I had maintained links with some of those with whom I had studied law at Cambridge and after. Two of the brightest of them were working in large City firms doing exactly this type of work, albeit in a subordinate capacity. I approached them and asked if they would like to 'moonlight' for me out of normal office hours and do the work for substantial fees in cash. They both agreed.

I was dining in a restaurant with my bank manager one Saturday evening and he was complaining what excessively short hours lawyers worked to make their substantial earnings. We finished the meal at nearly midnight and I drove him to the office. All the lights were blazing and not only were the two lawyers at work but three of the managing clerks were there as well, catching up on their backlog. He never complained about lawyers being lazy again.

The flotation was a great success and my enormous fee was paid by return. I was also given a substantial parcel of shares in the company. I gave both lawyers a bonus and was pleased to be asked out for a drink by them to celebrate. I should have guessed that there was an ulterior motive. John had a first in law at Cambridge while Fred had an upper second. Both degrees contrasted with my own miserable third but who was in the driving seat now? Drinks quickly transformed into job interviews with both asking to work for me full time as they were bored with their jobs in their big corporate firms. They had no clients of their own but I was confident, perhaps overconfident, that I could find them sufficient work of the right type and status to keep them busy. Thanks to the large fee just received, we were well ahead of our budget so there was something of a cushion while they became established. In addition, I had to recruit four more managing clerks and their secretaries to process the additional work coming from the Gages as they increased the lending of their bank. The landlord was happy to lease me extra offices and once again the place was alive all night with hammering, painting and polishing.

I liked occasionally to wander round the offices at night absorbing some of that well applied energy and then retiring to the comfortable swivel chair in my own room to think. On one occasion, the tiredness of the day overcame me and I fell into a deep sleep. I awoke, or so I thought, to see Sidney Bechet sitting in front of my desk just as any ordinary client would. He was surrounded by a cloud of dense and pungent smoke from the fat reefer that he held in his large hand. 'You have done well, boy, in this career you have chosen but is it the true life for Dick Gregory who can play jazz like an angel? Now listen to this.'

He whipped out his soprano sax and played me the opening chorus of *Sophisticated Lady* with heavy vibrato. I woke to find that I was much conflicted.

CHAPTER SEVEN

PUTTING ON THE RITZ

RICHARD. I always had great sympathy for my friends in the acting profession who never knew where their next job was coming from. It bred a sense of great insecurity. As the sole proprietor of a small but fast growing legal firm with regular bills to pay and only so much repeat business guaranteed, I felt similarly insecure. This feeling was increased at the firm's first Christmas party. As well as inviting the staff, I asked them to bring their wives, husbands or other appendages. Through the evening, I took stock of those around me and was overwhelmed by the thought of the sheer number of people, children added, who depended on me for their daily bread. It was a daunting responsibility.

I responded to it by beckoning to a rather tasty young secretary who had been giving me the eye for several weeks. When Mei's attention was distracted, I took her off to one of the empty and unlit offices. The door did not lock but I was in the mood to take a chance. She was a bit the worse for drink and completely cooperative. I lifted her up onto the desk, then we removed the essential garments and had an uncomplicated and very satisfactory screw. I gave her time to put herself back together and returned nonchalantly but on my own to the party. Nobody including Mei seemed to have noticed our absence. Why did I do it? Just because I could. It was a mixture of casual lust, a few drinks and the sense of power. I was exercising my *droit de seigneur*.

I had a surprise planned for the party which I was still not sure about. It involved bringing together the two separate parts of my life. While I had neglected the jazz playing side because of the need to build up the practice, I had the endorsement of the ghost of Sidney Bechet himself as to the quality of my playing. I was a little concerned that allowing the staff to see my wild other side might damage discipline, but I decided to risk it. I had hired a well-known jazz and folk singer and guitarist, Diz Disley, along with a bass player and drummer to entertain the party. I had also brought along my clarinet but I was still a little doubtful about playing, if only because I had practised hardly at all in the last year.

As soon as I heard the guitarist's opening chords, my doubts melted away and I produced my clarinet. I soon regained my confidence and the party went wild. Ted, the oldest managing clerk, was dancing an extraordinary jive with Tracey, the office junior. Everybody was joining in except for Mei Ling who stood on the side with an aloof expression on her face. Still, I was having far too good a time to worry about her and I continued to whip the party up to an ever greater frenzy with my red-hot playing. I could hear in my head the mellifluous tones of Sidney Bechet's soprano sax playing harmony and counterpoint to my lead. It was a good thing that the party was taking place in the office. There were no neighbours living near to complain and no restriction on the time we had to finish. The band and the dancers reached exhaustion simultaneously but there was no sign of Mei. I need not have worried about an adverse reaction from the staff. Morale after the party was sky high and they all seemed to view me with greater respect having seen that I had accomplishments outside the law.

***

MEI LING. There was an element of reckless and self-destructive stupidity in Richard's character that I found hard to understand. Everything was going so well with the new firm and also with our relationship. Our first Christmas party was supposed to be a celebration of all our achievements and he had to spoil it all by taking some little slut who had been making eyes at him all evening off to an empty office to do to each other who knows what.

Almost the hardest thing to bear for me was the insult to my intelligence that I was not aware of what was going on. Add to that the personal humiliation. Every office is a rumour factory and, while I did my best not to be obvious about our closeness, I did not fool myself that our out of office relationship was not the stuff of firm gossip. If he had been truly drunk, he might have had some excuse but he seized his opportunity almost as if it had been planned. Part of his plan might have been to send a brutal message to me. His behaviour that night made me finally realise that there was no long-term future in our partnership.

***

RICHARD. At my previous firm, I was constrained in what clients and work I looked for and accepted by the thought of the potential disapproval of the partners and staff combined with the fact that there was no pressing necessity. My ten per cent commission on the work foregone was never going to be all that much and I could soon make it up elsewhere. The situation was now very different. Driven as I was by my sense of insecurity, I felt that every penny counted. I no longer had any partners to keep me in check so I took risks.

There has always been a fringe element in the City and the members of it now beat a path to my door. To find a reasonably well established solicitor whose ethics were, shall we say, a little elastic, was a huge advantage. It was a bonus to find that the solicitor was also competent. It seems that elasticity and competence in this milieu rarely went together. I was not going to do anything so obvious as to jeopardise my hard-won practising certificate but I could often find ways of rejigging their nefarious enterprises to give them a cloak of seeming respectability. That was the case when I could understand their schemes and the objectives that they were seeking to achieve. Some of the proposals put to me were so fiendishly complex that they were way beyond my comprehension. If I went ahead and did as I was instructed, I was essentially flying blind. Needless to say, I never involved my lawyers, John and Fred, in these schemes. With their starchy City backgrounds, they would have run a mile.

One of the most elaborate schemes was put to me by two junior stockbrokers in one of the more blue-blooded firms. As they sat in my office in front of me, I was overwhelmed by the strobic effect of their attire. The broad chalk stripes of their well-cut suits were complemented by the broader multi-coloured stripes of their Jermyn Street shirts. Add the even wider diagonal stripes of their luminous silk ties and I reached for my sunglasses in order to retain my concentration and a semblance of sanity. The scheme they put to me involved the incorporation of no less than seventeen share dealing companies which I was to create and administer. Large parcels of government bonds were to be bought and sold between the various companies, creating artificial losses and gains partly depending on when interest was due to be paid on them. The timing of the transactions was all-important. The Inland Revenue was expected to repay large sums of tax on the notional losses even though no tax had been paid on the fictitious gains in the first place. I was comforted by the fact that no humans or animals were to be physically harmed by this business so I agreed with alacrity to act, especially when I was told the size of my fee which was entirely disproportionate to the small amount of work that I had to do. I shut my mind to the idea of being paid a premium for the risk undertaken.

***

TED. I had been looking after Richard from the first day that he joined the old firm as a wet behind the ears articled clerk. He soon found that what he had learned at the university was not of much use in the outside world. I saw that he had real promise so I took it upon myself to act as his mentor. The other partners looked down on us managing clerks and just treated us as underpaid dogsbodies to do their work for them. True, we had not had the advantage of a public school education but we had learned a great deal over the years in the school of hard knocks.

Richard was different. He absorbed everything I taught him like a sponge. When they made him a partner, his attitude towards us did not change one bit and I was happy to volunteer to do his work when he started bringing it in. When he announced that he was starting his own firm, some of the others had their doubts as he was still so young and inexperienced but I acted as his shop steward and persuaded them to join us.

What did worry me about Richard was a certain recklessness in the company he kept and the clients he took on. Because of our long time together, I very much had his ear and acted as his critic and sounding board but he was increasingly failing to take my advice. It was not a question of morality I assured him but merely of self-preservation. 'Some of these people are very clever and they will use you while they can and then spit you out when you have served their purpose,' I continually told him.

When you have spent your life working in the City as I have, you get to know who the villains are even though new ones are always coming up. I was sad to see too many well-known crooks in the client lists. Richard thought he was smart enough to control them but I had my serious doubts. I could still go into his office at any time and tell him what I thought, but he was no longer listening to me.

***

RICHARD. My more disreputable drinking associates from my jazz playing days had not forgotten me. Everybody needs a lawyer and they were no exception. As I have already indicated, I have a weakness or even a preference for low company and when Michael and Eileen Cassidy invited me and my chosen partner to be their guests for a weekend in Paris I gladly accepted. I had been working far too hard and needed a break. The Cassidys had started a window-cleaning business in Kensington. In fact they cleaned my windows in Lexham Gardens. Michael had been a boxer, wrestler and nightclub bouncer in Dublin before bringing his talents to London. He believed in the economic principle of monopoly. By conducting a reign of terror, he soon put all his window-cleaning competitors out of business, especially after one well publicised leg-breaking incident. Those who remained either worked for the Cassidys or paid them weekly 'insurance' money. They had recently diversified into mortgage broking and I was trying hard to keep them out of jail as their methods included taking large non-returnable advance fees irrespective of whether there was any chance of raising the required finance.

Nevertheless, they were charming company. Mei happened to be in Malaya that week visiting her parents so I invited the new receptionist whom I had recently hired, having chosen her especially for her looks and sexual promise, perhaps with such an opportunity in view.

***

MICHAEL. There were elements of Dick Gregory's character and behaviour that truly worried me. He was a brilliant lawyer who had got us out of trouble any number of times. We did not concern ourselves in Ireland about the class system as they do in England but even I could not ignore the vast gulf that existed between us in terms of education and profession generally. Eileen and I lived by our wits while Dick represented the establishment which was our natural prey. Why was he so happy to spend so much time in our company when he could be spending it with educated people of his own background? I needed to stop asking questions and just enjoy what we had, Dick's excellent company and friendship.

I also could not understand his attitude to women. Mei was a wonderful girl and a perfect partner in business and in life. She obviously adored him. Dick though took her for granted and continually hurt her. He was wasting his time now in chasing empty headed little Susan who worked for him as a receptionist. He should have remembered the old saying that my grandmother taught me – that you do not shit on your own doorstep or, if you do, not with those at the bottom of the pile.

Nevertheless, Dick was great company and when I came into possession, don't ask me how, of someone else's American Express card there was no question that Dick would be our first choice to join us on our trip to Paris even if we had to put up with Susan's vapid conversation.

***

RICHARD. We all met at the Golden Arrow platform at Victoria and the trip started promisingly with Michael ordering a magnum of the best champagne. As we reached Dover, Michael produced his American Express card like an ace from a hand of poker. While the waiter's back was turned, he casually announced that the card was stolen. I nearly choked on the last swallow from my glass. It seemed that the whole trip had been conceived and constructed around the stolen card. Michael could afford to be generous. He was not paying unless indeed his luck ran out and he was caught. He would then pay with his liberty as I feared would I.

I was very nervous accordingly throughout the weekend but Michael played the part of the wealthy Anglo-Irish aristocrat beautifully and no questions were ever asked. There must be something particularly erotic about the motion of boats and trains as by the time Susan and I checked in to our magnificent suite at the Ritz we were both ready to explode sexually. 'It can't go on as well as this,' she announced prophetically. We got up, dressed hurriedly and met the others in the dining room for a magnificent meal.

Michael had asked the concierge to book us the best table later that night at the Crazy Horse, although we were in competition with the hordes of lecherous Asian businessmen who seemed intent on undressing with their eyes the incredibly sexy performers who were already nearly naked, as well as creeping ever closer to photograph them with their long and phallic camera lenses. Predictably, after the show, Susan and I found that our batteries had been recharged and we enjoyed another magnificent sexual bout. Next morning, we woke simultaneously in the unfamiliar but luxurious surroundings and sunk into each other voluptuously yet again. It couldn't go on like this, as Susan had previously indicated. She detected a spot on her face and in no time she was covered all over in a nasty nervous rash. For the rest of the weekend she would not let me near her which gave me the chance to realise how dull and boring she was. Michael, always the perfect host, albeit with someone else's money, assessed the situation, took me on one side and offered to hire me a substitute. However there was no chance to put the plan into practice as Susan clung on unrelentingly throughout the rest of the weekend. I was never so glad to say goodbye to someone when we reached Victoria on the return.

Before then, Michael and Eileen ensured that we saw the best or at least the most expensive of Paris. Every lunch and dinner was at the finest restaurants. I felt sated with rich food and privately resolved to exist on a diet of baked beans and chips for weeks when we returned home. The Crazy Horse was followed the next night by the Moulin Rouge and then by the Pigalle. On each occasion we were treated like visiting royalty with Michael adding enormous tips to the bill, paid of course with the ubiquitous stolen American Express card. It is the mark of the true criminal to be unfazed by his actions. Michael never turned a hair. I, by contrast, a mere accessory after the fact, was a quaking lump of jelly each time he tendered the offending piece of plastic. I was not truly cut out for a life of crime.

CHAPTER EIGHT

HIGH SOCIETY

Once they had returned to London and her nervous rash had died down, the affair with Susan resumed. She had a room in a house off Gray's Inn Road and a deaf landlady. Susan kept normal office hours while Richard left much later as befitted the boss of the business. He would take a taxi to her place; they would normally go to a nearby pub for a couple of drinks and a pie and then back to bed for an hour or two. Mei said nothing, but she had resumed sleeping in her own room which was something of a relief as he was finding it difficult to give her the sexual attention that he thought she still needed.

The firm had reached its first year end and the figures were spectacularly good. Not all the profit was yet in the account but Richard went to see the bank manager with the draft accounts and borrowed the money to buy himself a fine but relatively old Rolls-Royce. He also bought a personalised number plate – RG1 – to go with it. He had read somewhere that when the chairman of a company adopts a personalised number plate it is the beginning of the end, but he knew that this could not possibly apply to him. He very much enjoyed driving around the City in his new glory. He felt that he had now arrived and really counted for something.

***

THE BANK MANAGER. I was pleased that my faith in lending to Richard had been justified and that the firm was doing so well. While his business plan had guaranteed nothing, these draft accounts showed all the signs of solid and serious success. However, I was disappointed how he chose to reward himself for that success. Every little East End scrap metal merchant who makes a bit of money wants to go out and buy a flash Roller to show his friends that he has arrived.

Richard should have been different. I looked up to him for his university education and the way he had seized his opportunities, but at rock bottom he was just another shallow spiv. None of that culture had rubbed off on him. He should have shown a bit more class and originality in how he behaved. At the end of the day, he was no better than the rest of them.

***

John and Fred had contributed substantially to the figures with their billings but Richard was disappointed to see that it was almost exclusively on his work. They had introduced almost no clients of their own. Nevertheless, to encourage them he put their names on the letterhead as salaried partners and increased the percentage of commission that they would receive on their own introductions. Richard Gregory & Co. now looked like a more substantial entity with the introduction of two more partners' names. Gage's Bank had also had a very good year and Larry told him that they were leasing a spectacular new banking hall in Lombard Street in the heart of the City. There was a spare floor above which he offered to Richard at a nominal rent. Richard was concerned that the world would see his firm merely as the in-house lawyers of the Gage group but, once he had satisfied himself that the offices were apart and with a separate entrance, he accepted the offer with gratitude.

One piece of adverse news in an otherwise perfect world was that Mei was leaving. She gave him three months' notice and announced that she had taken a similar job with a large law firm in Singapore. He knew that she was virtually irreplaceable and wondered whether he could have done more to keep her by a greater display of fidelity. He also realised that he should not have mixed business with pleasure. To some extent he had sensed Mei's feelings but not their intensity. Everything had been moving so fast and in such a concentrated fashion that he had had no time or opportunity to seek his sexual satisfaction in any other environment. His life had become a battlefield and Mei was just one of its casualties He resolved in future to be a little more relaxed about work and to build himself a social life outside the office.

Mei swiftly found a replacement to look after him at home. This was also a Chinese postgraduate student but a singularly ugly and unattractive one. In her own quiet way perhaps Mei was getting her revenge. Her last job for him was to supervise the move to their new offices which she accomplished brilliantly and smoothly so that the day-to-day work of the firm was hardly disturbed at all. She also helped him recruit a new office manager but he did not have the same faith in Percy that he had always had in her. Percy was the Victorian ideal of an office manager with his high starched collar and gold-rimmed pince-nez, but Richard felt that the firm ought to display a more modern image to the world.

***

MEI LING. Stupid, insensitive, hurtful Richard! He had no idea how he was destroying me. I felt that my influence over him was declining daily. I was fast becoming just another efficient functionary in one of the back offices of his firm. I was still living in Lexham Gardens, but doing my best to see that our paths crossed as little as possible.

I wrote to my former fiancé, Kim, whom I had completely neglected while my affair with Richard continued. He had not found anyone else and was happy to start life with me again. As a chartered accountant in an international firm, he was completely mobile and could join me anywhere. I knew how lucky I was to have such a devoted man in my life but he would never compare with Richard in so many respects.

I asked Richard for a reference which he absentmindedly gave me. I expected him to ask me why I wanted it but he was too busy to care. I was lucky enough to be chosen as office manager by one of the largest and best law firms in Singapore. I am sure my experience in London with Richard helped me get the job. Richard's reaction when I gave my notice was muted. I expected some show of emotion on his part. I was having great difficulty in controlling my own but there was little reaction from him.

I had to find someone as a replacement for myself at Lexham Gardens though the day-to-day work was now done by a daily cleaner. I have to say that I took particular delight in appointing the ugliest postgraduate Chinese student that I could find. I was far more concerned as to who would take over my role as office manager. I conducted the search in conjunction with Richard but there was no longer any spark in our working together. We chose Percy as the best of a bad bunch. He was the classic elderly retainer from the old-fashioned style of law firm. He did not really fit the youthful and progressive image that Richard was seeking to convey but he had the right experience, good references and seemed honest and capable.

***

It was not difficult for Richard to create a new social life. On the face of it, he was a very eligible bachelor. He engineered himself an invitation to a weekend house party in the country and after that the invitations followed regularly. The object of these parties was quite clear; suitable mates were required for the daughters of the wealthy. He soon learned the rules. Virginity was still largely prized so flirtation leading to heavy petting was in order but he must not try to go too far. This was all rather frustrating for someone used to total fulfilment and Susan during the week was pleasantly surprised by his increased ardour. There were rumours about a few girls who were branded as 'fast' and went all the way but he did not initially have the good fortune to come across any of them.

By coincidence, he first met Heather at the Gages' new country mansion. They had spent their first year's profits as a bank by buying a superb Georgian palace in Wiltshire. Richard was invited for the weekend to celebrate the purchase. Heather was just one of a number of eligible young county girls present. In general he was becoming a trifle jaded at the repetitive and mundane nature of their conversation coupled with the ritualistic form of the pseudo-courtship routine. He longed for the serenity and experience of the type of older woman on whom he had honed his sexual skills. He could not see that Heather initially differentiated herself from the pack or had very much to offer. She was average in height and in every other way with fairly attractive features and dark blonde hair cut in a fashionable bob. She seemed happy to twitter with the other starlings.

He was wrong. He had met his very first 'fast' girl. She was hot in every sense. She radiated pure energy and he felt it from the moment that they had their first conversation together on a one-to-one basis. She was burdened, if that is the right word, with an extreme sexuality which she found difficult to control. In certain circumstances, she would have been branded as a nymphomaniac. She saw something in Richard that she did not see in the other men present. Of course they indulged in the usual pointless and polite conversation but they were eyeing and assessing each other continually on a completely different level. There was definitely a hidden agenda. He found himself involuntarily becoming as aroused and hot was he knew her to be.

**

HEATHER. If it were not for my parents' wealth and reputation, I would long ago have been dropped from that set. Scandal seemed to follow me everywhere. The trouble was that I was too sexy for my own good. I had developed the 'itch' between my legs at a very early age. At boarding school, I could never concentrate because I spent half the night playing with myself. As a result, I was not much good at sport and did badly in exams. When the other girls caught up with me sexually, we played a lot of games together in bed at night until we were caught by one of the mistresses. I only avoided being expelled because Daddy by a strange coincidence – Ha! Ha! – was persuaded to pay for the new science block and I was given a bedroom on my own apart from the other girls. What the headmistress did not realise was that she was giving me a great opportunity. The only man in the place was the head gardener. He looked old and past it but I caught a gleam in his eye when he looked at my tits which were developing nicely. It wasn't difficult to make a date and drag him up to my room. The fact that I was well underage worried neither of us. I didn't bother about condoms in those days and after a few weeks of nightly sex the inevitable happened. Mummy arranged a discreet and expensive abortion for me in Harley Street and I never went back to that school. Mummy also gave me an early Christmas present: a diaphragm. Once bitten, twice shy!

The problem was that nice girls didn't. This girl did and wanted to do it all the time. Most of the boys were useless and as scared of knocking up some girl as the girl herself. I did screw a few quite satisfactory fathers who got my message but the risk of being found out was enormous. I did not suffer from class prejudice where satisfaction of my sexual need was concerned. There was a series of butlers, footmen and others. However careful we were, rumours started to fly around.

At home, it was worse. Mummy and Daddy were sick and tired of me dragging home unsuitable men whom Daddy wanted to horsewhip. My only criterion for selection seemed to be the possession of a stiff cock – and then I saw Richard.

He was tall, dark, perhaps a bit too dark, and handsome. I had seen him arriving in his Rolls-Royce and his clothes hung well on him. There was an inner intensity and also an outward appearance of relaxation about him. I instantly melted when he turned his eyes on me. This man knows how to satisfy a girl, I thought to myself. I'm going to marry him.

***

He sat next to her at dinner and tried not to touch her. He could see that she was making a similar effort as any physical contact would have been too much. She told him where to find her room and then made her excuses to the hosts, pleading a headache. Richard left the table as soon as discretion allowed. He tapped on her door but it was already ajar. She was naked except for a red bandanna wound round her head. They ripped his clothes off and fell onto the bed. There was no need for any preliminaries. The last two hours were nothing if not foreplay. She was so wet and open that he could not feel very much inside her. However, they were both so fired up that they came simultaneously in a great burst of fireworks. Their exhausted collapse was short and they were soon stroking each other again as a prelude to the second round. This was more measured and relaxed, though equally purposeful. He employed some of the tricks of the trade on her and he had never before had a woman who was so receptive and responsive to them.

This time their orgasms were not simultaneous. In fact they were long and deeper and in her case multiple as a result of the initial release of sexual tension. After two such explosions, the tiredness of the week was beginning to catch up with him and he was ready for sleep but the urgent little fingers on his thigh indicated that more was required of him. Her insistent mouth soon brought him to life again. As ever, he was responsive to a woman's needs. This time, his orgasm would have been mere routine if he had not experienced her animal excitement which had an inspirational effect on him. He now did need to sleep but it was not to be for long.

It was the Bechet dream again. Richard had offered his clarinet to Sidney, who was playing an increasingly beautiful tune on it. The dream gradually faded, to be replaced by reality. It was not his clarinet which was being played and it was Heather's rather than Sidney's lips and tongue that were drawing forth such a magic response. She was in the middle of a slow and languorous blues but her tempo soon quickened to end in a magnificent crescendo.

The rest of the night passed in a haze of exhausted rest followed by ever more frantic action. He did not know how many times he came. It reached a point where the effort became too painful and he was physically sore. He now knew how women sometimes felt. She still wanted more and his mouth and fingers were fully sufficient to keep her happy. It was amazing that she in her turn did not get sore like most women he had known but continued throughout the night to produce copious floods to keep her lubricated, particularly during orgasm when it was ejaculation after ejaculation. At last, they both fell into an exhausted sleep which lasted until nearly lunchtime. He was saved by the fact that she had a family engagement at home in the afternoon and he dragged himself back to London in the Rolls, looking forward to enjoying a few days of celibacy, though he believed that he had not seen the last of Heather.

CHAPTER NINE

TEA FOR TWO

RICHARD. I was sitting at home the following Thursday evening with papers strewn all over the dining-room table. I was working on an important case due to be heard in the High Court the following week. Physically, I felt completely drained and every muscle still ached. Nevertheless, I could not restrain the occasional smile when I thought about the extraordinary antics of last weekend. I had told Susan that I could not see her while I was working on the case. Making love to Susan, if I could manage it at all, would be like eating a sandwich after a banquet.

Suddenly the doorbell rang. I was expecting nobody and it was Teng's evening off. I went to the door. There stood Heather, quietly demure in an elegant frock and a nice little pink hat. Her smile was a bit nervous but it radiated confidence. She was clutching what looked like a weekend bag in her gloved hand. It hadn't been difficult for her to get my address from our hosts of last weekend but I chided her for failing to telephone me first. She answered that she thought I might not want to see her again because of her forward behaviour. She had obviously had previous bad experiences. I assured her that I was very glad to see her and gave her a small demonstration of just how glad I was.

She told me that she would like to stay the weekend. I answered that I had to go to the office tomorrow and spend time on paperwork on Saturday and Sunday. The former was no problem she assured me, as tomorrow she was meeting Mummy who was coming up to town to go shopping while the latter was not too difficult as she would be quiet as a mouse. Digressing for a moment, I had always previously hated girls who referred to their mother as 'Mummy' as if nobody else had one not forgetting those inanimately lying swathed in their sarcophagi in the British Museum. However, coming from Heather it sounded rather sweet, as did later references to 'Daddy' where I usually had a similar objection. She was having tea with Mummy at Fortnum's and asked if I would care to join them. Clearly Mummy wanted to give me the once over and I made no objection.

We had both eaten and as I had done enough on the papers for the time being it was bedtime. Despite Saturday night or perhaps because of it Heather was extremely sexually hungry and so to my surprise was I. During that night, I taught her the tricks of the Bangkok brothel and I found her an excellent and enthusiastic pupil, almost too enthusiastic on some occasions as I had to warn her against excessive use of her sharp little teeth. She appreciated that I had to work the next day so our activities were not too prolonged. I woke first and she looked very attractive spread wantonly and stark naked on the crumpled sheets. I could not resist the temptation to taste her. There is something wildly erotic about the taste and aroma of the stale and mingled juices from the previous night's lovemaking with someone to whom you are very attracted. Conversely, with a woman with whom you are only casually involved it can be a complete turn off. In this case, I became very aroused. Heather slowly woke and joined completely in the spirit of things. I had to keep one eye on the clock. She rose sweetly and padded naked into the kitchen to cook me some breakfast. This she did very obligingly but rather incompetently. Apparently it was always done by servants at the 'Hall'.

***

AMELIA. I was dreading meeting Heather's latest man. I had been a bit wild myself as a young girl but I had had the good sense to make an excellent marriage with Arthur. The problem was that Arthur indulged her totally. With him she could do no wrong, although he was very fierce with the motley crew of unsuitable men whom she persisted in dragging home. She seemed to have no sense of what we expected of her as the only child of rich and well established parents. Hers was to be a sizeable inheritance and neither Arthur nor I wanted to see it thrown away on some down at heel fortune hunter who happened to tickle her fancy.

I took time to fathom out Richard. He was not one of the county set though he was not out of place within it. He was very much a self-made man, as of course was Arthur when I first met him. He was a bit too smooth and anxious to please for my liking. He was clearly deeply attracted to Heather. You could see it in his eyes every time he looked at her. She was the same but I wondered whether this was the basis for a long and stable marriage once the initial sexual thrill wore off. For reasons outside my control, Heather had not had the education that I would have liked for her. Richard by contrast was a Cambridge graduate and a solicitor. I decided that was their problem to work out. She wanted to marry him as she always did with the man of the moment. This one was better than the others. Let her get on with it was my view, for fear of the next one being worse.

***

RICHARD. Lady Anson was everything that I expected. She was an extremely large pillar of the local Conservative Party, the Church and the Women's Institute. In fact, no serious female activity took place in her corner of Somerset without at least her tacit approval. I might have expected a cool and questioning approach but she was surprisingly warm and friendly to me. Afterwards, I was able to put two and two together and realise that, following a long line of wildly unsuitable men produced for scrutiny, I was the first to pass muster even moderately and was therefore the designated suitor, once Heather had expressed her choice. The mother was well aware what a hot little property her daughter was and how driven she was by her extreme sexuality. I wondered idly for a moment whether she inherited her talent from her mother but I could not see it. For a moment, I considered whether Heather might start to resemble her mother sooner or later but I dismissed the idea. I ticked enough boxes socially, financially and

81

professionally while clearly being able to keep her happy in bed.

I was looking forward very much to spending the following two days in London with Heather. I was not disappointed. I completed my work, we made love often and with increasing fervour, toured London as tourists and talked. Since Mei had left I had had nobody in whom to confide my hopes and fears. It was a great relief now to unburden myself. Heather was a first rate listener. She had followed the conventional educational path for girls of her position, so she told me, including Swiss finishing school and secretarial college in London. She had always been burdened by her obsession with sex which she had first discovered by herself at the age of eight. Constant masturbation meant that she was always tired and behind with her studies. Then followed various lesbian flings until she was willingly deflowered Lady Chatterley style by the elderly gardener in her fourth form year. She quickly acquired a taste for the rigid penis and was in and out of trouble for the rest of her educational career. She was superficially well educated but there was no depth to it. For example, she had a superb French accent but little French vocabulary.

We talked about her family and Daddy in particular. She was an only child and her father was fiercely but impotently protective of her. Lady Anson had several times stood in the way to prevent one or other unsuitable boyfriend sustaining a horsewhipping at his hands. Sir Arthur was now one of the great men of the City. A self-made man, he was big in finance, investment and insurance while sitting on the board as chairman or at least as a non-executive director of any number of prestigious public companies. It was only a question of time before his peerage followed. I realised that if he was so minded he could advance my career tremendously. This was only a very minor reason for my continued courtship of Heather. Primarily, I was fascinated and enchanted by her sexual responsiveness.

During the week, I was not surprised to receive a telephone call from Lady Anson – or Amelia, as I was urged to call her – inviting me down for the weekend. The case went very well so I was in a euphoric mood as I motored down on Friday evening in the usual slow traffic. The Hall made the Gages' place look like a garden shed. I was shown to my single room. Heather had already warned me that we would have to exercise much discretion over the weekend so I was looking forward to making love outdoors.

We dressed for dinner and fortunately I had been told to pack my dinner jacket. The butler who took me to my room informed me that I was expected sharp at 6.30 pm in Sir Arthur's study. I had seen his picture spread enough times across the financial press not to be surprised how the appearance echoed the achievements of the man. He was the very embodiment of the successful modern capitalist. His eyes pierced right through me as he shook my hand in a strong grip and then returned to sit in his large leather swivel chair behind his enormous antique desk. I was left standing in front of him as there was no chair for me. I would have seated myself even unbidden but I made the best of a bad job and stood there as relaxed as possible while he picked up one of his telephones and entered into a detailed and interminable conversation with his broker about selling some unwanted Japanese shares. I was immediately taken back to one of the many fraught interviews with my headmaster at school. I distracted myself with lascivious thoughts of the last time that Heather and I had made love.

I was brought back sharply from my reverie by a sudden question from Sir Arthur barked at me in parade ground fashion: 'What makes you think that you are better than all the others and fit to marry my daughter?'

I would not say that it was a completely coherent and persuasive answer but I put together a fairly comprehensive reply without blowing my own trumpet excessively.

'If I let you marry her, which at the moment seems very unlikely, you'll find she's a hot-arsed little bitch. Are you up to it?'

This was a change of tactics that I had not anticipated.

'I would do my best to make your daughter happy in every possible way,' was the best I could manage.

He seemed reasonably satisfied by my reply.

'If I were to let you marry my daughter, you could expect no help from me.'

He named his lawyers, two of the top firms in the City, who

would continue to receive all his legal work come what may. A condition of any marriage would be my entering into a marriage settlement under which I would receive not one penny if the marriage ended prematurely. He clearly saw me as a worthless opportunist and gold-digger, an opinion which I used at least partly to hold myself but had begun to discard based on my recent success in a world not all that far removed from that which Sir Arthur inhabited. He now turned his attention from me to his bank of telephones so I assumed that our encounter was over and left the room without another word. On reflection, I reckoned that our contest ended in a tie without extra time being played. I felt that the penalty shootout was yet to come.

***

ARTHUR. Oh God, I thought. Here comes another one. I was sick and tired of Heather bringing home totally unsuitable young men to meet me. She had been well indoctrinated by her mother as to her place in the marriage stakes and each successive little twerp was supposed to ask me for her hand in marriage. I never used to let them get that far but kicked them out of my room before they could get to the question. This one was a bit different. My view was that it was too early for Heather to marry. She was far too immature and needed more time at home. Besides having her around was a delight.

I liked the fact that he was not put off by my direct approach. I had done my homework as usual and knew he was a reasonably successful lawyer with his own practice who would give his back teeth to get his hands on some of my legal work. I told him he had no chance and I liked the way that he took it from me and stood up to me. He was not the usual snivelling fortune hunter. After I had dismissed him, I thought it over. If Heather was to get married and Amelia's pressure to achieve that object was unceasing she could do a lot worse than Richard Gregory.

***

RICHARD. Partly to spite him, as I knew he detested the thought of me as his son-in-law, with the sun shining on my naked back, in a grassy hollow and Heather spreadeagled under me, immediately after our mutual orgasms, I proposed to her. She instantly and joyfully accepted. Lady Anson expressed delight while Sir Arthur grudgingly accepted the inevitable. The date was set by mother and daughter for a few months away in the local church. There was no reason to delay and I comforted myself with the thought that henceforth we need not bother with any form of contraception and the diaphragm was ritually consigned to the top shelf of the bathroom cabinet. Heather stayed with me in London again the following weekend and I took her to one of London's best-known jewellers to buy her a ridiculously expensive engagement ring. I now had the opportunity to heal the split with my mother. Since the unpleasant row over Mei Ling and the possibility in my mother's mind that I might marry Mei, we had hardly spoken. I drove Heather up to meet her with no idea as to what reception we would receive. I need not have worried. We were greeted with open arms. I had often found my mother's obvious snobbery irksome but here it smoothed the path to acceptance. The fact that Heather's parents were titled was the key to an effusive welcome. From doing no right, I had become the son who could do no wrong.

***

BELINDA. When Richard telephoned to say that he was bringing his fiancée to meet me, at first I was upset that he had made the decision to get married without referring to me. I then remembered our last terrible row and I could understand. He told me a bit about Heather's background and as soon as the call was finished I popped down to the public library and checked out the Anson family for myself. I was delighted by what I read and so happy that my son had found a truly suitable bride. I welcomed them both and was looking forward to going up to London to buy my outfit for the wedding. I was slightly worried about how I would be received by Heather's family as a person of mixed race. I reckoned that they were sufficiently grand not to worry about such things. I was absolutely delighted to be proved completely right. I never felt the slightest embarrassment in my dealings with them in that regard.

***

AMELIA. Heather had warned me that Richard's mother was of mixed blood. Of course, that partly accounted for Richard's good looks, although you would never have guessed his heritage from looking at him. I was a little worried that the Indian strain might be more obvious in the next generation. I discussed my misgivings with Arthur who told me not to be a damn fool. With Heather's track record, we were lucky not to be saddled with a raving fuzzy-wuzzy. As it was, as is so often the case with her type, Belinda tried far too hard to be more English than the English. She was definitely not going to be a problem and it helped that she lived so far away in the Midlands. We would not be seeing a lot of her after the wedding.

***

ARTHUR. I might have guessed that Amelia would come up with some sort of stupid nonsense before the wedding. She found out that Richard has a touch of the tar brush. To be precise, his mother was half Indian or something like that. Having spent some time in India myself and met and fucked a few of the Anglo-Indian women, I had no problems whatever with the situation. They were usually very beautiful and I fancied that our grandchildren would benefit from the strain. I told Amelia to shut up and not be so silly. When I met Belinda at the wedding, I saw how right I was and enjoyed dancing with such a good-looking woman.

***

RICHARD. From then until the wedding day, apart from time spent in bed whenever we could, I did not see much of Heather,

86

who was busily planning the wedding with her mother. All I had to do was choose the best man and ushers together with the relatively small number of guests that I was permitted to invite. The choice of best man and ushers was not too hard as I could select from old friends at Cambridge, but my guest list was very difficult. I first wrote out all the potential names, then crossed them off in ever increasing numbers. So many of my close friends and associates were entirely unsuitable to be invited to a county wedding. For example, I could not trust Michael and Eileen Cassidy to resist the temptation of selecting a choice piece of the family silver as a souvenir of the occasion. As a result, my list was rather short.

They had chosen a fine day for the wedding. The sun shone and I sweated heavily in my Moss Bros hired finery though it could have been from nerves as well. I knew no more than thirty per cent of those present and a sense of alienation was steadily creeping over me. Heather looked conventionally beautiful in her lace dress, white of course, and carefully designed to conceal the slight swell of her three months' pregnancy. Yes, ceasing to use contraception had had predictable results. Sir Arthur bore up well, though if you caught his countenance in repose, it carried an expression of ferocious disappointment. Lady Anson was in her element and as I continued to swill the vintage champagne I had the ridiculous thought that she was some sort of pagan priestess and I was her human sacrifice. My mother, characteristically, was behaving in a sickeningly snobbish manner, but nobody seemed to mind.

The best man's speech was sufficiently near the knuckle to make Sir Arthur look as if he had swallowed a red hot chilli pepper. Frankly, I do not remember a word of it. I did my duty ritually by dancing relatively in rhythm with Heather, her mother and my mother. Then, taking exception to the pedestrian playing of the clarinet player in the expensively hired orchestra, I seized his instrument from him and proceeded to lead the all too willing musicians in a wild melange of styles from Benny Goodman to Artie Shaw to Barney Bigard to Johnny Dodds to Jimmy Noone and, above all, my hero and object of my dreams, the great Sidney

Bechet. In an off-guard moment, I caught a glimpse of Sir Arthur's face. He actually seemed to be enjoying himself and I almost felt a bond of sympathy between us

***

ARTHUR. I was delighted to find that there was so much more to my new son-in-law than I had anticipated. When I saw him guzzling my champagne, I feared the worst, though I had a pang of sympathy for him, trapped as he was in the jaws of the social nutcrackers with which my wife and daughter were squeezing him. I was anticipating an undignified collapse under the table but I was very pleasantly surprised when he leaped onto the bandstand and grabbed the clarinet from the lips of the player whom I had hired at considerable expense and who up to that point had been playing syrupy muck. I had always loved jazz and one of my great pleasures in life when I was home was to get away from the chatter of the women who surrounded me and seek refuge in my record collection.

Richard clearly was very drunk but it in no way affected his playing which was of the highest professional standard. I knew from my enquiries that he was a pretty good lawyer but this was something different. For the first time since I handed the caterers their enormous cheque, I was enjoying myself. I was sorry when Richard eventually collapsed at about midnight as I had agreed with the band leader to pay for them to continue playing beyond the scheduled close for an extra fee.

I did not envy Richard when he had his next encounter with Heather, my wife, or his equally formidable mother. There'll be a hot time in the old town tonight! He had disgraced himself totally but I loved every minute of it!

***

RICHARD. I collapsed finally, I am told, at about midnight. My sleep was disturbed by yet another Bechet dream. He was smiling broadly at me and indicating his approval.

'That's what those high society cats need, a bit of jazz in their bones to shake 'em up.'

The wedding night, spent in the bridal suite of a nearby hotel, was a total washout. I recall waking at one point to find Heather masturbating frantically beside me but I was too far gone to join in. We were hardly speaking the next day as we were driven to Heathrow and flown to Nice for our honeymoon at the Carlton in Cannes. I had a monstrous hangover and all I wanted to do was sleep. At least Heather spared me floods of tears and I did my best to close my ears to her icy sarcasm.

'Is this going to become a regular event and should I instruct the maids in future to leave a plastic bucket by your side of the bed?'

CHAPTER TEN

OUR LOVE IS HERE TO STAY

He had a lot of ground to make up with Heather after his display at the wedding. Their corner suite at the Carlton was huge and incredibly luxurious, with fresh flowers everywhere. It had two bedrooms. On the first night, they slept apart using one each. The sun shone and the sea sparkled seductively across the road from their enormous picture windows. To her credit, Heather soon came round and they both started to enjoy themselves. They spent most of the day on the beach, being careful not to soak up too much sun. The normal rule on the hotel's beach is that as newcomers you are given deckchairs in the rear rank and gradually move forward as time passes and those in front move on. A large tip to the attendant ensured that from the outset they were seated in the front row, dabbling their toes in the sea. They both swam inexpertly but could not fail to enjoy the experience. Deep massages in the health club ensured that they were ready to guzzle the champagne nestling in its ice bucket in their sitting room. He carried his bride over the threshold into the main bedroom and they at last consummated their marriage with great mutual enjoyment. Without realising it, the sexual tension had been building up over the last few days so both experienced a feeling of enormous release followed by huge euphoria. They were also very hungry.

Room service was swift and the oysters and lobsters they had ordered, washed down with a vintage chilled white burgundy, had an aphrodisiac effect. They did what honeymoon couples are supposed to do and went back to bed. Over the next two weeks, they swam and sunbathed, made love, explored the restaurants of Cannes big and small, shopped and particularly window-shopped on the Croisette and in the Rue D'Antibes, hired a car and drove up into the hills, bought glass in Biot and perfume in Grasse. A jarring note was struck in Monte Carlo. Heather, who had never had to earn a penny in her life, enjoyed the gambling in the casino and lost far too much money. By contrast, Richard, who had had to earn his own living from an early age, could not bring himself to throw good money away, as he saw it. He preferred to watch in fascination the habitual gamblers at work, particularly the elderly dowagers whose concentration would not have been broken if a bomb had exploded in the square outside. He realised how great were the cultural differences between Heather and himself and how hard he would have to work to bridge the gap.

The return to London was an anti-climax. He had assumed that the Lexham Gardens flat would be their matrimonial home but Heather and her mother had other ideas. They moved into her family's grand and gloomy apartment in one of those large red brick and terra cotta Dutch-style houses in Hans Crescent behind Harrods in Knightsbridge. As far as the family was concerned, it was surplus to requirements as Lady Anson rarely stayed the night now in London while Sir Arthur preferred his company flat in the City. Richard was worried that the rent would be astronomic but he was assured by his mother-in-law that it was a wedding gift. He felt a little like a kept man but on reflection decided that he rather enjoyed the status.

They were seeing a lot of Amelia. In fact, communication between mother and daughter seemed constant. Rarely an hour went by without them talking on the telephone. He was finding it irritating and he was also horrified at the thought of the phone bills to come. The scheme of the moment was the preparation of the nursery for their forthcoming arrival. It amused him that they would have to wait for the final painting until it was actually born as its sex would control the ultimate colour. Then again there was the booking of a suitable nanny. He sat in on the interview with the first battle-axe to appear but then decided that his time could be better employed in earning the money to pay her no doubt exorbitant salary.

Recent events had led to him to spending far less time at work than before but he was very pleased how well things had gone in his absence. Strangely enough, the move to better offices in Lombard Street had attracted an entirely superior class of clients. His firm was now acting for more and larger companies rather than working for individuals. He reflected on the stupidity of man in concentrating on the outward appearance while the quality of the service was no better than it had been before. There was also a subtle change in the nature of the personnel delivering the legal services. Several of the managing clerks were approaching retirement and he made no attempt to replace them on a like-for-like basis but was in process of recruiting bright, young, qualified lawyers who had been trained in the City and were impatient with the hierarchical structure of their large firms. The quality of the type of work was also improving. They were getting more City-style corporate and banking jobs. He now felt sufficiently relaxed about the forward momentum of the firm to be more careful in choosing the new clients and work that they were prepared to undertake. He had also increased the fees that they were charging and this had the effect of encouraging certain of their older clients whose work was no longer economic to seek less expensive legal representation elsewhere.

Their social life was also undergoing considerable changes. Amelia had prepared a self-contained suite for them at the Hall and they were expected there at weekends unless they had special arrangements in town or elsewhere. He found the life of a part-time country gentleman rather appealing. His tailor ran him up a few sets of tweeds and he enjoyed walking the grounds. You would never get him on a horse, despite his previous membership of a famous cavalry regiment, as the horse and he had a long-standing and mutual antipathy. However, he enjoyed resuming shooting, although the type of gun used and the nature of the target were very different from his previous experiences in Malaya. The pub in the village, the Coach and Horses, ran a nice little jazz session on Saturday nights. The band lacked a good clarinet player and the village considered it quite a coup that the young gentleman from the Hall had become its leader.

In London, Heather took to organising regular dinner parties which in their turn ensured that they were invited back to their guests' homes for similar events. The problem was the boring nature of those attending and especially their conversation. Initially, he tried mixing in a few of his friends but they stuck out like sore thumbs. He gently suggested that they could use their dinner parties to help his firm's marketing activities but Heather dismissed the idea as vulgar. She had a network of fellow displaced county folk who considered that they were still living in the country even though they spent at least five days out of seven in the town. The women all seemed to be former pupils of a small group of girls' public schools, better known for their social value rather than their academic achievements. The men were from that stratum at their public schools where there was no question of them having a chance of a university education. On one occasion, he tentatively introduced the subject of music into the conversation. Nobody showed the slightest interest. In the middle of the noisy and inane chatter he often felt very lonely even if he sometimes castigated himself as an intellectual snob.

He was pleased and surprised to receive a letter from Mei Ling in Singapore. The job was going well and she had married Kim, her former fiancé, who had joined her there. They were having a delayed honeymoon and planned to spend a few days in London. Richard told Heather and suggested that they have them to dinner in the Knightsbridge flat. With practice, Heather had become a reasonably competent if unimaginative cook but she flatly refused to cook for, as she put it, 'one of Richard's former tarts'. They had a big argument but for once Richard would not back down completely. He compromised by bringing in the chef from the office to provide and serve the meal. It was a difficult evening.

***

MEI LING. I was so much looking forward to seeing Richard in his new home. I knew he had married well but my first impressions of Heather were not favourable. I made allowance for the fact that she was pregnant and probably not at her best but she struck me as a typical spoiled, undereducated and snobbish child from the southern counties with nothing very much to recommend her. I had met a few of the cleverer examples of this type at the London School of Economics but this woman had neither brains nor any particular beauty. I assumed that Richard had not married her for her money. He had no need to, as I knew that the practice was going well. It had to be, knowing Richard, due to some initial and extreme sexual attraction which looked as if it was already fast fading.

My feelings surprised me but I felt sorry for him. He had made a bad choice. I could not see her in any way contributing to the success of his practice. All she would ever do was spend his money, and would she stand by him if things went wrong? Somehow, I doubted it. I contrasted all this with the life Richard and I could have had together. Ours would have been a genuine and progressive partnership on all levels. I was happy with Kim and would not now wish to make a change, but life could have been so exciting and different if only Richard had been able to see what was in front of his nose.

***

HEATHER. I hated Mei Ling from the moment that she entered my flat. Of course, Richard had told me about all his previous lovers just as I had told him about some of mine, but certainly not all. I did not trust her one bit. Kim, her husband, was nothing but a washed out little wimp of a man, much older than her. I could see her casting her oriental eyes on my Richard and wishing that she could take my place. She showed off by talking about Richard's business. Boring as hell. I never could be bothered to understand it. So long as Richard brought home the money, how he earned it was of no interest to me. I sulked for much of the evening. Mummy had warned me about the power that former lovers can still have over men. Here it was hard to miss. I was very wary of her. Thank God the evening at last came to an end. At least in bed Richard was all mine and not hers. That night I made sure I drained him of everything that he had to give.

***

He had heard of men being put off sex with their wives during pregnancy. On the contrary, he found Heather increasingly desirable with her ever more swollen breasts and stomach. Fortunately, pregnancy made her even more randy. They had to avoid certain positions but this led to some most inventive and satisfying alternatives. The problem was that the baby never seemed to arrive. There were any number of false alarms, followed by mad dashes to the very expensive and fashionable nursing home that her mother had chosen for the great occasion but each time they returned home with the baby getting ever bigger, still inside Heather. Richard arrived home one evening starving hungry to find Heather for once on her own at home with no food in the kitchen. She was as usual clutching her stomach and complaining that the contractions were well under way. He had heard that story too many times before so insisted that they get a taxi to his favourite Indian restaurant on Old Brompton Road. Half way through a particularly delicious biryani, he looked up to see that Heather was not eating but had gone very pale and was suffering quite violent contractions. He quickly called for the bill and they dashed outside to find a taxi to get them to the nursing home in time. When they arrived, Heather was rushed away and his job was to phone Amelia who arrived amazingly quickly, almost as if she had been hanging around outside waiting for the call. She radiated disapproval at Richard's callousness in putting the needs of his stomach before those of his wife's. When Heather was being prepared for the birth she was asked when she last had intercourse.

'Just a minute: let me look at my watch. It was after lunch when I was feeling in the mood so I phoned Richard to come home for a quickie. I suppose it was about six hours ago.'

Amelia marched in to her daughter's room to be an active presence at the birth while he was left in the waiting room. Just as she passed out of his sight through the swing doors she turned her head and barked at him: 'Just wait there until you are called.'

He spent endless hours perusing tired copies of the *Tatler* and *Country Life*. When he was eventually admitted into the flower-stacked room, he was enchanted by the little bundle that was their daughter, Isabelle, and felt an enormous surge of love and gratitude for Heather, lying sweaty and exhausted on her bed.

It was fortunate that they occupied a large flat. Not only did they need space for the hastily pink painted nursery and the nanny with her bedroom and private sitting room, but Amelia had taken up seemingly permanent residence. The new order at home was not much to his liking. He seemed to be separated from his new daughter by defensive and concentric rings of doting women. There was of course Heather herself who seemed to be continually breastfeeding. Then there was the new nanny, extremely broad of beam who radiated disapproval towards him, whether personally or as a representative of the male sex he neither knew nor cared. Lastly and most discouragingly of all, there was Amelia herself who seemed to occupy vast areas of space around mother and child as she fluttered about being eternally helpful. Nobody had a moment to spare for the father and he felt totally surplus to requirements and without a role to play in his personal exclusion zone.

***

BELINDA. I had been happy that Richard had married into such a good family but now I was realising that there were disadvantages as well as the obvious social benefits. As no invitation to see my granddaughter was forthcoming, I invited myself up to London. I had telephoned and spoken to Heather's mother. Her response had not encouraged me.

'How lovely to hear from you. It would be wonderful to see you but I just don't know how on earth we are going to fit you in.'

There was no room for me in the lovely flat that Richard and Heather occupied but this was hardly surprising with the new nanny and everything else going on. I noticed that Lady Amelia was firmly settled there and very much in charge. I would not say she was rude but she gave the appearance of being so busy that she had no time for me. I felt sorry for Richard. He clearly doted on Isabelle but he was hardly allowed near her. It was as if, having done his duty in fathering the child, he was now no longer required. After a week in an expensive hotel, I went home with a heavy heart. I did not think that I would be seeing too much of my granddaughter and I realised that there was a price to pay for marrying into the upper classes. Richard to his credit did his best to keep me informed and regularly sent me photographs of Isabelle and later William as well.

***

As there seemed to be no role for him at home, he took refuge in the office and in work. He understood that the birth had been difficult and that Heather would be sexually off limits for a considerable time. On the other hand, Susan the receptionist was looking particularly attractive. When he had started seeing Heather he had arranged for Percy, the office manager, to give Susan a substantial salary increase as compensation for her exceptional performance. He knew he could be accused of pensioning off his surplus mistress but she was also a particularly efficient receptionist and a number of clients had told him only half-jokingly that they made appointments to see him so that they could have the chance to chat up Susan while they waited. He resisted temptation for a couple of days, then thought that it would do little harm just to ask her out for a drink. He needed a friendly face to chat to rather than feeling a stranger in his own home. Predictably, after a few drinks they ended up in her bed. He felt enormous relief and no great guilt. When he arrived home, nobody asked where he had been or paid any attention to him. He did however have a few minutes holding Isabelle. She was absolutely delightful.

Life gradually returned to a semblance of normality. Sir Arthur came to collect Amelia and gave Isabelle the once over. He smoked a cigar with Richard in the drawing-room and Richard almost sensed a bond between them, surrounded as they both were by a monstrous regiment of women. The almost palpable hostility of the nanny to Richard did not diminish and created a horrible atmosphere at home. She was clearly an enthusiast for virgin birth and saw no use for any man in the child-rearing stakes. He did his best to avoid a direct confrontation with her as he felt that he was by no means certain to be the winner if one occurred. He diffidently suggested to Heather that they should change the nanny but he was assured that she was a treasure and quite indispensable. He was eventually readmitted to the matrimonial bed and sexual relations gradually resumed but with nowhere near the same enjoyment and intensity on either side. They took no precautions which at least gave the event some spontaneity but they miscalculated. All too soon, Heather announced that she was pregnant again. This time, by tacit agreement they ceased having sex. Susan was the immediate beneficiary and theirs was a raging affair once again.

***

ARTHUR. I felt sorry for Richard.

'How does it feel not to be master in your own house?' I joked with him. 'Perhaps you should spend some time on the golf course.'

Why will women never learn to show a little common sense and include the father in what is going on after a new birth? I had seen Richard with his daughter and he clearly was crazy about her as any new father should be. However, all these women were so busy rushing around looking after Isabelle that he was completely cut out. It creates a very dangerous situation as I know from personal experience, believe me. I suffered the same exclusion when Heather was born. Amelia and her mother together with the then nanny kept me away from my baby. Very few people know and Amelia is not one of them, even though she thinks she knows everything, but Heather has a half-sister about a year younger who lives in the village and whom I support. It was nearly the end of our marriage.

William was born without too much fuss, though Amelia once more took over the household. Richard now had a regular jazz gig in a pub in Covent Garden on Wednesday evenings. As he waited to perform his solo, he went through in his mind all those tired jokes about mothers-in-law and realised how much they were based in truth.

***

Home life was no longer a comfortable existence. Fortunately, he had his pleasurable distractions elsewhere. It did not come as too much of a disappointment or surprise when Heather announced that she had been talking to her mother and they both thought that it would be better and particularly healthier for the children to be brought up in the country. There was plenty of room at the Hall and even a ready-made nursery suite. He of course would join them all for weekends. After a show of false reluctance, he happily agreed to the proposal and felt nothing but a sense of relief. School was out!

***

AMELIA. I never thought that London was a healthy place to bring up children. Good country food and air were what they needed. Also, with the nanny and all the daily help available in Knightsbridge there was little for Heather to do and with her track record I was worried that she might get up to mischief, especially as Richard worked such long hours. At home in Somerset, she would have sufficient work to do with the children and I could keep an eye on her. Richard would come down at weekends and absence in the week would make the heart grow fonder. This was the pattern of life that Arthur and I had successfully followed throughout our marriage. It had worked for us and I saw no reason why it should not work for them. I knew of course that

Arthur had kept a string of mistresses in the week in London but I said nothing. They never troubled me. I anticipated that Richard would follow the same path with similar results.

CHAPTER ELEVEN

STRANGE FRUIT

RICHARD. I rather enjoyed my new life. In the week I had the Knightsbridge flat to myself, except for the cleaning lady who came in daily but whom I never saw as our times did not coincide. The flat was far too large for me alone and I resolved to move into something smaller which was my own but I never got round to it. I was able to devote all the time I wanted to work and I no longer had to rush home to host Heather's ritualistic and inane dinner parties. I had joined a second band which played on a superior London circuit of clubs and pubs. I found that playing regularly with better musicians was pushing me up into a higher league. I was no longer just the amateur outsider who did as he was told but was treated as a seasoned and senior member of the group who was consulted on all matters of content and style. Susan normally came along to hear me play and came back to the flat afterwards, though she rarely spent the whole night with me.

***

MRS GILKES, THE CLEANING LADY. I felt sorry for Mr Gregory. There he was on his own all week rattling around in that huge flat and working such long hours at his office. If I was married to him I wouldn't leave him on his own all that time and not expect him to get up to mischief. Who could blame him? We did not meet and I never actually saw the lady but he was careless and left plenty of traces. I even found a pair of her knickers once in the bed. I knew they were not his wife's as they were not nearly expensive enough. Lady Amelia was paying my wages and I had strict instructions to report to her each week on what he was up to. I did not like to do it but you don't get such a good and easy job every day of the week so I did as I was told.

***

RICHARD. I would drive down to Somerset on Friday evening to find as far as Heather was concerned that absence had made the heart grow fonder. She was now well over the birth of William and had regained her spectacular sexuality. As soon as I arrived I was dragged off to bed. We would get up for family dinner only to go back to bed as soon as politely possible after the meal to continue where we had left off. It was like our early days again to the point that I had to abstain from Susan on Thursday nights in order to have enough sexual energy from Friday onwards to meet Heather's urgent demands.

The odious nanny was given the weekends off so I was able to spend lots of most enjoyable time with Isabelle and William. I had no idea before how I would take to being a father but I found the concentrated time with them at the weekends sheer pleasure. Perhaps it was mere relief but I found no difficulty in abandoning my role as a grown-up and becoming a child once again. I had no problem in seeing life through their eyes and interacting with them on their level. I would try to bring a new toy down with me on each visit. The ideal was one which appealed equally to both of them and required all three of us to be deeply involved in its construction and afterwards. If I could not find such a toy, then it had to be one each and I had to be careful to split my time equally between them as they were both obviously rivals for my full attention.

Heather very much left me to look after them and spent most of her time in bed resting and recovering from our lovemaking and in preparation for more of it. I suppose she did have responsibility for them during the week so it was only fair that I should be in charge at the weekend. Nevertheless, she had the nanny to take control of them and I had a sneaking suspicion that she was not the most maternal of mothers and was far more interested in her own life than in theirs. If I had them for seven days a week I suspect that my patience would snap and I was glad that child-rearing was basically a woman's work. I felt as if I was a member of a public library taking out a couple of most entertaining books and giving them back when I had had enough of them.

The band at the Coach and Horses welcomed me back for the Saturday night sessions. I was amazed a few weeks later to see Sir Arthur ensconced in a corner of the smoke-filled saloon bar with a pint of ale in front of him. We walked back to the Hall together and he told me that he had been a jazz lover since his teens. He had a great record collection and he took me back to his study for brandy and cigars, playing me some particularly choice stuff from the twenties, thirties, and forties. That evening and for many after, Heather had to wait simmering with impatient desire while her father took me on a jazz pilgrimage through the lesser known bands of Chicago, New York, New Orleans and elsewhere. He had spent a lot of money with skilled sound engineers having the original recordings cleaned up and freed from their constant and irritating hiss. I had listened to a lot of his material before but I was now able to appreciate artistry and subtlety which previously was lost in the poor quality of the originals.

***

ARTHUR. I was increasingly viewing my son-in-law as a kindred spirit. We both had our work which absorbed us so much as an antidote to our second-class status on the home front where our women sought to control us totally. Now that Heather was married and technically away from my control, I was able to take a much more detached view of her. I realised that I had spoiled her by giving in to her every whim. There were excuses. As she was my only child, I had wanted her to have the best of everything. Then again, I felt guilty for my long absences, although it was Amelia who engineered the situation whereby I spent the week at work in London while she and Heather had a country existence. When I saw how Heather treated Richard under her mother's influence, I reckoned that I had not done such a good job as a father after all. She viewed him as little more than an errand boy, dancing to her tune and supplying little luxuries from Harrods and Fortnums on demand.

Like me, Richard was a self-made man though he had had a far better education. He had built up a good law practice and obviously had an excellent business brain. I do not think much of lawyers generally and view them as parasites. I wished that Richard had a more positive career but unlike my wife I was not seeking to change him. He was a brilliant clarinet player and we both enjoyed the same types of jazz. I had never learned to play though I could lose myself in the recordings of those who could. I seemed to have little opportunity to seek out live performances before Richard came on the scene I would spend my evenings at home shut in my room listening to my music. I now had a well-informed companion to share my passion. I also liked going down to the Coach and Horses on Saturday night and hearing Richard play with the band. He was a vastly superior musician but I liked the way that he used his talent to coax the best out of the other players and never showed impatience at their mistakes.

***

HEATHER. Mummy was absolutely right. Life in the country really suited me and the children. They ran wild on the estate while we could not let them outside the front door in London. Mummy had recently been elected to the county council and I helped her with her correspondence and filing. I took up riding again. Going like the wind made me feel much healthier and very sexy. I could take care of myself in the week until Richard arrived on Friday evening. An old boyfriend put in an appearance and said he wanted to make love to me like in the old days but I told him to push off. I really gave Richard a good time over the weekends. I hooked up again with Gill, Molly and Mary, old school friends, who all lived within easy driving distance and also had husbands working in the week in London. We all had children about the same age and we met for coffee or tea at each other's houses and let the children play together. It was important that they should mix with children of their own class rather than pick up bad habits and heaven knows what diseases from the village kids. On Thursdays, we left the children with one of the nannies and had a day out shopping in Bath or Bristol. We ended the day with drinks in a pub so we had quite a nice social life. Nanny had given six months' notice as she wanted to return to London and nurse babies again. Mummy and I decided not to replace her but to make do with local girls as mother's helps instead. There were plenty available in the area and some of them were quite well educated so as not to speak with the local accent.

***

RICHARD. When Sunday evening arrived, I would kiss the children goodbye, take Heather back to bed for one last orgasm and set out for London. Susan always came over to greet me and it amused me to go straight from Heather's hot and greedy demands to Susan's quieter but none the less passionate style of lovemaking. I always slept well on Sunday nights and awoke fully refreshed and looking forward to the working week. Perhaps luckily, my fortune-telling skills were not well developed.

We had just finished our third financial year which I judged in my seat of pants fashion to have been more successful than the one before. Turnover had increased substantially and we had recruited so many new staff to cope with the increase in work that we were bursting at the seams. I was a good practical lawyer but a classical education left me very inadequate where maths and figures were concerned. I needed management training as I was now running a successful and growing business which happened to be providing legal services. I just about knew the difference between a balance sheet and a profit and loss account but the subtleties and details were totally beyond me. I was far too busy to seek out the type of academic course that was probably not readily available anyway or at very least a suitably qualified mentor.

As a result, I relied very heavily on Percy who, despite my initial misgivings, had turned out to be a treasure as office manager and cashier. His devotion to work exceeded all others. He never took a day off sick and, though I urged him to do so, took no holidays. Whenever I needed information, he provided it to me in the format of an idiot's guide that even I could understand. One problem which I put down to our rapid growth was that there was never enough money in the bank as we were investing so much in new staff and equipment. In addition, some of the clients were slower in paying their bills than I would have liked. I knew that it would all work out eventually as the new lawyers in time became fully productive and profitable.

I viewed the firm's audit as a necessary evil. The Law Society demanded it anyway. Percy was fluttering round the office like a nervous hen making sure all the books and papers were laid out for inspection like troops on the parade ground. Young men in suits descended on the office, ticked endless columns of figures, asked stupid questions and chatted up the female staff. It was all rather disruptive but had to be endured in order to achieve our annual clean bill of health.

I was surprised to receive a telephone call from the senior partner of the rather prestigious firm of chartered accountants who conducted the audit. Normally, we lunched each other twice a year with a view to seeing how we could share each other's client base but that was our only contact.

'I think you have a problem,' he began with the minimum of polite preliminaries. 'We need to talk.'

I sensed that the matter was urgent and offered to come round immediately to his office.

'No,' he responded, 'let's meet this evening out of the office after work.'

I had recently joined the Cavalry Club in Piccadilly. Despite my aversion to club life, it was useful to have a base in the West End where I could see clients. Over a brandy and soda, he produced a list of invoices of some of the suppliers of goods and services to the firm. They were all shown as limited companies registered in

England. The total was substantial but I did not recognise any of the names. That by itself was not conclusive of anything wrong as there was no reason why I, as proprietor of the firm, should concern myself with the nuts and bolts and know the names of the many entities which supplied our needs to keep us running.

'We have made some enquiries ourselves and here are company searches on all the listed suppliers.'

The results were shattering. The majority were not listed at all at Companies House and therefore did not exist. Those few that were registered had been established in the last two years and had filed no accounts. They all had the same directors and registered offices. They were clearly dummy companies. He then produced a list of payments from our office account after the closing date of the audit.

'These are payments,' he announced, 'which are not covered yet by invoices. What business pays money out without first receiving a bill?'

The inferences were all too obvious as we both knew. There was only one person in the position to perpetrate this fraud. I thanked him profusely for his staff's vigilance in uncovering the crime. I was not over impressed by his parting remark.

'I hope you will be able to settle my firm's bill at the end of the month.'

I hurried back to the office to confront Percy but he had left for the evening. I found his home address in the personnel records and set out for Ilford in the Rolls.

It was an undistinguished council flat in a shabby block. I rang the doorbell and was admitted by Percy's overweight and dowdy wife into a conventional scene of domestic bliss but initially without Percy. She was obviously in the middle of washing up the supper dishes. Two large teenagers were slumped on the sofa watching television. Mrs Percy rushed to put the kettle on and get out the tea things. She gave all the conventional signs of terminal panic at the unexpected appearance of her husband's boss but there were no indications of guilt or complicity. At that moment, I heard a lavatory cistern flush and Percy appeared blinking in the light and pulling up his trousers. The sight of me was enough to make him almost drop them again. He went white and started shaking violently. I had to suppress an overwhelming desire to throttle him.

'We can't talk here,' I began.

Without speaking, he led me into an adjoining and unused dining room, the sort of room that is kept polished and ready for entertaining the Queen who sadly never comes. Frankly I had now reached boiling point and I did not care if the whole family heard our conversation.

'You have betrayed me!' I shouted.

He collapsed like a jelly. In floods of tears, he told me that he was a closet homosexual. He had picked up a man in a public lavatory and gone back with him to a flat. They had been in the middle of sex, both completely naked, when a third man came in with a Polaroid camera and took pictures. Percy was then badly beaten up and robbed. It was a classic blackmail sting. Stupid Percy had all his identity documents on him which gave his home and work addresses and the demands began first by telephone and then in writing. He had sold his house to satisfy them initially before moving into the council flat and had eventually started stealing from me to prevent his secret becoming known to his family and his church. It was a pathetic story and there was clearly no chance of recovering any of my money. I told him not to come back to the office and that I would consider overnight whether to report the matter to the police. I could not wait to get away from him.

Not surprisingly, I did not sleep well that night. I dreamed that I heard the sweet sounds of Bechet's soprano saxophone getting ever nearer as I walked down a long corridor. There he was, surrounded by a Creole rhythm section. When the number, *Summertime*, came to an end he greeted me.

'Didn't I tell you no good would come to you from working with lawyers? You should have done what I said and played up here with me where the air is purer. Let the man go. He has troubles enough.'

I decided that Sidney was right and that there was no point in a prosecution. Besides, I did not want the police trawling for evidence and crawling all over my office. I was surprised when I arrived there the next morning to find an urgent message to ring Ilford police station. Percy had hanged himself in the night. Clearly, he could not face the disgrace of a trial for theft and fraud or being unmasked as a blackmailed homosexual and a possible trial and prison for that. He had truly been between a rock and a hard place. I arranged for the auditors to provide temporary accounting cover and to put in place systems that would ensure that a similar situation could never happen again.

The tragedy of course extended to Percy's family. Had he been a good employee, I would have felt obliged to give financial help to the widow, but he had already stolen from me far more than I would ever expect to offer her as a gratuity or a pension. At the same time, I felt angry that in my ignorance I had become so dependent on one man. I resolved that it would never happen again and that, in future, I must take an active and informed interest in what happens in the engine room.

I was also concerned as to how Percy's death would affect the firm's morale. Clearly there would be an inquest and a great deal of publicity, at least locally. I agonised as to how to handle the situation. It would soon be known that the firm was not supporting Percy's family and therefore the staff needed to know the reasons as I did not want us to have a reputation for meanness. I therefore put out a very simple announcement:

Private & Confidential. To All Staff
Percy Harris was yesterday dismissed with immediate effect for serious and ongoing theft from this firm following a thorough investigation by the auditors. Unable to face the consequences of his crime, he took his own life.

Signed: Richard Gregory, Senior Partner

There was a good deal of animated discussion for a time together with a great sense of shock but things were back to normal surprisingly quickly.

CHAPTER TWELVE

AFTER YOU'VE GONE

LARRY GAGE. I could not understand the attitude of the clearing banks: Barclays, Lloyds and all that lot. They were content to lend us money at six per cent and see us lend it on to our customers who were also their customers at eighteen per cent. They could have cut us out completely and made huge profits for their shareholders. We were making vast sums for virtually no risk. Gage's was much more conservative than some of the other secondary banks who were our competitors. They were taking share stakes in their builder clients. I refused to do that as I saw it could lead to conflicts in future.

I had reduced the number of developer clients to whom we lent to half a dozen. They were all the top builders in prosperous areas. Everything they built sold like hot cakes. I tied in with a few building societies so that loan packages were available to the ultimate purchasers. It was a very efficient operation which was making us all a lot of money.

I could have dropped the second mortgage business but we were lending to a nice quality of customers who gave us breadth. Brokers knew that we only accepted the best. We even lent to a High Court judge who wanted to extend his greenhouse and there were numerous city solicitors and accountants using the growing equity in their houses to raise extra capital for their firms.

In the midst of all this well-controlled growth, I am afraid that I was rather sharp with Richard when he started urging me to be cautious on the basis that the market was overheating.
'I don't try and second guess you on the legal work. Please stick to what you know and leave me to do the banking.'

***

Richard needed to be careful with what he spent. Despite their last year having been extremely successful after a great amount of hard work by everyone in the firm, he had no profits as Percy had stolen the money. This made him all the more determined to do well in the new financial year. There was plenty of work about but he worried as always about the fact that Gage's was far and away their largest client. Richard liked there to be a balance of work between the property department and the litigation and corporate lawyers but this balance was lost in the housing boom. They were in the middle of a runaway property explosion and he was well aware that his business was as subject as any other to the wild swings of the nation's economy. The trend was to buy the most expensive home you could nearly afford, borrowing as much as possible from a bank or building society, all of which were falling over themselves to lend you far too much. Prudence had been forgotten. Property prices were rising ever higher. Otherwise intelligent people cashed in their gains and bought something even more expensive with bigger borrowings.

The ever-upward spiral made him feel dizzy and very uncomfortable. Running an expanding law firm reminded him how ignorant he was of basic economics. His reading now consisted of the *Melody Maker* for jazz and the *Financial Times* for its economic and business coverage. He had no time for the legal periodicals. There was talk in the *FT* of previous housing booms that had ended in bust and certain commentators were raising the spectre that the conditions were right for it to happen again. He tried to warn many of his clients but he felt like Cassandra, the prophet of doom, whom nobody heeded. Everyone was too busy getting rich quick.

The first signs of trouble were reports from estate agents that sales were slowing down. As a result, determined sellers were having to reduce their prices to find willing buyers. Those with little equity in their homes suddenly found that they had none or, even worse, owed their lenders more than their property was worth. Some handed back their keys and walked away in the hope that they would not be sued for any shortfall. The change in the industry was like a sudden storm. Lenders stopped lending as they lost confidence in their borrowers' ability to repay. The market swiftly ground to a complete standstill.

Richard received a call from Larry Gage who had recently become chairman of the bank as the last of the older generation of the family retired. He sounded a very worried man and asked Richard to come down and see him immediately. He was white and shaking. Gage's was in a completely exposed position as a result of the property crash. The typical example of its commercial clients was a builder developing a number of residential estates simultaneously. The best estates were funded at relatively low interest by the builder's clearing bank which insisted on a substantial cash injection from him. The worst were funded by Gage's with a minimal or even nil contribution from the builder. Up to now, it had not mattered as everything sold so quickly and easily. Gage's had made huge profits by charging higher rates of interest to reflect their perceived extra risk. Now nothing was selling. A typical personal customer borrowed from the bank against the ever-increasing equity in his home to fund improvements rather than move to a bigger and better house or maybe just to pay for a holiday. Now there was no longer any equity to cover the security as the value of the property shrank.

To fund its rapid expansion, Gage's had borrowed short-term from the first-line banks, was due to repay substantial sums and no longer had the cash flow to meet its obligations. Richard asked Larry about the possibility of extending the bank's credit but he told Richard that their lenders were panicking and demanding their money back immediately. In the recent property boom, many secondary banks like Gage's had flourished. Now they were all in the same boat. Richard knew that they had to approach the Bank of England as the lender of last resort. The problem as he saw it was that there were any number of secondary banks all asking for assistance at the same time and only so much money to go round. Those first to apply had the best chance and those who had been least imprudent were most likely to be helped. He thought that Gage's were unlikely to fall into the latter category so he urged

Larry to make an appointment at Threadneedle Street as soon as possible and offered to go along to hold his hand. The danger was that the establishment might seek to make a public example of the most profligate secondary lenders by letting them sink unaided into bankruptcy. He did pause for a moment to consider whether he should have expressed his own disquiet more forcibly to Larry about the runaway nature of the economy, but he reckoned that Larry would still have brushed off his concerns as the usual worries of an over cautious lawyer. After all, Larry was the experienced businessman with the impeccable track record who was merely following in the footsteps of so many City great men.

Once again, he felt as if he was a naughty boy entering the headmaster's study.

'Don't sit down, Gregory' resonated in his ears.

At least on this occasion he was there only as the lawyer representing his clients but he still felt the customary sinking feeling in the pit of his stomach. Larry had prepared and distributed detailed figures of his bank's plight in good time before the meeting. There was much tutting and shaking of heads while the Bank of England officials concentrated on the papers in front of them. He was becoming steadily more pessimistic of the chance of a rescue operation. Theirs was indeed an extreme example of reckless lending persistently over a long period of time.

'Here's a nice can of worms,' was one comment that he inadvertently overheard.

Unfortunately Richard was not wrong. Their application was summarily and rather brutally rejected. As they walked out, Richard realised as he should have done before that Larry was completely out of his depth.

'What do we do now?' Larry asked.

'You call in the liquidators,' Richard replied.

He had no experience of a corporate failure of this magnitude, particularly one with which he was so closely involved. The liquidators brought in their own solicitors and suddenly Gage's was Richard's largest ex-client. He had a rather stiff and difficult meeting with the legendary insolvency solicitor acting for the liquidators.

'Say goodbye to your clients, Mr Gregory,' was his opening gambit.

'What do you mean?' asked Richard.

'Say goodbye to your clients because from now on they are my clients.'

Richard could only swallow hard. His firm was allowed to keep a few ongoing matters but the business of enforcing repayment of the loans and disposal of the securities went elsewhere. He and his staff also had to spend an inordinate amount of unpaid time dealing with endless queries from the liquidators and their lawyers. Larry and Richard had always talked about formalising the occupancy of the law firm's offices which were let at a rent way below market value but somehow they had never got round to it. Richard knew that the firm was vulnerable and would soon have to seek new accommodation. He also had to face the problem of the personnel who were previously employed exclusively on Gage's work. He had nothing with which to replace it and they would have to go. Richard set about the unpleasant task of organising mass redundancies.

Bad news travels fast and the atmosphere at the Hall that weekend was very different. The sex with Heather was still hot but the overall attitude towards him on the part of Heather and her mother was distinctly cool. At the outset, he thought that he was being over-sensitive but as the weekend progressed he decided that he was not. By contrast, the more hostile towards him his wife and mother-in-law became the friendlier was the welcome that Sir Arthur gave him. They stayed up late on both Friday and Saturday nights listening to Sir Arthur's jazz records and drank far more brandy than was good for them. Just as he was leaving for London on Sunday evening, Sir Arthur greatly surprised him by taking him on one side and asking Richard to let him know if there was anything he could do to help.

'At least you've hung on to the Rolls so far,' was his parting shot as he saw Richard off down the drive.

***

ARTHUR. I knew about Gage's failure on the City grapevine virtually the moment that it happened. I was aware what an important slice of his practice their work represented and wondered how Richard would take it. He seemed tired and pale but overjoyed as usual to see the children and they him. Where Amelia got her information from I never knew but both she and Heather very obviously were giving him the cold shoulder, presumably because they had heard about his reverse in business. I had been lucky enough in my own career after we were married not to have any financial setbacks or at least any that were publicly known about. I wondered cynically whether I would have been for the scrapheap if I had failed to provide financially for my family. It looked to me that Richard could be destined for that fate if things got worse. I resolved to keep an eye on his situation and do what I could to help.

***

Susan was visiting her mother in Wales that weekend and was not due back until late on Monday morning. Richard returned to a large, cold and empty flat. As he cooked himself a simple omelette, he reflected how well things had been going but how suddenly the changes had taken place. He was the same person now as he was three months before but events were pushing him in a different and decidedly unpleasant direction. He realised that despite his pride and pretensions he was merely a plaything of a higher power.

CHAPTER THIRTEEN

OUT OF NOWHERE

RICHARD. I did not sleep well that night. I was worried about the future of the firm. I was going to have to make some big decisions in a limited time frame. I also sensed that all was not well in Somerset. Did I have a wife who would stick by me in the lean years as well as in the fat? I had just dropped off into a deep and troubled sleep when I dreamed that there was an urgent ringing on the doorbell. I gradually woke to find that the bell was indeed sounding constantly and it was now supplemented by loud and persistent knocking. I looked at my watch and saw that it was about seven o'clock. I put on my dressing gown and slippers and hurried to the front door. There were six men crowded in the lobby by the lift. The first handed me a piece of paper which I blearily examined. It was a police search warrant signed by a magistrate. They all produced police identity cards, filed past me as though I was not there and spread out to search the flat almost as if choreographed as dancers in some elaborate ballet.

I had no idea why they were there or what they were looking for. My questions to that effect were ignored in grim silence. They seemed fascinated by a children's printing set which they found in a disused cupboard in what had been the nursery. I hadn't noticed its existence. At that moment, the phone rang. It was a friend who had kindly agreed to let his house be used as a registered office for one of the companies owned by my clients whom I had christened the 'strobic stripes brigade'. He too had plain-clothes police swarming all over the place. Other similar calls followed in quick succession. The last was the one I was dreading. I had foolishly used my mother's home as one of the registered offices. I was worried that the shock of a police raid might kill her as she was becoming increasingly frail. I need not have been concerned. She phoned me in high spirits to tell me that the police had indeed arrived in strength but she had sent them about their business with a flea in their collective ear

***

BELINDA. What fun! I knew it had to be something to do with Richard's business and it was wonderful to help him by sending the police packing. I knew that Richard would do nothing dishonest so it all had to be a silly mistake. I had just switched on the wireless in the kitchen while the kettle boiled for my early morning cup of tea when the front doorbell chimed. They were so obviously plain clothes police that it was almost laughable. Fortunately, I had no lodgers that week so their search warrant did not worry me.

'Search away,' I announced, 'and let me know if you find anything interesting.'

They soon got bored and started to leave. My natural instinct was to offer them a cup of tea but I suppressed it as I did not think they deserved it. I gave them a good sending off as they went down the garden path.

'You should be ashamed of yourselves bothering an elderly lady over absolutely nothing so early in the morning and wasting taxpayers' money. Be off with you and catch some criminals!'

***

RICHARD. I suddenly remembered how the police love their cups of tea and put the kettle on. The search seemed to be coming to a natural end and my offer of tea changed the atmosphere completely. They eventually left, triumphantly clutching the juvenile printing set but with nothing else. I was handed the card of Detective Chief Inspector Charles Holton of the City Fraud Squad and told to phone him in about an hour's time. He was obviously too senior to be one of the early risers. I phoned my office to say that I would be delayed and set about tidying up the mess that the search had created.

I was quickly put through to DCI Holton. He had a rough, gravelly voice which reminded me of the regimental sergeant major at our Officer Cadet Training Unit.

'Mr Gregory,' he began, 'when I authorised the raid on your apartment, I did not know you were a practising solicitor. I need to know the names and addresses of your clients behind the following companies,' and he listed all seventeen.

'I cannot tell you,' I replied, swallowing hard. 'I am bound by my rules of professional confidentiality.'

'Really?' He paused for a long time. 'If you do not tell me, I will assume that you are not acting for clients and are in fact the principal of a dishonest scheme designed to cheat the tax authorities. I will apply for a warrant for your arrest on the grounds of fraud.'

His words put me in a state of shock but I managed nevertheless to think quickly.

'Look, give me time to seek advice from the Law Society and I will phone you straight back.'

'Alright. That seems reasonable,' he replied.

I collected my thoughts, dialled the Law Society and asked to speak to someone in the Professional Ethics Department. As soon as I told my basic version of the story, I felt a great sense of relief rather like a Catholic in the confessional. What I was told also served to lighten my mood.

'If your clients have used your services and your offices as a vehicle for fraud, your professional retainer is at an end and you are free to give the police the information that they seek.'

'It certainly looks like it,' I answered and thanked my saviour profusely.

I phoned DCI Holton back and sang like a canary.

I now had time to reflect on my situation. Through my greed and stupidity I had taken on unsavoury clients operating an obviously dubious scheme which I had never tried fully to understand. I knew that as many as seventeen seemingly unconnected and arms' length companies which in fact were all under one ownership were trading huge parcels of gilt-edged securities with each other. These securities were borrowed cheaply from one of the respectable stock jobbing houses. Some of the companies were then making vast paper losses which were reclaimed from the Inland Revenue. It was all about the timing of the deals involving interest either payable or not, but I had been too lazy or uninterested to find out more. Suffice it to say that due to a technicality only the Treasury was paying out large sums of public money with no justification whatever. One man sitting behind a desk with a bank of telephones operated the whole scheme. They were anything but commercial transactions.

I had accepted fees which were totally disproportionate to my work involved year after year. It was true that the clients had produced the nominee directors but I had provided the separate registered offices in an obvious attempt to make it appear that the companies were not linked when in fact they were. I did not know what criminal offences my clients had committed, if indeed they had committed any, but whatever they had done I was an accessory to it and one who as a sophisticated lawyer ought to have understood and kept away from situations like these. Worse still, I could be accused of being responsible for devising the scheme. I worked out that I desperately needed help.

I telephoned and made an urgent appointment to see a well-known solicitor who specialised in white-collar crime. It was an erroneous description in my case as my collar was already almost black with sweat. Clearly, in his eyes the very fact that I had consulted him meant that I was guilty and he made no attempt to hide his contempt for me or disguise his view that I was a prominent member of the criminal classes. What I needed to do in his view was play down my involvement in the scheme by claiming that I was a complete idiot and had been duped from first to last. He advised me on no account to contact the clients. He read out from the law books with considerable relish the possible penalties for conspiring in tax evasion. If I felt bad before, I felt worse now.

As it was, there was no prosecution. I was expecting a parcel from the toy department of Harrods to send on to the children so I was not surprised when the doorbell rang and I had to sign for a large package. I was surprised when I found that I had been served with formal papers summoning me to appear as a witness on oath before a Stock Exchange Inquiry. I was naturally concerned at its possible implications for me and returned to see my hostile criminal solicitor. He booked a consultation with leading and junior counsel specialising in this area of law. As we sat in their opulent waiting room in the Temple I notionally totted up how much all these accumulated legal experts were costing me hour by hour. I reflected that now the boot was on the other foot. I had made a good living for years out of my clients' plight and uncertainty. Now it was my turn to suffer.

The threat to me was more subtle than direct. I had to be careful how I answered the questions of counsel for the tribunal not to incriminate myself. I could also expect a roasting from counsel acting for my former clients who would be seeking to deflect blame from them onto me and depict me as the mastermind of the scheme. The danger was that the tribunal would make adverse findings of fact against me in its judgement. These findings would be passed on to the Law Society which could in its turn take disciplinary proceedings against me. The ultimate possible sanction was to be struck off which would end my career and comfortable livelihood as a solicitor.

Many months passed and I almost forgot the uncomfortable experience that I was due to face. The first day of the tribunal hearing however eventually dawned.

There was a lengthy and unpleasant wait on the morning it opened, rather like waiting to go out on patrol in the Malayan jungle. On that first morning, I arrived surrounded by my legal team and sat there for the next three weeks hardly able to see what was going on because of the mountains of paper in front of me. Every morning before proceedings started, we met to plan our strategy for the day. Every evening after we finished, we met again to review the day's events. I was desperate to spend time in the office to look after my clients who were being neglected and earn the fees to pay for all this. I was not getting enough sleep and living on black coffee and cigarettes. I was about to enter the witness box for my examination and I had a lot of preparation to do. I had done some acting at school and the skills learned then came in useful. After three days in the witness box, I was assured by my legal team that I had acquitted myself quite well.

Meanwhile, communication with Somerset was frosty to say the least. I could have done with the solace of a wife at my side but I realised that Heather's place was in the country with the children. During this difficult time, there was no question of my breaking away to make a visit so our dealings were confined to the telephone and far from satisfactory.

'I so much wish you were here by my side to comfort me through this difficult time.'

'Oh God no. I'm far too busy here wiping bottoms and cleaning up snot to get away.'

'Let me tell you how things are progressing. My lawyers have uncovered some interesting possibilities.'

'Spare me the details. You know I have never had a head for that sort of thing.'

'How are William and Isabelle?'

'As well as can be expected with an absentee father. Must go now. Molly is at the door and we are off shopping to Bristol. Bye!'

Eventually, the meandering proceedings came to an end and the bills started to arrive. I was fully occupied in running the practice and trying to make the money to pay them. So much so that when after some months a thick envelope containing the tribunal's findings arrived it caught me by surprise. I had been so busy with current work for active clients that I had forgotten the ordeal that I had experienced before the tribunal. Inevitably I had been heavily criticised for hosting blindly the companies that were at the core of the scheme.

Now was the time for some more sleepless nights. I had to wait in trepidation to hear from the Law Society. I knew its deliberations would be slow but what would be its verdict and was I due to face another tribunal, this time as the sole accused rather than as a significant witness? It is amazing though how the combination of time elapsing and being frantically busy blunts even the most acute fear.

***

ARTHUR. They say that troubles never come singly. I had a personal interest in the outcome of certain tax avoidance schemes being sold around the City. I was always reasonably conservative about those in which I invested but I had become used to looking at the fate of their more extreme offshoots as the Inland Revenue was beginning to adopt an unpleasant habit of following through from the more outrageous schemes to the blue chip ones if they bore even the slightest similarity. I learned through my contacts about the police raids in relation to one such bond-washing scheme. I was dismayed to learn that Richard was involved as the lawyer and pleased when I heard that there was to be no criminal action. Unfortunately, the protagonists of the scheme were licensed stockbrokers and there had to be an official Exchange enquiry. Richard was an important witness and did not come out too well. I knew that the next stage was a reference to the Law Society and he was going to fare badly in the subsequent disciplinary proceedings.

Jimmy Clifford, the Law Society's Secretary General, was a member of my Masonic Lodge and well known to me. I telephoned him and arranged to give him lunch at my club. The world is indeed a small place. It transpired that Richard and he were old boys of the same school. Jimmy knew him quite well and liked him. We agreed that we had to find a formula to save Richard's reputation but to keep him out of similar problems in the future. After all, we had to think of the best interests of the public as well. We agreed that Richard could be trusted to keep his word so his undertaking not to practise any more as a corporate and commercial lawyer would be enough. We thought he would do far less harm as a divorce lawyer and I resolved to myself to help him set up in his new practice if, as seemed likely, his recent reverses had greatly depleted his cash resources. After all, I rationalised my decision by the fact that I was merely helping to make sure that there was bread on the table of close members of my own family. It might even encourage Richard to spend more time on his jazz playing. I asked Jimmy not to let Richard know about my involvement as I planned to tell him myself when it was appropriate.

***

RICHARD. When it eventually arrived, the Law Society's verdict came in a surprising form. James Clifford, the Secretary General of the Society, was an old boy of my school. We had spent time pleasantly getting drunk together at a number of its functions. He unexpectedly phoned me. After making sure that I was on my own and the call could not be overheard, he told me that I could be struck off but the Law Society was inclined not to take disciplinary action against me if I closed my present practice and informally undertook in future not to involve myself in corporate and commercial work.

'Look, Dick,' he continued. 'You have a reputation as a bit of a ladies' man. Why don't you take up divorce law?'

Formal notice to quit the offices came the next morning from Gage's liquidators so I set about the painful process of sacking all the staff except my secretary and receptionist and winding up the practice. Sitting down with people like Ted was the hardest of all. He had been my mentor since the day I became an articled clerk. He had acted as my recruiting sergeant when I started the firm. He had kept me out of trouble time and time again by pointing out that certain clients whom I was proposing to take on were undesirable. He was approaching retirement and was burdened with a bedridden wife. He had virtually no chance of finding new employment and I knew that he needed still to work as his pension arrangements were inadequate. I had let him down so badly that I could hardly look him in the eye as I gave him the news. I was now desperately short of money, knew little or nothing about divorce law and had not much idea how to start a new practice by myself. I wished that Mei Ling was still working for me.

Help came from an unexpected quarter.

CHAPTER FOURTEEN

DOWN BY THE RIVERSIDE

RICHARD. At last, the unceasing sense of panic was coming to an end. I felt that I could not take any more emergencies or disasters in my life. I craved a semblance of normality and I was badly missing Heather and the children. This very English ideal of the family living in the country while the father toils away during the week in London is all very well while things run smoothly and he can get away at the weekends to resume family life. However, when disaster after disaster hits the breadwinner in the eye on a continual basis so that he cannot get away, the situation becomes entirely unsatisfactory. I would have liked to have had a loving and understanding wife to come home to while my business and professional life was unravelling around me. Then again, the presence of the children would have been a welcome distraction. As it was, I came home exhausted to a cold and empty flat. Heather was not a great communicator at the best of times and our snatched and infrequent telephone conversations were no substitute for real family life.

I desperately wanted to get back on track. There was nothing to stop me going down that coming weekend but I wanted to hear first in Heather's voice that I was welcome and she missed me just as much as I missed her. I planned my call carefully at a time when I knew she would have bathed the kids and put them to bed. She was likely to be relaxing in front of the television with a glass of wine. We got off to a bad start:

'Hallo, darling.'

'Oh it's you. I hardly remembered your voice it's been so long.'

'How are the kids?'

'You mean you remember that you have some.'

'You know how busy I have been and how worried for us over the past weeks.'

'Spare me the gory details.'

'Anyway, I'm coming down this weekend.'

'Bully for you but you won't find me here. I'm spending the weekend with Janet in Bath. She's back for a few days from Rhodesia and it's our only chance to get together. Still, that will give you a good chance to spend time with the kids and get to know them again. I'll be back late on Sunday afternoon and will see you then.'

I kept my disappointment to myself but I was sure that we would make up for lost time when she did get back. Despite her offhand tone, the sound of her voice made me feel randy and I could not wait to get her into bed. It had been far too long.

Having made arrangements, unsatisfactory though they were, for the weekend, I was pleasantly surprised to receive a telephone call from Sir Arthur, the first in our relationship.

'Hello, Richard, this is your jazz loving father-in-law speaking. I'm stuck in some smelly telephone box in Heathrow on my way to Paris for a board meeting. We need to talk. Can you manage lunch on Friday? One o'clock. My club, the Carlton. See you there.'

I responded weakly but positively to his flow of words. I wondered what was up.

***

HEATHER. What did Richard expect? He knew how hot and needy I was. He had not been down to Somerset for months and I was going mad with frustration. Doing it to myself was not enough. I needed a man. He talked on the phone about some problems in the office but I was not really interested and anyway it was all too complicated for me to understand. I was out with the girls one Thursday night in a pub in Bradford on Avon when I noticed a man at the bar giving me the eye. He was big and rough looking. He reminded me of the head gardener at school who I had had such a good time with. He grabbed me on my way back from the ladies. His name was Joe Reynolds and he told me how much he fancied me. I told him that we girls were about to leave but that I would come back to the pub to see him. Fortunately, we all had our own cars so I zoomed off and returned as soon as the coast was clear. Joe wasted no time. We were in the back seat of my car in an unlit corner of the pub's car park in a jiffy. He smelt of booze, cigarettes and stale sweat but I loved it all. He sensed my need and was as rough and strong as I wanted. The frustrations of the past weeks melted away as I came and came and came again. Frankly, sex with Richard had become a bit boring. It was all a bit too clever and clinical for me, just like Richard himself. He was always so much in control. OK, it was all designed to see that I had a good time and I did, don't mistake me, but what I wanted was to be the object of a man's sheer lust. Let him just take his pleasure and leave me panting along in his slipstream. With Joe it was very dirty and basic. I loved it and wanted more.

***

Following Arthur's call, Richard resolved to confide in him and tell him his business problems. He felt that he needed advice and he had nowhere else to turn. When Richard started to tell Arthur his sorry tale, the latter motioned him to stop.

'I know all about it,' he said.

Richard asked him how he had obtained his knowledge and he replied that the City was a small place. In his position, all sorts of news came to him. If he was interested in a particular matter he had only to ask and all the information he required was made available.

'Naturally, when I heard about your involvement in the tribunal, I wanted to know more. Before Jimmy Clifford contacted you we met to discuss how to handle the situation. I told him to go easy.'

Richard thought he knew how the world worked but clearly he still had a lot to learn.

'This new divorce practice of yours,' Arthur continued, 'you will need some premises and some start-up capital. A company which I control owns a freehold in Wimpole Street. It mainly lets to doctors as consulting rooms but the top two floors are empty and you could move in tomorrow. You can live on the top floor as in any event you ought now to be moving out of the Knightsbridge flat and the floor below will make excellent offices. No need to pay rent for the moment. When the business gets profitable we can talk again. As for a loan to start you up, go to my bank and mention this conversation to the manager.'

Richard was astonished and deeply grateful. He remembered all too well their first meeting and Arthur's attitude towards him. While their mutual interest in jazz had brought them closer, it did not justify such a complete volte-face. Now was not the time to ask his reasons but merely for Richard to express his thanks. Arthur had a meeting to attend so Richard was sent off into St James's Street to count his good fortune. It did not end there. When Richard got back, he received a telephone call from some brash young lawyer in the West End who had heard that he wanted to dispose of his practice – was there anyone in London who did not know all about his business? – and was prepared to offer a nominal sum to take it off his hands, what was left of his clients and staff included. Richard did not haggle but immediately accepted. He planned to move his personal belongings to Wimpole Street the following week.

He had plenty of time to reflect on his past and future life on the way down to Somerset in the comfort of the Rolls. At least he had been able to retain that so far. Arthur was staying the weekend in London for business meetings. Heather was away in Bath with her girlfriend. By the time he arrived, the children were asleep in bed and the frigidity of Amelia's welcome left him in immediate need of a scalding hot bath. Warm again, he chose a book from the library and had an early night. Spending Saturday with the children was pure pleasure. After a little shyness at first because of his long absence, they were delighted to see him. Not surprisingly, it was Isabelle, the older child, who was hardest on him.

'You naughty daddy, where have you been? We missed you so much.'

'I've been to London to see the Queen,' and he thrust an imaginary crown on her head.

After that they all rushed around the estate like lunatics. Heather had arranged for a local girl from the village, Esther, to help Richard. They kept catching each other's eye giving one and other appraising looks. She was dark, very attractive in a gypsy fashion and Richard was consumed with pangs of sudden lust. He realised that he had not had a woman for months. He had even neglected Susan who had taken a job as a receptionist with a dentists' practice in despair. There had been no opportunity while he had been so occupied in dealing with emergency after emergency at work and the inclination had subsided at the same time. The inclination was now rising with a vengeance.

While the children were having their afternoon nap, he learned that Esther's boyfriend was a serving soldier who was currently away on a posting. She was missing him a lot. Richard told her that he was playing that evening at the Coach and Horses and invited her along. She said that she would bring a girlfriend which he privately felt might have a dampening effect on later activities but he need not have worried.

***

ESTHER. I could have told Richard a lot about his wife's affair but it wasn't up to me to make trouble. The children were a bit shy with him at first. After all, he had not been down to see them for months and I think Isabelle particularly wanted to punish him for having been away so long. However, he was really good with them and soon brought them round. I had done a lot of child-minding for the local gentry and I knew what a lot of stuffed shirts the men usually were. They treated me like a piece of the furniture. Richard was different. He was not a snob at all and was genuinely interested in me and my life. I told him about Rob being in the Military Police and how we were saving up to get married. He was away for six months in Germany on an important investigation and I was missing him a lot. When his tour finished, his time in the

130

army would be up and he was planning to join the police where he thought his experience in the Special Investigation Branch would give him speedy promotion. I was able to talk to Richard like one of my own friends.

He told me about some of the problems he had been facing in London and I could see how pale, stressed and thin he looked. All this time as we talked, the children were rushing round us but he was increasingly taking control of them and I could just leave him to it which was a pleasant change. He was very good looking and I realised that I fancied him a lot. With Rob away, that part of my life had shut down. I fantasised about making love with Richard and I got a real thrill when I caught him giving me the glad eye when he thought I wasn't watching. I was so happy when he asked me to come along and hear him play jazz that evening at the Coach and Horses. I was also pleased that he looked disappointed when I asked if I could bring Peggy along as well. I reckoned that he knew how to give a girl a good time.

***

The band was glad to have him back and he was happy to lose himself in playing again. This was another pleasurable activity which he had abandoned in his time of crisis. He could see Esther at the rear with her unremarkable friend – why is it that beautiful women choose to go around with plain companions? – but by and large he kept his distance as too much familiarity might breed questions. He did however play a particularly soulful 'Petit Fleur' with his eyes fixed on her and the clarinet pointing at her in a very obvious manner. In the interval, he went out for a quiet cigarette and she followed him, pressing herself briefly against him but he was cautious of prying eyes. Amelia was at home babysitting but everybody knows your business in a small village, rather like in the City of London!

When the band packed up, he repeated the process and went out for a smoke again. Esther was quickly at his side. 'Let's go,' she urged. They ran hand in hand to his car and she directed him to the local lovers' lane. Clearly, this was not the first time she had been there but he liked his women experienced. They got into the back seat which was built to accommodate a dowager or two and hence far more suitable for lovemaking. They were very needy and passionate. Their clothes flew in all directions and the windows soon steamed up to spoil the fun of any lurking voyeur. They both ended up completely satisfied. With much more difficulty than when they had taken them off they dressed themselves and made themselves look as presentable as possible. He started the engine but could not move the car. The extra weight of the Rolls had caused the wheels to sink into the marshy river bank. A smaller car would not have had this problem. There was perhaps a moral here. They decided that calling the local garage to tow them out would cause more reputational damage than they could handle.

There was only one thing for it. Rubbing off the steam from the side windows, Richard saw that while they had been amorously distracted a whole fleet of cars had arrived and the occupants were similarly engaged with windows steamed up and much shaking up and down on the shock absorbers and springs. With profuse apologies, they went from car to car recruiting men to help push them out of the bog and their predicament. Richard tapped nervously on the window of the first car:

'What the fuck do you want?' An extremely belligerent male face filled the aperture as the window was wound down.

'My car's stuck in the bog and I can't move it.'

There followed bellows of laughter.

'Just a minute. Let me get my trousers back on. I'll come and help you. That's what you get from screwing too hard.'

He could have written a social study about the reception that they received from the occupants of the cars. It ranged from outright aggression and physical threats to abject fear and panic at being caught in a compromising situation with an inappropriate partner. When their problem was explained to them, tears of laughter replaced aggression and panic. They were soon on the road again with many thanks to all their clandestine helpers. Richard dropped Esther at the end of her lane and retired without being accosted to his bed at the Hall with a satisfied smile on his face.

On Sunday, Esther phoned in with a headache, although Richard doubted if it was that part of her anatomy which was sore. He did not mind at all as it meant that he could get even closer to Isabelle and William. They played wonderful and exhilarating games. He fed them and put them to bed for their post-lunch nap. In the middle of it, Heather returned and he was fully prepared for them to go straight to bed for a 'quickie', but her attitude towards him was icily cold and completely disinterested. He would have liked to talk to her to find out the reasons but the children woke and needed their full attention. The only adult member of the family who welcomed him was Arthur. There had been a complete turnaround. He told Heather and her mother who had just appeared that he had to go back immediately to London. Neither could have cared less.

He thought about the situation on the way back. Understanding Heather as well as he did, he knew that she could not live without sex. She was not seeking it from him; therefore she was getting it from someone else. He needed to know who it was so he resolved on Monday to instruct a private detective to follow her, using the money that he had received for his former practice as his down payment. He thought it ironic that the first divorce that he might be handling in his new career could be his own.

CHAPTER FIFTEEN

MAKIN' WHOOPEE

ARTHUR. I had a reputation in the City as the man who saw problems before they arose and solved them so smoothly that most people did not even recognise their existence. I knew that Heather and Richard's marriage was about to become one such problem and that I had to move fast to defuse the situation and achieve the desired results. I blamed myself a great deal for what had occurred. Amelia and I should have had more children but she was advised after Heather's birth that another would put her life at risk. We talked about adoption but it all seemed too difficult. I was continually distracted by the demands of work so we never got round to it.

As a result, Heather was brought up like a little princess whose every whim I rushed to satisfy. I doted on her. I regularly sabotaged any attempts that Amelia made to discipline her and I now had to face the fact that I had created a monster. At least I did not run my businesses like that. More by luck than judgement, she had hitched herself to a thoroughly decent man. Richard had successfully survived my initial attempts as with all her suitors to blow him out of the water and as time passed I got to like him increasingly as my regard for Heather faded.

My intelligence network did not fail me. Amelia dropped many hints as to what was going on between Heather and Reynolds and the landlord of the Coach and Horses who was my company sergeant major in the Territorials filled in any gaps. I knew that Richard was soon going to find out and how explosive his reaction would be. He had all my sympathy. Just when he most needed a loyal and loving wife, he was going to find himself saddled with a treacherous slut who was going to deprive him of his children.

My job was to make him so dependent on me that he would not divorce Heather messily as the guilty party but would follow my wishes to the letter for the sake of our family's name and reputation, particularly for his children. I was weaving a cunning web but I believe that I was doing it for the greater good.

My staff worked overtime to set up Richard's office. It did not take a financial genius to realise that the combined hits he had recently experienced would have left him drained of money. When I saw him last, I formed the view that he was in shock and unlikely even to think of all the things that had to be done, let alone carry them out. I only hoped that he would recover sufficiently quickly to make a success of the new venture.

As I have already indicated, I needed Richard to be thoroughly indebted to me. I knew exactly what his reaction would be when he found out about Heather's antics and my first object had to be to keep him under control to protect the family name and all we stand for. In no way did I want the 'Penny Dreadfuls' to get hold of the story and splash lurid headlines all over the place. That was not my only motive. I genuinely liked Richard the more I saw of him and I was keen to make up to him a little for the degenerate conduct of my daughter.

***

RICHARD. I needed to get to know my new home and office as soon as possible. The ground floor housed a rather grand waiting room for the patients of the hordes of doctors whose names appeared on the well-polished brass plate beside the front door. I was surprised to see a separate and rather discreet brass plate with my name and description as a solicitor already in place and with my own front door bell underneath. The doctors' receptionist had keys waiting for me and I ascended in the lift to the third floor which was as far as the lift went. I was amazed to find that the whole place was fully furnished down to headed note paper and envelopes in the office. When I climbed the narrow staircase leading upstairs, I found cutlery and crockery in the kitchen and sheets and blankets on the comfortable double bed. I was in what had been the old attics of a once rather grand private house, probably the servants' quarters. They had low and sloping ceilings together with dormer windows and were very stylish and attractive. I had my own sitting-room, bedroom, bathroom and kitchen. The offices were ready to open for business. All I needed were clients' papers to put in the shiny, new filing cabinets. I had been dreading the expense and time that it would take to set myself up and I was overjoyed that it had been all done for me. Two journeys by taxi were sufficient to move my meagre belongings from the Knightsbridge flat. I was happy to leave my keys with the porter and depart the place. The only thing missing in my new premises was a shrine to my great benefactor, Sir Arthur Anson. Although religion had played little part in my life, I felt like falling down on my knees and loudly giving thanks.

I spent most of the week thinking how to market my new practice, bearing in mind the Law Society's continuing ban on advertising. A number of my journalist friends rallied round and promised articles and mentions about me and my new speciality. The best was likely to be a spread in a coming edition of a glossy magazine for women. The legal grapevine worked efficiently. I received a phone call from a contemporary at Cambridge who wanted to close his practice and emigrate to Canada. I went round and extracted those files relating to divorce matters. They were all large and extremely untidy bundles of papers. That evening, I sat down and started to read the files and thus make the acquaintance of my first new clients. They were all on legal aid and the narrative seemed to meander on inconclusively for ever. Frankly, I had no desire to be a legal aid practitioner as the economics of legal aid would ensure my permanent poverty. However, they would do to start me off and I resolved to bring these cases to a conclusion as quickly as possible.

Normally, I hate the divided English legal profession of solicitors and barristers with its separation of power and responsibility. So much seems to slip between the cracks to the detriment of the client who pays two lawyers to do the work of one inefficiently. The English system is not one followed in most parts of the world and the clients there do not seem to suffer as a result. In fact, as soon as most countries in the British Empire received their independence, one of the first things they did was to abolish the distinction between barristers and solicitors and fuse their legal professions into one. However, for my purpose in learning quickly about a new branch of law it was ideal. I would bundle up the papers, send them to counsel, sit at his feet and learn how it was done. I resolved that as soon as possible, when I knew the ropes, I would cut out the middleman, the barrister, and take all the fees for myself. I was convinced that the clients would not be the losers from this change.

I also saw my first fresh clients. I found that my attitude towards the men was entirely different from my attitude to the women. It was hard for me not to despise the weak, mummy's boys who so often typified the male clients. Unable to make decisions of their own, having their manhood serially eroded by the women in their lives from mothers to girlfriends to wives, they had rightly in my opinion been discarded by their spouses. I was reluctant to help them get out of the mess that they had created for themselves. It was only the thought of the fees that I needed to earn that roused me from my antipathy but I felt deep down that I was not serving them well. Now was not the time for self-analysis but I wondered whether I was in a way celebrating my own lucky escape. If I had let her and not fought back fiercely on every occasion, I too could have been the victim of a dominant and pushy mother settling into a pattern of behaviour to be repeated in all my subsequent dealings with women. Perhaps I should have been thanking my lucky stars rather than castigating those of my fellow men who did not make it.

By contrast, almost every female client was a damsel in distress and I was Saint George slaying the dragon on her behalf. Sympathy flowed between us from start to finish. By instructing me to act for them, they were doing the best possible thing to ensure a satisfactory outcome to their cases. I loved the sense of control that the lawyer/client relationship gave me. It was just the same as the ideal sexual relationship which I was always seeking, based on my being totally in charge as some kind of involved observer.

I was waiting for the enquiry agent's report on Heather's activities. I had time to think and contrast my behaviour with that of Heather. I was not blameless. I had had my affairs but I had conducted them discreetly. I had done nothing to jeopardise our marriage and had always been ready enthusiastically to satisfy her sexual needs. In addition, I had been a good and loving father. I had behaved like many men I know and that behaviour mirrors that of countless men throughout the generations. I was prejudging it before seeing the detective's report but I felt that Heather's conduct was disloyal in the extreme. She was a fair-weather wife only. While my professional life was going well she was fully prepared to enjoy the financial fruits of it. As soon as things took a turn for the worse, she was no longer interested in the marriage or me, did nothing to give me comfort and seemingly sought her sexual satisfaction elsewhere. I had married the wrong woman for the wrong reasons. She was not a suitable consort for me.

I was not sleeping very well. The day before, I had had a visit from my mother. I tried putting a brave face on the recent series of catastrophic events but she wasn't stupid, and eventually it all came tumbling out. The biggest shock to her, I could tell, was not Heather's seeming behaviour but the perfidy as she saw it of the upper classes. Heather and her mother had used me to make an honest woman of her and give her two lovely children. As soon as the going got a little tough, instead of supporting me, they abandoned me. I had been dreading my mother's visit but I found it strangely comforting.

That night I had another visitor. I woke to the sounds of *When the Saints Go Marching In*. There was Sidney flanked by Tommy Ladnier on trumpet and J.C. Higginbottom on trombone, all in shining white.

'Didn't I tell you? No good could come of that law business. If you had done as I said, you would be up here playing with us and not have all that woman trouble. A jazz man loves his woman when he's with her until he leaves her. Then he forgets her and goes on to the next. That's the life for a cat who moves from city to city. No ties, no commitments.'

He handed me a clarinet.

'Now play,' he commanded me.

I obeyed.

***

BELINDA. My heart went out to Richard. I knew that he didn't want me to visit but I also knew from his tone of voice in our weekly phone conversation that all was not well and that he needed me. Why had a given up his big offices and large staff in the City to live and practise from an attic flat in the West End? Where were Heather and the children while all these changes were going on? He tried to make out that everything that had happened in his life was for the best but he could not fool his mother. Eventually, he told me the whole sad story. I wanted to hug him but I could see that he was not ready for that.

I confess I was happy when he first told me that he was marrying into such a good family. I thought that unlike in India, where you knew your place and stick to it, life in the home country must be different and there genuinely was social mobility so that my handsome and talented son, whatever his background, would be welcomed into county society as an equal. I did not expect the same treatment for myself although I would have liked a little more kindness and acceptance. But their treacherous dismissal of Richard as soon as all was not well when he needed their support justified the very worst warnings that my own family gave me when first I married Matthew and later when I sailed with him to England.

I said as much to Richard but he was full of praise for his father-in-law who he told me had been a true friend throughout his difficulties. I warned Richard not to be too trusting as I felt they were all alike.

***

RICHARD. The report when it arrived confirmed all my suspicions. Heather was indiscreetly conducting a raging affair with Joseph Reynolds, a car salesman in Bath, a man in the motor trade. Reynolds' background was unsavoury. He had deserted his own wife and three children. She had divorced him and he was substantially in arrears with his maintenance payments. He also had a considerable criminal record which particularly concerned me, bearing in mind the fact that if their relationship continued he would undoubtedly be close to my children and have influence over their lives. The list included two years in prison for grievous bodily harm, disqualification for drunk driving and driving uninsured as well as several minor convictions as a juvenile. Heather had clearly not distinguished herself in her choice of a mate to replace me. He was accustomed to pick her up in his car in the lunch hour and take her for a quick bout of lovemaking down the same lovers' lane where Esther and I had so much enjoyed ourselves. I was almost too upset to appreciate the irony of the coincidence. There were some accompanying photographs shot with a telephoto lens through the car window, which although rather grainy were clearly of a half-naked Heather in an embrace with a man who was not me. He also met her almost every evening and took her back to his lodgings in one of the poorer suburbs of Bath. If I had thought about it and not been so consumed with lust for Esther, I could probably have obtained most of this information from her, as she was Heather's regular stand-in with the children while she was off with Reynolds, thereby saving myself the detective's considerable fee.

I was sitting drafting my petition for divorce on the grounds of Heather's adultery with the aid of a precedent book, when the phone rang. It was Arthur, who asked me if he could come round and see me in my new habitat. In view of his extraordinary generosity I could hardly refuse. After a brief conducted tour, he sat down comfortably in front of my desk and I told him about the contents of the report and my intention to divorce Heather on the grounds of her adultery.

'No, that's not the way we are going to do it,' he announced with authority. 'You have to think first of the family. We must above all protect your children, my grandchildren. Look, I have no time at all here for Heather. She has behaved throughout like the slut she is, but she is the children's mother and nothing we can do will change that. You have to do the honourable thing. Give evidence of your own adultery so that she can divorce you. That way, the whole stinking mess can be buried and forgotten as quickly as possible.'

I sat there with my mouth opening and closing like a landed fish. I wanted to protest. None of this was right. Did I deserve this? Then I stopped and collected my thoughts. I could only admire Arthur's Machiavellian manipulation. He had planned it all down to the last detail from the very beginning. I knew I was beaten and would comply with his every wish. I could only learn at the feet of the master. We discussed details. The children would live with Reynolds and Heather. She would have custody but I would have generous access. I would of course pay for every penny of the children's upkeep.

The scene was set in a shabby room in one of the myriad of small private hotels that are to be found in the Victoria area near the station. I had picked her up in the bar below. She was a pale, emaciated, peroxided woman covered in a shabby, fake leopard-skin coat. I had no possible interest in her except for this particular purpose. There was a timid tap at the door and a little weasel of an enquiry agent entered, clad in the obligatory dirty raincoat. He recited his mantra in a monotone and I then admitted adultery with the creature sitting beside me, a woman whose name for the record I was not prepared to reveal. In truth, I did not even know it. He wrote all this down laboriously and I then signed it. I paid and over-tipped my companion in pseudo-adultery then left the place as quickly as possible. The divorce went through smoothly and speedily but my troubles were only beginning.

CHAPTER SIXTEEN

COME TO ME MY MELANCHOLY BABY

Reinventing himself as a successful divorce lawyer proved far easier than Richard had imagined. The quality of his competitors was not high. The best solicitors seem to be drawn to the commercial and corporate fields, while those of impeccable social credentials and few brains chose high-level divorce. Once again, the division of the legal profession into two creates weak solicitors. Even if you could think for yourself at the outset of your career, the safety first approach ensures that you go running to a barrister to do it for you, so the ability for independent thought soon atrophies. Richard, by contrast, coming from the intellectually superior school of corporate and commercial law, only ever went to see a barrister if he had been a naughty boy.

The judges, almost all former barristers, go out of their way to reinforce the Bar's supremacy. On one occasion, Richard felt that he knew his client's rather complicated financial case so well that it was pointless instructing a barrister who would find difficulty in grasping its ramifications. He therefore decided to take on the advocacy himself. He arrived early in court with his client to find the judge discussing last weekend's mutual golf round with his opponent, the standard member of the Bar.

'Ah well, I suppose we should get started,' he began. 'Appearing for the applicant is my learned friend, Mr Snodgrass.'

He then turned to Richard. 'What did you say your name was?'

Of course, he had a piece of paper with Richard's name prominently displayed before him. It was a classic put down designed to show not only Richard but also his client his lowly place in the natural scheme of things: thus embarrassing him in front of her and making sure that in future Richard did not deprive barristers of their livelihood.

His approach to his clients' difficulties was entirely different from that of the other divorce lawyers. Among the wealthy, where he wished to concentrate his practice, he realised that the real battle was about financial matters, the division of assets and income. As a former commercial lawyer, he was better qualified to deal with those issues and negotiate successful outcomes than those who were mainly concentrating on the grounds for divorce or problems relating to the children. He became a firm believer in the concept of competitive edge to achieve his professional success which is best illustrated by the story of the two Canadian hunters tracking a moose in the wilderness. A huge grizzly bear appears lumbering towards them. One of the hunters gets out his running shoes.

'Why?' asks the other hunter. 'You can't outrun a grizzly!'

'No, but I can outrun you.'

He perceived that his ideal catchment area for clients were the very social circles in London which he had frequented during his ill-fated marriage to Heather. Her current liaison rendered her persona non grata so that a confrontation with her was unlikely. Any possible stigma against him for being an adulterous respondent was overridden by the fact that he was the hostess's ideal guest, a presentable newly-single man with excellent social skills, ready and willing to make up the numbers even at short notice. He also gave off that slight frisson of danger with unanswered questions as to what really happened between him and a former prominent member of their social set. It was easy for him to get across that he was a sympathetic divorce lawyer. If those he met were not currently in need themselves, they had friends who were, whom they were happy to introduce to him. The prospect of divorce seemed to be on every mind. Couples had been together too long and boredom had set in. He also became a founder member of a new and smart nightclub for the very rich, Abigail's, off Bond Street, where he had a regular table every Friday night. This became an informal office where those in need came to consult him. After giving them initial advice, which was quite difficult considering the volume of noise from the over-loud music, apart from the obligatory time wasters he would tell them to come and see him in his proper office on the following Monday. Most of them did.

He had learned many lessons from building his last practice. If potential clients could not pay his ever increasing fees, he turned them away. This way he avoided indiscriminate expansion. Space constraints at Wimpole Street allowed him to take on only two lawyers to help with the flow of work that he was introducing. He chose carefully. They were both women to whom he could pass the male clients in the knowledge that they would be far more sympathetic to them than he would be himself. They were well trained in divorce law and one of them indeed was a former practising barrister. He could look to them for help in supplementing his lack of technical knowledge. The fees were coming in and he was beginning to make money. He entertained Arthur to lunch and they agreed a rent for the premises that Richard started to pay immediately. He had already eliminated the overdraft that Arthur had arranged.

'I greatly miss the Saturday night jazz sessions at the Coach and Horses and our record nights afterwards. I wish we could find a way of reviving them,' said Arthur.

Richard did ask him for news of current life at the Hall and the children but Arthur was evasive in his replies and did not seem eager to discuss them.

Richard's experiences with Heather had changed his attitude to the responsibilities of parenthood. Hitherto, like so many men, he had viewed sex as a recreational activity only. He was now compelled to recognise that creating children caused long-term consequences that could not be blithely ignored. Heather and he had irresponsibly brought two children into the world. Now that they were divorced, the children had to be with one or other of their parents. Richard was convinced that he was the more suitable but no court would grant him custody in view of his confessed adultery and the bachelor life that he was leading. In the brief time that he saw Heather when he went to collect and return the children for his access, he could see that she was neglecting herself and the children as well. Their hair was lank and unwashed and their clothes dirty and wrinkled. She always had a cigarette either in her mouth or dangling from her fingers. She had done nothing to bring Joe Reynolds up to her station in life but had all too readily descended to his. He could not care less what she made of her life but he was extremely concerned for the children. When he had seen Arthur he sensed that he had similar feelings about them and that he wanted Richard to maintain contact and have influence over their lives. At first, Heather made it easy for him to see them but problems soon arose.

He hated having to pick the children up and return them to the squalid little bungalow at the end of the barren cul-de-sac where Heather and Reynolds were living. In a moment of inspiration, he suggested that Heather leave the children with their grandparents at the Hall when he was coming down for access. This obviously gave Heather more freedom as to timing so she jumped at the idea. It did have one benefit when Heather changed the arrangements at the last moment without telling him. When this happened at her home he was faced with the frustration of an empty house with no communication and the prospect of a lonely drive back to London. On one occasion when he arrived at the Hall after a gruelling drive, he found Arthur on the front step, who greeted him with the words: 'Sorry, old boy, she's just buggered off with the kids without telling us. Better come in and have a beer and a sandwich. It's a long drive back.'

He sat there at the kitchen table with Arthur making small talk and Amelia, who had just appeared, making it apparent that she wished him off the premises as speedily as possible.

***

ARTHUR. Richard had no idea of the difficulties I was having with Heather over the children. Now that she was with Reynolds, she had gone completely native. She could not see any importance in the children having contact with their father and his having any influence in their lives. Amelia was no help. She took the view that if Heather was happy that was all that mattered. At the same time, she was careful to cut Heather and the children out of any social contact with our friends and neighbours. Once a snob, always a snob! I tried to point out to her the schizophrenic nature of her attitude but to no avail. I wondered if she was beginning to go bonkers. For some reason, she had taken against Richard and seemed to have little problem with the children running around with a gang of council estate kids. I wanted more in life for my grandchildren and for them to have the education and position to which they were entitled. I fought and argued with Heather to make sure that Richard had a place in the children's lives but she was besotted with Reynolds and had little thought for anyone or anything else.

***

AMELIA. What Arthur did not know was that I had had a series of hideous confrontations with Heather. As she stood there with her face contorted into a grimace of hatred and with her eyes blazing, I could not believe that she was the daughter whom I had reared. She presented me with an ultimatum: either I supported her in her continuing battles with Richard and Arthur or I would never see her and my grandchildren again. There was no doubt that she was serious and meant every word she said, so I had to come up with some way of persuading Arthur at least that I was happy with the new way of life that my daughter and her children had adopted even though every instinct shrieked to the contrary. I knew that Arthur would think that I had become senile and demented but the risk of failing to support Heather to my mind was too great. I exaggerated the fact that I despised Richard for his failure to keep his business together and for neglecting Heather so that she chose another man's arms.

Arthur was far from perfect but at least he was strong and looked after me financially. I had no time for weak men and I put Richard somewhat in that category. Whatever other people thought, and I know Richard's mother was of that opinion, I was not totally obsessed with class and privilege. Keeping the family together to me was more important. If Heather wanted to bring the children up at the standard of life that Joe Reynolds offered, we had to accept it. They could probably be just as happy rolling in the dirt as being brought up as privileged, upper-class little darlings. I had seen enough of life not necessarily to equate happiness with the trappings of the establishment. Arthur was fighting to preserve the status quo but it was not a battle that I dared join on his side.

***

Richard's new social life was designed solely for the purpose of bringing in new clients. He had no desire to bed any of the women whom he met, whether married or unmarried. It reached a point where one evening his hostess who had had far too much to drink accused him of lacking interest in women and in fact of being homosexual. He nearly responded to her goading but he let it go as it was more important for him to retain his reputation as the smoothest of guests in order to keep the dinner invitations flowing. He reserved the weekday evenings for his marketing activities and had regular gigs with different bands on Sunday nights. This was his great relaxation of the week when he could forget that he was a practising solicitor with the pomp and circumstance that the status brought with it and lose himself in playing and listening to the music that he loved. This made him feel at least for a short time like a free spirit. His sex life currently was non-existent but there were signs that spring might once again be approaching.

The clients for whom he acted personally as distinct from those assigned to the other lawyers in his office were exclusively women. He did not set out to ensnare them but mutual sexual attraction and sympathy seemed to be essential components of his lawyer/client relationships. He found the subject of this mutual attraction academically interesting and began to have lengthy discussions over a drink with a clinical psychiatrist who had consulting rooms below. The problem of transference was particularly well known to psychiatrists. It was a mixture of the dependency of the client/patient, the intimacy of the professional relationship and the perceived lack of love in their existing life coupled with the understanding flowing to them from their professional adviser. For the first time, as it was seen, their problems were being sympathetically understood and it was far too easy to view that understanding as love and respond to it with love of your own. There was extreme vulnerability on the part of the client/patient, of which the practitioner had to be well aware and take steps to keep at an appropriate professional distance without damaging the sympathetic link. Sometimes the skills of a circus tightrope performer were required.

After his previous professional problems Richard was determined not to transgress again and often found himself metaphorically pulling away vigorously to counteract what was a powerful magnetic force. He was not helped by the fact that an increasing number of his clients were in fact the sexual aggressors and, like the doctors below, he had to make sure that there were members of staff about him effectively acting as chaperones when they visited the office. He had become deeply suspicious of clients who wished to make appointments out of normal office hours. He learned his lesson early. An existing client who had already made her interest apparent claimed she needed to see him urgently. He could only see her at seven o'clock after work. All the staff had gone for the day and the front door below was locked. When the bell rang, he had to go down and let her in. In the lift she pressed herself against him and left him in little doubt of her intentions. When she told him why she needed to see him he realised that it was merely an excuse and that she had an enormous crush on him. The whole episode turned out to be very embarrassing for both of them as she expected him to be responsive and he was not. He was not surprised to receive a letter from another solicitor about a week later to say that the new solicitor was now acting for her. Richard wondered if she had had any better luck with his successor. There were in fact clients who told him that they had never paid cash to their previous solicitors. They had only ever made payment in kind. He assured them that by contrast he expected his bills to be paid in the conventional manner and promptly at that.

His downfall eventually came indirectly as the result of an article in one of the superior Sunday newspapers about divorce and the best lawyers to go to. The writer had been his client. The case had gone well, the bill had been reduced and the payoff was the very flattering words written about him. Several new clients had already come as a result of the article and the discount on the bill was covered several times over. Harriet was new client number five from the newspaper article. She was coming up from the West Country to see him. Her train was delayed by flooding and it was after six when she phoned him to say that she had arrived at Paddington. It was Friday and he could not meet her on Saturday as he was driving down to pick up the children. He decided he had to see her that evening which meant breaking his self-imposed new rule.

In terms of professional propriety the meeting was a disaster from first to last. He fancied her as soon as he opened the door to her. She was small, blonde, blue eyed and big breasted, a combination impossible for him to resist. Having had no interest in a woman for some months, he felt an enormous sexual urge consuming him. She, whether she liked it or not, and he was sure that she did like it, was caught up in the same fire. He pulled himself together and went properly through the professional motions of summarising and noting down her story. Her husband had left her for another woman. Richard privately thought that her husband must have been mad. He could hardly wait to finish their business. He ascertained that apart from checking in to her hotel she had no arrangements for the night but she had to be home on Saturday afternoon to look after her children.

It was all very easy. He invited her upstairs to his flat for a drink and opened a bottle of champagne which they both decided was more practical to finish. The first kiss was tentative and he liked the taste of the drink on her mouth. They progressed to a deeper exploration of each other's mouths as the wine took hold, and from there events followed naturally. When she was half unclothed he picked her up and carried her into the bedroom. She was surprisingly light although well built. Their lovemaking was a wonderful release for both of them. Neither of them had realised how frustrated they were by their previous deprivation, hers caused because her husband had abandoned her and his of a more voluntary nature as no woman had caught his fancy for a long time.

Suddenly he realised what he had done. He felt terrible. He had completely let himself down professionally. He had done what he swore he would never do. He had taken advantage of one of his clients and made love to her. However, she in no way seemed to share these feelings of guilt and he did not think it appropriate to communicate them to her. In fact, she was enjoying herself greatly. She was gently stroking him back to life with the intention of having more. Who was he to disappoint a lady? The second time was even more delicious than the first. As they lay on their backs afterwards smoking the cigarette of contentment, she brought the conversation round to her forthcoming divorce. He found himself giving post-coital legal advice and he realised that he could not possibly charge for his time. This was another and previously unpublicised reason for not sleeping with one's client, perhaps an even more persuasive one

They both felt ravenously hungry so wrapped themselves in bath towels and made for the kitchen. There was no great supply of food in the place but they managed to put together an improvised meal from various cans and packets. At least the wine was excellent. They retired to bed for some more lovemaking and carried on happily throughout the night, alternately dozing and rousing each other. At one stage she was so demanding that he felt like serving his own petition citing cruelty to solicitors. In the morning, they cooked breakfast, went back to bed for a quick one and then he drove her to Bath, where she could pick up a local train. He was glad of her company as her sharp elbow regularly applied to his ribs ensured that he did not drop off to sleep as was his inclination after their busy night. They resolved to meet again as soon as possible and he drove away to collect his children.

***

HARRIET. I must say that Richard's profile in the newspaper that I picked up in the hairdressers intrigued me. He sounded so dashing and glamorous and also of course extremely clever and competent. I was half in love with him before I even met him. The local solicitor I had consulted had been no match for Henry's expensive Lincoln's Inn lawyer. I needed to fight fire with fire. 'The Six Top Lawyers to Go to for Divorce' was just what I needed to read and Richard's name was the first of the six.

It had been a terrible shock when Henry announced that he was leaving me to go and live with his secretary. I may have been a blind fool but I sensed nothing wrong with our marriage. Henry was just as attentive or inattentive to me at the end as he had been for many years. I was accustomed to his long absences. As export sales director of a big steel company, they were part of the job. We always had a rapturous reunion when he returned from a trip and this continued to the last. I must say that I was missing the sex as well as the presence of a man beside me in bed.

Richard was everything that I expected and more. He was so understanding and quick to assess the situation, unlike Mr Stokes who seemed far more at home with his musty piles of documents. I told Richard my story and he swiftly analysed the strengths and weaknesses of Henry's position. Here was a lawyer who would fight for me and not give up until he had got everything he could. He was so handsome and well-dressed that I was sure he would want to get rid of me as soon as our business was finished and go off with some perfumed society woman. I was very pleasantly surprised when he asked me up to his flat for a drink. I had no sense of danger. I was actually hoping that he would make a pass at me. When your husband leaves you and you are stuck in a tiny village with two small kids, your social life goes out the window as well as your sense of self-esteem. To have a good-looking man be attentive to me and perhaps fancy me made me go weak at the knees and gave me flutters in my stomach.

After the first glass of champagne, when he offered a refill I knew he was going to make a serious pass at me and I welcomed it. It had been so long. His first kiss was a bit schoolboyish but I led him on. By now, the drink was talking and I wanted more. No false modesty for me. As a grown woman I knew what I needed. Richard was as sympathetic and knowing as a lover as he had been before as a lawyer. He satisfied me totally. In fact, he seemed almost as needy as me. Afterwards we went to the kitchen to get some food. It was a typical bachelor's lair. There was very little in the fridge but I put something together. After the food and some good wine I wanted more of him. I felt a bit bad about asking him for more advice on my divorce while we lay in bed. Poor man, he had had a tiring week. Still, I couldn't help myself. My divorce was preying on my mind.

By sheer luck, he was going to my part of the country the next day to see his kids and offered me a lift. This meant that we could really make a night of it and it was lovely to get rid of all my pent-up frustration, a lot of which I didn't even know I had. Not only had I found a lawyer to fight for me but a lover to satisfy me. I couldn't wait for the next visit to town. I was sure I could manufacture an excuse for a trip and find somebody to look after my children.

CHAPTER SEVENTEEN

*JUDGE, YOUR HONOUR, GOOD KIND JUDGE,
SEND ME TO THE 'LECTRIC CHAIR*

RICHARD. Put it down to my restless nature but I was not enjoying the professional part of my life. When it went well, my time spent with Isabelle and William was the high point of the week. I was increasingly looking forward to being with them which was somehow becoming more rewarding with each successful visit. Early on, a pattern developed. Heaven knows what propaganda they were subjected to in the week from Heather and to a lesser extent Joe Reynolds but there was always the initial ice-breaking period where I had to overcome their strangeness and, yes, shyness with me. My sheer delight at seeing them soon did the trick and they would be gabbling away and telling me in minute detail all that they had done in the week. I was careful not to be seen to 'buy' them with expensive gifts, although my financial circumstances were slowly once again becoming so much better than those of the household where they spent the majority of their time that it was quite difficult to restrain myself.

Strangely enough, Reynolds was little problem and he seemed to welcome the fact that I was taking the burden of the children off them and giving them free time. Initially, he did strut around a bit as the cockerel in possession but, when he saw that I was not in any way trying to pull rank, he visibly relaxed. No, the problems were all with Heather. Perhaps my visits unsettled the children but she was sour in every respect towards me. This sourness extended to the odour of her body and her clothes. If she was in the vicinity and the children were aware of it as the time for my visit was coming to an end, they would begin to be nervous and the conversation between us would become stilted and awkward. On each occasion, I had to make a new beginning.

All too often however, things went wrong. Sometimes, Heather would phone me late on Friday evening to tell me casually that one or other of the children or perhaps both were unavailable as they had a more pressing engagement. Life in Somerset seemed to consist of a constant stream of reciprocal children's parties. Then again, the children seemed to suffer more than their fair share of sickness. If I was prepared to risk contact with their juvenile germs, I did not see why Heather must deprive me of the pleasure of their company at the first sign of a runny nose. As it was, on several occasions I came back from Somerset having caught something quite nasty from them which lasted me the rest of the week but I was prepared to take the risk for the increasing pleasure of their company. They were developing as separate individuals. William was the less talkative of the two and keen on all sports. He was inclined to think long and hard before rushing into anything. Isabelle, by contrast, was madly enthusiastic and impulsive. She was a very loving child and I could see that the problem of having 'two daddies' worried her as she wanted to give them both all her love.

Heather took to changing the hours of collection and return and abbreviating my time with them. She now insisted that I collect and returned the children at her home. She had no concern for the length of my drive down to see them. It was even worse on a few occasions when I arrived to find her house empty and realised that I had made a completely wasted journey. She had either forgotten our arrangements or could not be bothered to contact me to tell me of the changes. I could not understand her bitterness and hostility towards me. After all, she had got the man she wanted in Joe Reynolds and she did not seem to miss the life that she had led with me and her parents.

The problem was exacerbated by the unequal nature of our bargaining power. Possession truly was nine tenths of the law. Theoretically, I could have gone to court to enforce my access rights but it was an expensive, cumbersome and lengthy process, beset with long delays, where the judge usually took the mother's side in any event and I risked alienating Heather still further. I could always cut off the children's maintenance but that would put me in the wrong and she would easily and quickly get a court order to enforce payment. Furthermore, the children were likely to be the main sufferers in that event. I could not win.

I went to see Arthur to discuss my problems. He offered sympathy but nothing more. Heather had always been difficult and wild and the one person whom he could not control or manipulate. Her mother was no help as her only interest was Heather's happiness and it seemed that Heather was happy in her life with Reynolds. A problem was looming over the children's schooling. Arthur and I wanted to have the best possible private education for them and fortunately I was in a position to pay for it. By contrast, Heather had no such ambitions and wanted to send them to the local state school. Whenever I saw her and our encounters were always brief I wondered what I had seen in her. Her face and body had coarsened and bloated. She obviously took no interest in her clothes and appearance. She looked as if she drank heavily and she certainly smoked too much. She now spoke with the local accent and all her refinement had gone out of the window. I was worried as to how I was to have any influence over the children's future.

***

ARTHUR. I would so much have liked to help Richard with the children as we were in complete agreement about what should be their upbringing but my hands were tied. I did not tell him about my conflict with Amelia over the matter and her newly discovered socialist principles, as I called them. So far as I was concerned, Heather was a lost cause. She might come to her senses at some unknown future date and kick Reynolds out but I told Richard not to count on it. Meanwhile, all he could do was to be patient and hope that there might be changes for the better in future. We both viewed it as important that he maintain as much contact with the children as possible. He had to resist the temptation to throttle my daughter, an impulse which I have to say I was feeling increasingly myself.

One chance encounter that I had with Heather typified how impossible I was finding it to get through to her. She had come over to see Amelia but she had chosen a day when Amelia was off doing good works in the local community.

'I am afraid you have had a wasted journey but sit down, have a drink and tell me about life on the wrong side of the tracks.'

My jocularity went down like a lead balloon. Heather had lost whatever sense of humour she had once possessed.

'Wouldn't you like William and Isabelle to have a similar education to yours?'

That approach was clearly getting me nowhere.

'A fat lot of good it did for me, except for screwing the head gardener. Let them take their chance in the world.'

'Doesn't their father have any say in this?'

'Don't talk to me about that pathetic loser. Joe Reynolds is twice the man he ever was. I don't know why I put up with Richard creeping round the place at all. He'd better watch out or I'll tell him once and for all to go to Hell.'

This discussion was getting us nowhere and I was in danger of making things worse by losing my temper so I abruptly left the room. I pitied Richard for having to deal with this unpleasant shrew. Where did we go wrong?

***

RICHARD. Whenever Harriet came to London to see me for a consultation, we ended up in bed. I cursed myself for my weakness. Paradoxically, I felt that she was taking more advantage of me than I was of her. She was getting plenty of gratuitous legal advice by way of pillow talk, a free place to stay in London and the sexual satisfaction that she needed. I often asked myself who was in control of the situation. What would happen if I told Harriet that we were finished? Through my weakness and stupidity I had given her the perfect tools to blackmail me.

I would often combine my visits taking the children out with spending Saturday nights at Harriet's place. That was a good arrangement but subject to the demands of Harriet's ailing and despotic mother who lived far too near her daughter for my comfort. We unexpectedly came face to face on one occasion when I was dropping off Harriet after a steamy night in London. The mother gave me a look which I am sure she reserved for errant under-gardeners. She clearly had no illusions about my double role. I pitied her late husband who had had the good sense to die prematurely.

Unusually for me, I was in a monogamous relationship. I suspected that it was unlikely to last.

My work was not giving me the same satisfaction as before. I suppose that anybody who had school reports which repeatedly stated 'easily bored' or 'the leopard has not changed its spots' is heading for problems of this nature throughout his life. The flow of new clients was now well established. Most of them came from the recommendations of past and current satisfied clients, the best form of marketing. Strangely enough, hairdressers were also an extremely profitable source of new introductions and always received a reduction on their own bills. Perhaps their power was created by the decline of organised religion. The priest had been replaced by the hairdresser as the true confessor. I was therefore able to cut down my attendance at those very boring dinner parties which allowed me more evenings to play jazz. There were always bands that were happy to have me as a member. I had given up the Saturday night gigs in view of the demands of the children and Harriet but I reckoned at least the musical part of my life was in balance.

It was the work itself which was becoming boring. There were a maximum of six possible scenarios leading my clients to consult me. As soon as I had identified which one it was, I could let my mind drift, paying only sufficient attention to make the client think that I was fully on her case and taking the appropriate notes. Very occasionally, as I let her drone on I would leap to full attention as she said something which did not fit that particular scenario. What accounted for the anomaly? Suddenly, I was very interested, if only for the moment. Often the answer was that the client was lying and I probed to get the true picture. I could not imagine spending the rest of my professional life engaged in such limited activities, however lucrative they were for me personally.

I still had to have recourse to the wretched barristers whom I despised for their pomposity and pretensions. Even with a simple undefended divorce a bewigged and begowned barrister had to go in front of the judge to put the case before the decree was granted. It took all of ten minutes and the judge must have been as bored hearing the case as the advocate presenting it. On one particular morning I had seven similar cases with the same barrister before the same judge in the same court. At the end of the session, the barrister remarked to me that each petitioner had told the same story.

'I know,' I replied, 'I wrote the same script for all of them.'

The other problem was personally more worrying for me. The conquest of Harriet had been so delightfully easy that I fantasised about repeating it, not just with one client but with all those whom I found attractive and somehow, in the close surroundings of my office, taking into account the intimate nature of our discussions, I was finding myself drawn to more and more of them. I even considered putting myself in the hands of the friendly psychiatrist downstairs but I did not want to confess my weakness to him. I knew how destructive my impulses would be if I gave in to them, like an innkeeper drinking the contents of his own cellar but I was becoming increasingly obsessed. I tried taking out a few of the women whom I met at dinner parties and who were not clients but these attempts all ended in failure. The worst encounter was very embarrassing as having simulated great ardour and persuaded the lady in question into my bed, I was limply incapable of achieving the penetration that obviously was expected to follow.

***

MONICA. I had known Richard since he started going out with that tart, Heather Anson. Everyone knew that she was man-mad and it was a big surprise when she hooked someone much too good for her. It was no surprise when she went off with some garage mechanic. She was no longer welcome in our set but I saw Richard a lot at dinner parties and around the scene generally. He seemed more interested in working the room and selling his wares as a divorce lawyer than in shacking up with some new woman.

I was very surprised at one particular dinner party where he was suddenly all over me. We were both singles and I found his attention very flattering as I had always fancied him in a distant kind of way. He took me out to dinner the week after and I could not help feeling that his ardour was a bit forced. We ended back at his flat both a little tipsy. I have been around long enough not to show false modesty and I had no problem ending up in bed with him on the first date. After all his enthusiasm I expected lead piping but all I got was limp spaghetti. It is not the first time that this has happened to me and will probably not be the last. At least he did not break down and cry on my shoulder. He was very apologetic and took me down to the street afterwards and paid for my taxi home. He had something on his mind, but whatever it was he was not telling me.

***

RICHARD. I had to do something to relieve the pressure on me. I saw an advertisement in the legal press inviting applicants for the post of part-time junior judges or deputy registrars in the Divorce Registry in London. I thought that such a change of status, even partial only, would necessarily distance me from the clients, making it much more difficult for me to convert my obsessive fantasies into reality. I applied and was accepted. I had to attend a training weekend at some country house. It was a mixed group and I was astonished at the nocturnal activities which took place. I could hear footsteps, beds creaking in rhythm and doors banging until daylight arrived. I suppose that illicit sex between the judges was some sort of antidote to the demanding nature of their work in solving bitter and destructive matrimonial disputes. None of the women judges or candidates took my fancy so I had an early and celibate, albeit sleepless, night.

I found that I was good at the work. Most lawyers talk too much and find the transition from active advocacy to passive judging difficult to achieve. I had always been a good listener and had been told that it was one of the qualities that attracted many of my clients to me. What was hard was to remember my need to be impartial when one party was so obviously more attractive and also more deserving, invariably the woman, than the other. I reduced my workload in the office and even hired another lawyer as my assistant to take on some of the women clients, particularly those who felt more comfortable talking to a woman lawyer, although frankly that had not been much of a problem for them or me so far.

Time passed quickly in my new role and I received a formal letter from the Lord Chancellor's Department asking me to attend my first yearly review as a judge. I felt as if I was taking part in an Ealing Studios comedy. The setting was the anticipated Whitehall office with a smouldering coal fire beneath an imposing marble mantelpiece, rows of chipped filing cabinets and a large but uncluttered Victorian desk. The middle-aged man sitting behind it in his black coat and striped trousers was a comic caricature of a civil servant with his gold framed pince- nez. He went through my appraisal in detail. I had done well. He then changed gear.

'Well, Mr Gregory, you must find it difficult to combine running a busy legal practice with the demands of judging in the Divorce Registry. Do you have any particular hobbies by way of relaxation?' '

'Yes,' I replied, 'I play music.'

'Classical, I assume,' he responded.

'No, I play jazz.'

'Do you perform in public?' was his next question.

'Yes, I do.'

'In concert halls, I presume.'

'No, in clubs and pubs.'

He paused to let my words sink in and then slowly replied: 'I do not think the Lord Chancellor would approve of that.'

He terminated the conversation and ushered me out. I slowly realised that our whole dialogue had been a charade, stage-managed by him from start to finish as a warning about my future conduct. He knew perfectly well before the conversation started that I played jazz in clubs and pubs which was considered disreputable behaviour. This was advice with the maximum dramatic impact to change my ways. It was done in a manner worthy of Arthur himself. Needless to say I resolved instantly to reject the advice.

The building was something of a Victorian labyrinth and I went down a staircase too many on the way out, finding myself in an ill-lit basement. There was a hunched figure at the end of the corridor with his back to me tending the boiler. He turned and I saw that it was Sidney Bechet dressed as a janitor.

Papa don't allow no clarinet playing in here.

I sang the second line: *Papa don't allow no clarinet playing in here.*

We were now joined by my original interlocutor who must have been attracted by the noise. The duet now became a trio:

> *We don't care what papa don't allow,*
> *We'll play that clarinet any old how.*
> *Papa don't allow no clarinet playing in here.*

In the depths of winter, the drive down to Somerset to see the children was no picnic. This particular weekend, Heather at the last moment had advanced the pick-up time to ten o'clock in the morning. This meant that I had to leave Wimpole Street at half past six. I listened to the weather forecast as I dressed. Conditions on the road would be foul and there was danger of patches of fog and black ice. I could not disappoint the children so I set out. I had played an excellent gig the night before in a smoky pub of which the Lord Chancellor would not have approved but I had slept well. I did not find the road difficult and the Rolls was the ideal car for this type of journey. Just before Bath, disaster struck. I must have dozed off. There was a tremendous bang and I regained consciousness to find myself in great pain, hanging upside down, held fast by my seatbelt in the overturned car in a ditch. I was trapped between the front seat and the steering wheel. The radio which I had previously turned off was loudly playing Humphrey Lyttleton's *Bad Penny Blues*. The counterpoint was provided by the ticking sound of overheated metal as it gradually cooled, together with the hiss of steam escaping from the fractured radiator.

CHAPTER EIGHTEEN

RUNNING WILD

RICHARD. When I next woke up, I found myself in intensive care in the Royal United Hospital in Bath with tubes connected to every conceivable orifice. I had been unconscious for quite a few hours. Apart from a mangled left leg, broken ribs, concussion, lacerations and bruising I was in pretty good shape except for waves of pain whenever I tried to move. Luckily, no other car had been involved. They thought that I had nodded off and skidded on an ice patch. All might have been well if I had not subsequently hit a mature oak tree with a certain amount of force. I wondered how the tree had fared.

I was worried about disappointing the children but was in no fit state to call Heather myself. I gave her number to one of the nurses who returned visibly shocked. It seemed that Heather had no concern about my condition but was badly upset about the disruption to her schedule. I drifted in and out of consciousness for several days. When I eventually was able to keep my eyes open for more than a few minutes, I was surprised and happy to see Arthur sitting at the end of my bed. In fact, he was my only visitor throughout my stay in hospital. I did not even tell my mother about the accident. I just could not tolerate her fussing around me in my weakened state and I was also concerned how she would take the news of my injuries as advancing age was clearly causing a deterioration in her faculties. Before the accident, each of our telephone conversations had become a more difficult medium of communication.

***

ARTHUR. Being well connected in local affairs has its advantages. I received a call from Bath police to tell me that my former son-in-law was in the Royal United Hospital badly smashed up after a nasty accident. At least nobody else was involved or hurt.

When I heard this, I decided to visit him at once. I was still reeling from the shock of a meeting called by Amelia in a private room in the Royal Crescent Hotel in Bath. I had received her summons a few days before. All that she would tell me was that it vitally concerned Heather and the children. I had little idea what to expect.

As well as Amelia and Heather, Reynolds also turned up. I had to be introduced to him formally as I had refused to meet him up to now. I had had first-hand experience of Heather's shocking deterioration generally. I did not know whether it was just for this meeting but she had pulled herself together and cleaned up her act. She almost looked and behaved like the Heather of old. I was pleasantly surprised by Reynolds. He was articulate, clean-cut and quite forceful. There were few prospects for him locally, if only because of his criminal record. However, an old friend of his had migrated to Australia and done very well as a sheep farmer. The friend was now offering Reynolds not only a good job as a manager on his estate but also a new home and life for his family. Reynolds needed my help to smooth his path with the Australian authorities and also my approval to take my grandchildren to start a new life so far away.

I took a great deal of persuading. I was thinking very much of Richard and what this news would do to him, particularly bearing in mind his devotion to his children and the recent setbacks in his life. They were all lined up against me and it was the fact that Amelia was prepared to sacrifice the opportunity to see her grandchildren grow up close at hand which finally swayed me. However, before I made my decision, I needed a few words alone with Amelia to make sure she fully appreciated how this move was going to break up our family.

'Do you realise what this decision means for our family? We are not likely to have any more grandchildren with whom we have any connection. Speaking selfishly, I find it very hard to let them go.'

'I know,' replied Amelia through her tears. Now that we were alone, she could show her true feelings. 'But what chance do they have here? I don't want to give up being close to our only grandchildren either.'

I felt that I should widen the discussion. 'But what about Richard?'

'From what you tell me, he almost died and he's nothing but a mangled wreck. I can only thank God the children weren't with him. We don't want to risk that again. What good is he as a part-time father anyway, especially if Heather makes it difficult for him to see them? For once I think Heather may be right. A fresh start may be what the children need.'

I have to say that I was impressed by Reynolds's demeanour and I felt that he had a good chance of making a go of it. What chance did they have to better themselves if they stayed in England? They had to be given the opportunity to move on. This was a decision that was incredibly painful to make but was there truly any alternative? Richard's consent would be needed but he, poor fellow, was hardly in a position to object. I knew that I would have to break the news to him and it was a task which I approached with a heavy heart. I would have to choose my moment with care.

***

RICHARD. Arthur enquired about my health insurance. I had none. I had always been meaning to put it in place but there were so many distractions and other priorities. He told me that he was a director of one of the top companies in that field and it would be organised retrospectively, something I am sure that only he could do. As soon as I could be moved, he would arrange for my transfer to a private room in the London Clinic where I could gradually resume my practice. At the present time I felt completely incapable of doing anything but I hoped that my faculties would gradually return. He asked if I would like him to bring the children to see me. At this suggestion I looked in the mirror and all I saw was a gargoyle. We agreed that my current appearance was far too frightening. He became a regular visitor, until we decided that the cuts and bruises to my face had healed sufficiently for the children to see me, though I still had my left leg in traction.

165

'Well, Richard, look who we have here. I had to smuggle them out of the Hall past the sentries and the guard dogs.'

The children were very sweet and concerned. They presented me with get-well cards that they had specially made at school. Eventually, their naturally active nature reasserted itself and they were running frenziedly around the ward. Arthur saw that this was too much for me and took them off. He asked if he could return that evening as there were important matters to discuss. I wondered what they could be until I fell into an exhausted sleep.

Arthur looked very grave. 'You are not going to like my news and what I am going to ask you to do.'

Reynolds had received the offer of a good job in Australia and wished to emigrate with Heather and the children. I asked how the Australian authorities were prepared to overlook his previous convictions but it seemed that they had been smoothed over. I suspected the helping hand of Arthur at work yet again. My consent was needed for Heather to take the children out of England and Arthur asked me to give it. The alternative was for me to go to court to seek custody. Not only was I in no fit physical condition but I had no suitable alternative lifestyle to offer. I cried for the first time since my prep school. I was surrendering the children's future to Heather and Reynolds. I would have little or no part to play in their lives from this time on except to pay for their upkeep if I was able. Then again, I was having increasing difficulty in playing any other part under the present arrangements. Arthur assured me that Heather was prepared to make them available to me if and when I visited Australia but he did not meet my eye as he said it. We both knew that I was effectively abandoning them to whatever life Heather and her new husband were prepared to give them. With the greatest reluctance, I agreed.

I was offered a final visit but I thought it better not to accept. I could not trust myself to keep my emotions in check. That would be bewildering and distressing for the children. It was agreed that they would write regularly to me, sending me photos, and I to them. Shortly after I was declared sufficiently improved to make the journey to London in a private ambulance. I said goodbye to my ward mates and the doctors and nurses who had looked after me. I found the journey painful and I realised that I still had a long recovery period ahead of me. It was strange to be looking out the back window on a journey which I had made so many times looking out of the front windscreen. I felt like Alice in *Through the Looking Glass*. My private room was a great improvement as was the quality of the food. I slept much better and I had not realised how disturbed my nights had been in a public ward.

As soon as I felt up to it, I phoned the lawyers in the office. They had assured me that everything was running smoothly so I was not prepared for the large suitcase full of papers that my secretary brought round for me to deal with. It was almost two months since the accident but I was in no condition to start on the mountain of correspondence before me. Over the next few weeks, I went through it more or less methodically. My secretary came in daily with her shorthand book and I felt that I was getting things under control. Predictably, a number of clients had drifted away and gone to other solicitors.

The list included Harriet, which disappointed me. I phoned my assistant and asked her to prepare bills for the work done for the defectors which I would approve and sign. The wording of this type of bill is fairly standardised and is a summary of what had been done for the client, normal boilerplate stuff. I glanced cursorily at the typed bills, signed them and told my secretary to post them. A few days later I received a blistering phone call in my hospital room from Harriet.

'How dare you. What do you mean by it?'

I was completely bewildered and asked her to explain. It transpired that the bill contained the words 'numerous personal attendances', standard wording in this type of invoice but Harriet, with some reason as I conceded, had interpreted it as meaning that I was charging her for our time spent in bed. She eventually accepted my assurances that this was the last thing that I intended and paid the bill by return. I never knew and could not ask whether my assistant slipped in the offending wording with intentional malice, perhaps being aware of my affair with Harriet, or whether she had just blindly followed the conventional precedent without further thought.

My accountant came to see me. The figures were not looking good. My lawyers capably handled the work that was given to them but in my continuing absence the flow of new clients had reduced to a trickle. I suspected the lawyers were sitting around with lots of spare time on their hands. While the cat's away, the mice will play. The bank overdraft was rising alarmingly. I needed to get back to work as quickly as possible. There was no question of my being ready yet to leave hospital as my left leg was still a terrible mess but the clients could come and see me there.

I did not realise what a pathetic figure I presented. Throughout my adult life, I had always given the appearance of strength and masterfulness where women were concerned. I was accustomed to taking the active role and sweeping them off their feet. I discovered for the first time that I was an object of pity and brought out the motherly instincts in my clients. There seemed to be a new breed of women, hitherto impervious to my charms, who now wanted to get into my bed. I mean that literally. The first was an existing client with whom I had had a jolly, rather than a flirtatious, relationship.

'You poor thing,' she said, sitting as close as possible to me on the bed, although there was an armchair conveniently placed nearby for her. She kissed me lovingly on the lips and her hand snaked purposefully down under the covers to grasp me and bring me to an erection. There was next to no possibility of movement on my part. Perhaps that was the attraction for her. She brought me swiftly to a climax. I had not realised how deprived and ready I was and she tenderly wiped me down with a wad of tissues. We then managed to discuss her case.

***

SARAH. Richard brought out all my motherly instincts. He looked so sad and diminished sitting in bed in his pyjamas while at the same time advising me and reassuring me as he had always done.

I had rather fancied him in an academic way but the professional barriers were too high an obstacle between us for me to make an approach. Now he looked so pathetic that I just wanted to cuddle and comfort him. I instinctively gave him a kiss and immediately sensed his need. Maybe it was just a twitch of his hips under the blankets that did it but I was happy to relieve him of his burden. As a former nurse, it was not the first time that I had made a male patient content in this way. I have to say that I increased the number of my professional visits. Suddenly I seemed to need so much more advice! Also, I felt that I was playing an active part in Richard's recovery. We progressed to his doing wonderful things to me as well. We were like a couple of naughty adolescents giving each other simultaneous hand jobs. The fact that a nurse might come in at any moment and catch us in the act added spice. When I could at last help Richard out of bed we were able to be much more relaxed behind the security of the locked bathroom door. It was good for me and it was good for Richard too.

***

RICHARD. This proved not to be an isolated occurrence. Other clients followed a similar path. We even managed with a few contortions to achieve mutual satisfaction. Day by day, I was becoming increasingly mobile. One more adventurous client suggested that she share my bed and we have full intercourse. The bed was far too narrow and there was a risk of falling out which could have done me a lot more damage. There was also no lock on the door of my room. I was concerned that we might be disturbed by one of the nurses on her rounds. However, there was a lock on the bathroom door. We collected together all the pillows and blankets. She helped me out of bed and across the floor. I had not realised how much I had missed the feel of a woman's body against mine. It was a great release and my ribs were not too sore afterwards. Other women followed and the visit to the bathroom became a well-trodden path. By now, I hardly needed the helping hand as I could get around with the assistance of a metal crutch, although I still suffered a lot of pain. I felt that my life had completely changed. I had narrowly escaped death, my children had gone for good and there was nothing to prevent me from selfishly enjoying what was left of it to the full.

My room was well soundproofed. We therefore did not need to worry about how much noise we made with our lovemaking. Arthur, who seemed to think of everything, on one of his visits brought me in my clarinet. It was a great pleasure to restart practising. Once again, I did not need to worry about the noise I made. I could thus play day and night. On the next occasion, he staggered in with a large gramophone closely followed by several nurses carrying piles of his jazz records. It was like being back at school again when I used to practise obsessively in one of the music rooms, playing along with the records of band after band. This is how I originally learned to improvise. I was now playing to a far higher standard and could not wait to get out of hospital to resume my career as a jazz musician. If Arthur intended his gifts as occupational therapy, I could have assured him that they worked.

CHAPTER NINETEEN

DON'T GET AROUND MUCH ANY MORE

Eventually, Richard's consultant said he could leave hospital. There was nothing more that medicine and physiotherapy could do for him. On the positive side, he was entitled to disability benefit and free parking. As it was his left leg that was smashed up, he could in due course drive a normal automatic car. They had tried a few operations to improve the leg but he knew that he would be on painkillers for the rest of his life. He left the womblike comfort of the hospital and came back into the world on a sunny Sunday in May. Everything around him looked big and uncontrollable. He resisted with difficulty the urge to panic and run back to the safety of his little hospital room. Although his flat was only down the road, he took a taxi. He rationalised it as being necessary because he had to transport a considerable amount of clutter which he had accumulated during so many months in hospital. The true reason was that he did not trust himself to make it on his own, despite the hours of physiotherapy and stomping endlessly with his crutch up and down the hospital's corridors to get used to walking again.

The place was spotlessly clean but empty. Richard felt very much alone. He found it difficult to climb the flight of stairs to the flat and resolved to improve with practice. After unpacking, he sat down at his desk to study the books and bank statements. Richard needed to know just how bad the position was and what he had to do to try to put things back on an even keel. It was much worse than he had thought and with each passing week he was getting nearer to bankruptcy. He needed to sack his three lawyers and their secretaries immediately. They were no longer productive and they certainly were not profitable. Keeping them on was not a realistic option. He no longer had the drive and energy to provide enough work for all of them. From now on, the firm would consist of himself, as the only lawyer, his secretary, Dorothy and Barbara, the receptionist, who could act as their general factotum. By drastically cutting the overhead bill, he would not need to produce nearly so much by way of fees to bring the firm back into equilibrium and keep it there.

Monday was not a cheerful day. There was no point in keeping those members of staff who were due to be fired in the office a moment longer so he paid them off immediately and asked them to leave the premises. Those remaining looked apprehensive. After all, they had just lost close friends and colleagues. The remedy was to keep them busy and he produced as much work as possible for them. He felt very tired and dispirited by the end of the day. His final act was to write a letter of resignation as a judge. It had always been a vanity project only and he could no longer afford the distraction and time spent out of the office for not much pay.

He saw his first client the next day. He had been wondering whether he could get back to his old ways of professional standards and detachment but she was far too attractive. Zoe came through the door in a fragrant cloud of musky scent and looked far more like a stripper on her day off than the respectable housewife who Richard knew her to be. She was one of those with whom he had had sex during his last weeks in hospital. She clearly intended the sexual relationship to continue and Richard lacked the strength of character to deny her in response to her blatant desire. They got through the business element of her visit in a perfunctory way as quickly as possible. Theirs was not an in-depth discussion on the merits of her case.

The staircase to the flat above was luckily in the corner of his office. They could therefore go up to it without the staff being aware. His bad leg made him very slow and awkward but she did her best to help him. In fact, he pretended to be more incapable than he was. He lay on the bed and allowed her to undress him. He did make her a cup of tea afterwards. It was all so easy and he had made her very happy.

***

ZOE. Now that Richard was out of hospital, I was looking forward to visiting him in his office. I was wondering whether he would be all distant and formal as in the old days or whether we would carry on like it had been in hospital. I know which I hoped it would be and decided to help things along a little. I dressed in a short slit black skirt, my sheerest silk stockings held up by fancy garters, impossibly high-heeled shoes and a low cut, tight, red silk blouse which revealed and emphasised as much as possible. I also doused myself in my sexiest perfume. I saw Richard's eyes pop out when he helped me off with my coat. Poor dear, he hadn't a chance. I was getting wetter and wetter as we went through my case. I kept crossing and re-crossing my legs to relieve my tension and making a swishing sound as my stockings rubbed together. Every time I did it, I saw Richard becoming more and more distracted. I was ready to lie down on the rug in front of his desk and let him do it to me there. We finished and he asked me upstairs to his flat for a drink. His leg was giving him a great deal of trouble and I had to help him.

It was a nice apartment and I enjoyed a drink or two before we helped each other over the threshold into the bedroom. He really was in a weak state and I had to undress him. He just lay there helplessly and let me ride him. It's not often that I get the chance to be so much in control and I took full advantage. Nearly all the men I have known like to be the boss. Afterwards, he very sweetly made me a cup of tea and we vowed to meet again very soon.

***

HE HAD started a pattern of events and in the next few months client after client followed the increasingly well-trodden path to his bedroom. He had the good sense to take 'no' for an answer if 'no' it was, but he seemed to be able to select those who would say 'yes' by some innate sixth sense. There were one or two who insisted they make love before discussing their cases but with most they dealt with the business first before retiring for pleasure. In his more contemplative moments, he mourned the loss of his professional detachment. He also felt that he was no longer the objective and detached lawyer that he once had been. He was now far too involved though, as a counterbalance, his additional closeness made him fight all the harder for his chosen clients. In an attempt to get some balance back into his professional life he took on a few male clients, but the chemistry was completely lacking and they soon drifted away.

Addiction he knew could take many forms and he was addicted to sex with his clients. He could have looked for medical help but he was enjoying himself far too much and he seemed to be providing so much satisfaction and pleasure. Could he live without this new drug? He answered this question in the negative just as he could not live without the codeine tablets which masked his pain. This was his new life.

Fortunately, the number of clients he was handling was now a trickle rather than the previous flood. It was just as well as his constitution would not have been able to bear satisfying still more clients. He fantasised about ever increasing numbers and the difficulties his office staff would have in keeping them apart. He would have to introduce a colour-coded system for his files so that he could recognise at a glance those with whom he was having sex, say purple, those who were future prospects, red, and those with whom there was no chance, yellow.

***

CAROLINE. I have to say that I was a bit disconcerted the first time it happened. I had seen several divorce lawyers since Charles and I split but I had clicked with none of them until I met Richard Gregory. All the others talked down to me. OK, I know I did not make a big thing about having been to university but I did not expect to be treated like a child. As a model and actress, I am used to all sorts of men making a pass at me and several of the divorce lawyers made clumsy and obvious attempts.

My self-esteem was very low after Charles walked out on me for his child bitch, as I called her, and there was no current man in my life. Richard was different. His concentration on the needs of my case was total. His dark eyes seemed to burn right through me. For the first time in ages, I felt completely taken care of by a man. All I lacked was that man's arms around me and it was almost no surprise at all when he suddenly embraced me. I found myself responding passionately. There is nothing more seductive for a woman than having an attractive man concentrating one hundred per cent on her. The transition from office to bedroom was smoothly accomplished in spite of his impediment. I could not help the thought coming into my mind that he had done this before but it was quickly forgotten in the passionate onslaught that followed. Richard seemed to have an innate instinct as to how I liked to be loved. I was overwhelmed in a sea of pleasure.

It was only afterwards when I had left him and stopped at the Langham for my usual black coffee that it hit me. Richard, the lawyer, had taken advantage of me, the client. Still I had to admit that the overall results were highly satisfactory. I had received great legal advice and I knew that Richard would fight my case to the death. In addition, I was all aglow in those parts of a girl where she likes to glow and I could see the silly smile on my face reflected in the mirror opposite. He might be way out of line but of course I was going back for more.

***

He had bought a Mini Cooper automatic to replace the Rolls which was a total write off, using some of the insurance proceeds for the purpose. The rest he put into the business to pay off some of the more pressing debts and get the bank off his back. He was now able to get around and he revived a couple of his weekly gigs. The other members of the bands were glad to have him back. They seemed to think it odd and amusing that he had this rather unusual and absorbing other career as a society divorce lawyer. They were always seeking free legal advice or asking him for his opinion about a particular aspect of the law which they had read about in the papers whereas he knew no more than the average man in the street. Jazz playing does attract some unusual characters. He knew of other professionals, particularly architects and schoolteachers, who also played regularly as well as a few lawyers and doctors. Paradoxically, when they retired from their main activity they had more time to practise and thus became better musicians.

Professionally, divorce lawyers are supposed where possible to encourage their clients to reconcile. Richard had helped it happen before with his clients. Sometimes it occurred naturally but nearly always to his personal detriment. He eventually worked out the reason. When husband and wife get back together again, somebody has to be blamed for their original parting. The lawyers who acted for them are the convenient scapegoats. They readily overlook the fact that they only went to lawyers in the first place because of their unhappiness with the marriage. He publicly rejoiced when his clients reconciled but privately cursed because he knew that he would now have an uphill struggle in collecting his fees.

'Why pay the lawyer, who was the cause of our parting and who created so much pain and trouble for us in the first place?'

Two of his clients were reconciled with their husbands in the same week which in itself was something of a record. They were both clients whom he had been taking to bed regularly and he felt uneasy, although he could not put a finger precisely on the reason why. Suddenly, he received a telephone call out of the blue from one of the great and good, a very prestigious and well-known lawyer in one of the top city firms, not the normal type of opponent with whom he was accustomed to do daily battle. He asked if he could come and see Richard urgently on a delicate matter. The fact that he did not summon Richard to his office was in itself surprising. They arranged for the lawyer to come round at six that evening after the staff had left. Richard wondered what he needed to discuss with him in such a hurry.

The lawyer did not bother with preliminaries but got straight down to business.

'I have been consulted by five of your female clients.' He then named them. 'They all are current clients of yours with whom you have been involved sexually.'

Naturally, Richard's approach to each was that she was the only object of his desire and affection. Any other approach would have been completely counterproductive. He wondered how they had all got wind of each other's existence and made contact with each other. He immediately suspected Barbara, the receptionist, who had lately been acting somewhat strangely. He assumed that she had been bribed by one of the clients who suspected that she was not alone in Richard's affections to give the names and telephone numbers of the others. Once they started comparing their experiences with him, and especially if the husbands of the reconciled wives were involved, he was done for completely.

***

BARBARA. When I first started working for Mr Gregory I liked him very much. He was a man who had no religion in his life and I dreamed of taking him along to my church and saving him. We would sit hand in hand in the front row and the priest would bless us. I started to dress especially for him and had my hair done in a new fashionable style. But he took no notice of me and preferred those miserable society bitches who were his clients. He could not see all that I could do for him when I was right under his nose so I soon got to hate him instead.

It was disgusting what was going on. Right behind where I sat in the office was a disused hot-water pipe which led directly to Mr Gregory's flat upstairs. I could hear every word and every sound and, believe me, an awful lot did go on. I talked to Dorothy about it but I think she fancied him herself. She told me to mind my own business but it was my business what went on in the office. I was very troubled and upset by it and was having terrible dreams at night, living on my own as I did. I went to see my priest to ask what I should do but he was no help. I was determined to put a stop to it so I came up with the idea of sending letters to all the women in question giving the names, addresses and telephone numbers of the others. Each of them will realise that she is not the only one. They will then get together and that would put a stop to it, I thought. Then would be my chance and he would realise how much he needed me.

***

CAROLINE. When I received that foul letter I was in a real spot. I was sitting at the breakfast table opposite Charles who had left the child bitch and we were trying a reconciliation. Frankly, I was not shocked or concerned that Richard was having sex with other women clients but I was bowled over that there were so many. The surprise obviously showed on my face and I just had to show Charles the letter when he asked me to. The rest is history. He was on the phone immediately and as luck would have it quickly found another husband who had just got back together with his wife. Hell hath no fury like a reconciled husband! They quickly hatched a plot to get even with Richard and destroy him. I felt desperately sorry for Richard, who had given me so much pleasure as well as good advice, but our reconciliation was still at a far too fragile state for me to try to intervene.

***

RICHARD pretended to show his surprise and allowed the other lawyer to continue.

'I have good reason to believe that you have been conducting a sexual relationship with each of the women in question. None of those relationships are consensual but have arisen from the undue influence which you have exerted in the role of their legal adviser in the intimate matter of their divorce. Worse still, there are allegations also of rape and violent conduct to coerce certain of your clients to have sexual relations with you.'

All of this of course Richard knew was completely untrue. They could not have been more willing and enthusiastic participants.

'Investigations are continuing and we think it likely that other women will soon be adding their names to the list of complainants. As a lawyer yourself, you are aware of the gravity of the charges and the likely sequence of events if these matters are referred to the police. Your clients as the victims will retain their anonymity, a privilege which will not be afforded to you. In the first instance, your reputation will be ruined and a lengthy custodial sentence is the likely outcome of the inevitable prosecution that will follow. You will of course be struck off the roll of solicitors and prevented from practising further.'

Richard swallowed hard.

'However, your former clients are reluctant to bring these matters into the public domain if a satisfactory solution can be reached without that necessity. They are determined that your corrupt and immoral activities must cease forthwith if only for fear that you will continue to prey on other members of their sex. You must immediately close down your practice, cease working as a solicitor and leave the country. If you ever return, they will wish to reopen these matters and ensure that you are properly punished.'

Anonymity was an illusion. The ladies in question were keen to keep their affairs out of the limelight. He could already see the banner headlines in the popular press. Richard would quite possibly go to prison for many years but they would suffer social embarrassment for eternity. He also appreciated the irony of a cripple being accused of rape.

Richard accepted the offer which he knew to be a good one. His visitor clearly was glad that matters were concluded satisfactorily and left abruptly. Richard immediately turned his thoughts to closing down the practice. He would have to write to his clients, fortunately not as many now as there once were, and tell them to find other solicitors. He had to collect what was owed to him and pay off the firm's debts. His accountant could deal with this part in his absence. He would sell the car back to the garage and give away to charity those few personal effects that he would not be taking with him. He had to terminate the lease and he decided that Arthur, if only for his many past kindnesses, was due an explanation in person. He made an appointment to see him and all that remained to do was buy his air ticket.

He had not intended to tell Arthur the whole story but somehow it all came out. He was grateful that Arthur was in no way judgemental. In fact, they arranged that Richard would join him for a final dinner at Arthur's club the evening before he flew off. Arthur had news of the children for him including photographs and drawings. They were growing up nicely. Richard was ashamed to admit that he had failed to write to them for some time, distracted as he was, and made no complaint when not surprisingly they did not write to him. Arthur asked him what his plans were and Richard told him that he was going to try to make a new career for himself abroad as a jazz musician.

'In that event, you will be needing this.'

Arthur reached down beside him and produced a long, black leather case which he handed to Richard who opened it to find a bright new brass soprano saxophone.

'You have always admired Sidney Bechet. Now go and play like him.'

Predictably, that night as he slept the dream returned. *I Want Some* was the background melody. Mezz Mezzrow wailed his solo while managing to wink at him at the same time as Bechet held out his arms to Richard.

'Welcome, son, it has been a long and painful road for you. Now at last you are going to be what the good Lord always meant you to be. You ain't no lawyer. You play jazz. Join the club!'

CHAPTER TWENTY

DEAR OLD SOUTHLAND

Preparing to leave England was far easier than he thought it would be. He was excited by the possibilities that his new career as a jazz musician might offer. After all, he recalled, he had always been drawn to the world of jazz and his career as a lawyer had been nothing better than a rather shabby compromise. The threat of what would happen to him if he stayed silenced any strong feelings of attachment but he knew that he would have to see his mother to give her some sort of explanation for his precipitate departure. Belinda's health was getting worse with her advancing years but Richard was not prepared for the physical changes in her. His hectic life had very much restricted him to London and Belinda had not had the energy to visit for some time. They talked regularly on the telephone but each was careful to put on the best possible front so as not to upset the other. Even so, communication between them had become increasingly difficult and Richard had been reluctant to burden her with his problems, including his accident and its aftermath.

Richard was scheduled to sell his Mini as soon as he came back from the trip but he was looking forward to the drive and the chance to be alone and think about his past and future life. It was a woman grown old and a little careless of her appearance who greeted him. He did his best to mask his shock. As for Belinda, she still saw in her mind the straight-backed athlete of earlier years. She had to get used to this middle-aged and limping wreck of a man who bore so many of the marks of his suffering on his face.

'I'm giving up being a lawyer. I'm off to the United States to start a new career as a jazz musician. I'm very excited at starting a new life.'

'Yes, dear. That sounds very nice. Where did you say you were going?'

Richard was expecting a lot of probing and hostile questions based on her disappointment but she had no more to say on the subject. If he had not been so distracted himself about the future, he would have realised that her lack of engagement was due to the deterioration in her faculties caused by the onset of dementia. As it was, he was able with no great difficulty to cut short his visit and drive back to London that evening. It was a tender parting but neither of them was able to grasp the true significance of it.

***

BELINDA. I could not understand why Richard had not brought the children to see me. At the back of my mind was something about his not getting on too well with his wife. Perhaps she had stopped him bringing them. I kept meaning to ask him but each time I was side-tracked. Richard did not look too well. He was putting on weight but I was pleased to see him. He said he was giving up being a lawyer. I could not think why. All those years of training wasted. I also could not understand why he was going abroad. He did tell me where he was going but it slipped my mind. I hope he comes back soon. He gave me a record of some jazz music that he had made but I didn't like it. It was all too noisy and nothing like the waltzes we used to dance to in the old days.

***

HE ALWAYS knew what his ultimate destination would be but he wanted to make a slow pilgrimage to get there. He landed in New York but found the lack of an American Musicians' Union card an absolute bar to getting legitimate work. He did manage a few gigs in obscure and out of the way bars but the pay was poor and he was conscious that he had a finite supply of funds that would soon run out if he was not careful. New York was far too expensive and its frenetic pace did not suit his mood, which in turn was governed by his decreased mobility.

He took the train south to Washington DC. In its more relaxed atmosphere, he was able to get quite a lot of work. Thanks to Arthur, he now had two strings to his bow. It had always been awkward displacing the current clarinet player in established bands and it often caused resentment, particularly when he was seen to pick and choose the gigs that he played, usually because of the exigencies of his previous professional life. Now, he often did not need to displace the incumbent clarinet player but could augment the band by mainly playing his soprano sax. He was a long way from emulating his god, Sidney Bechet, but he was improving rapidly with practice. After all, Sidney himself had started on clarinet and only later in his career made the soprano sax his main instrument. Jazz buffs are on the whole a conservative breed and Richard found he was becoming increasingly popular and in demand by largely replicating Bechet's well-known solos as best he could. At the same time, he was introducing some ideas and themes of his own which he played sparingly as he did not want to surprise the audiences too much.

He found a cheap room on the edge of an insalubrious neighbourhood. Away from the biting cold of New York his aching limbs responded well to the comparative warmth. His timetable changed completely. He tended to sleep all day and work most of the night.

At first, the traumatic events in London had undermined his sex drive. He put that down to severe shock. Eventually the old itch returned. When he felt the need, there were usually some single women listening to the band play. If he fancied one, he would make eye contact, approach them in the interval and offer to buy them a drink. If the conversation went well, they would arrange to meet for more drinks when the session ended and they would then go back to his room. With his disabilities, he found it uncomfortable to spend the night in the same bed with a woman and he usually phoned for a taxi to take them home after making love. He reckoned that he was now getting this aspect of his life back under control after the crazy and indiscriminate seductions of the existence that he had just left.

Despite his busy nocturnal life, he was aware that he was living in the seat of government. He had kept in touch with Desmond, a Cambridge friend and a career diplomat now based in Washington. Eventually, Richard got round to contacting him and they arranged to meet for lunch. It was a painful occasion for both of them. They no longer had anything in common.

The encounter served as a mirror. Richard had not realised until now just how much his experiences had changed him. If they had met a year earlier, when he was still a lawyer in London, they would readily have talked about old friends and old times. They would both have come away from the lunch happy and looking forward to the next. Richard now found that he no longer had any interest in those people and occasions. He had moved on and away too far. His friend had not changed but Richard was now a different person and he could see that the changes in him made him unacceptable as a companion. There would be no more such lunches.

***

DESMOND. What a difficult encounter! I was really looking forward to meeting up with Richard and talking about old times and old friends. DC may be the centre of the universe, but diplomatic life can be a bit of a straitjacket and you see the same people at the same parties all the time. At Cambridge, Richard had been a bit of an original. I well remember his Teddy boy phase, which raised a few eyebrows, particularly among the ex-public school set. I always enjoyed his company, his rebellious though relaxed attitude and his somewhat unorthodox take on everyday events.

I was in no way prepared for the badly dressed, shambling wreck of a man who limped painfully towards my table. His old school tie bore traces of many breakfasts and his suit badly needed a visit to the dry cleaners. All in all, he was like someone from a different planet. He now spoke with some kind of mid-Atlantic accent and used a jargon that I found difficult to follow. I gamely tried to steer the conversation round to people we had known and situations we had shared, but to no avail. He seemed lost in a world of his own. I asked him about his life after Cambridge and he seemed unwilling to reveal very much. He had had varying experiences as a practising lawyer but, reading between the lines, things had not turned out well. I had always assumed up to this point that being a lawyer was a passport to success and a licence to print money. I know I lived a relatively sheltered existence in the diplomatic service where keeping up appearances was all important but Richard had let himself go and I could only assume that his appearance reflected an unhappy and unsuccessful life.

'I heard a rumour that things got too hot for you in England and you had to leave.'

'No. That's not so. I left of my own accord.'

I didn't believe him. Bad news always travels fast and I had heard this from a mutual acquaintance. After this exchange, our time together really dragged. He made no effort to make further conversation and I was glad to bring the lunch to an early end by pleading that I had to do urgent work on an important paper for my ambassador. I doubt whether Richard and I will ever meet again.

***

HE HAD reduced his baggage to manageable proportions for the nomadic life that he was now living. Richard felt that he had had enough of Washington. There was no real excitement in the music that was being played around him. He felt that he was going through the motions only. As a city, he was beginning to find it claustrophobic and he disliked the pretensions of its people. Everyone and everything revolved around Government. There was no reality about the place.

He paid off his landlady and took the train to Charleston. He remembered seeing *Gone With The Wind* with his mother when he was a boy. The film was so long that they took sandwiches to eat in the interval. The portrayal of southern life had impressed him greatly and he had always wanted to visit the city where much of the film took place. It turned out to be a strange experience. At the end of the Civil War, the North had punished the South with severe economic sanctions and they had continued for very many years. As a result, Charleston had not developed but at best stood still and at worst merely decayed. In other American cities, the Georgian heart had been ripped out and replaced by the buildings of nineteenth-century American prosperity. Sadly, Charleston's beautiful architecture had been allowed to atrophy. He dreamed that some future saviour with much money would come along and restore it to its former glory.

The people were very relaxed and he found himself as a limping Englishman an object of some curiosity and quite warmly welcomed. There was plenty of work for him in the bars and clubs and it was far easier to stay than continue on his journey. He discovered a tumbledown Georgian wooden house in an area which had once been prosperous but which had fallen on hard times. Labour was cheap and plentiful as full employment had not yet arrived. He spent much time in libraries and museums looking at pictures of authentic fireplaces, lights, door furniture and other fittings of the period. He then combed the antique shops and junk markets to find suitable specimens for the house. He did the same with furniture and other items. Slowly, and at no great cost, he re-created and restored his house to its original condition. Although he had planned to live an itinerant life, he was following some primeval urge to put down roots.

With his nightly gigs combined with work on the house, he was not getting enough sleep. That winter, he went down with a heavy fever but was nursed back to health by the wife of one of the richer businessmen of the town. She also spent considerable time in his bed. They had to be very discreet however, as not only was her husband a man with a ferocious temper but he was known for eliminating his rivals in business without mercy and was likely to behave in a similar fashion to anyone who threatened his personal life.

Spring arrived and Richard made a good recovery. He had heard about the hurricanes and other storms which ravaged the South but was unprepared for the disaster which hit Charleston that year. He thought the locals were scaremongering when they talked about the destructive nature of the storms that attacked the city. He saw no evidence of them but merely the results of neglect and decay all around him. Accordingly, in order to economise, he did not rebuild his house with the storm shutters and other protective and strengthening features which were recommended to him.

He was playing one evening in a rather superior inn outside the city. In the interval, he was approached by a burly man unknown to him who took him on one side.

'You've been fooling around with my wife, dickhead. Get outta my life and outta my city. You've got twenty-four hours. Stick around and I'll smash your other leg, you pathetic cripple. Here's something to help you think it over.'

He kicked Richard viciously in the stomach and walked quickly away. Richard collapsed and momentarily blacked out. He woke to find himself slumped in a pool of his own vomit and surrounded by the rest of the band, all greatly concerned. He cleaned himself up as well as possible and shakily played the second set.

As if that wasn't enough, that night brought a huge storm. The wind howled and the rain lashed down, accompanied by the deafening din of thunder and both fork and sheet lightning intermittently lighting up the sky. Tiles flew off the roof and cascades of water entered his lovingly restored rooms as the windows blew in with terrifying force. He wrapped himself in all the blankets he could find, with a waterproof on top, and snatched a few hours of sleep. He dreamed that he awoke to the sounds of 'Sweet Lorraine' played by Sidney Bechet with Muggsy Spanier. Bechet came towards him.

'Will you never learn, Dick? Get outta this town. No houses, no ties, no roots. We're cats and we stay on the move. This man that kicked you, you going to shoot him first, maybe? If not, get out of here pretty damn quick. Move!'

At first light, he surveyed the damage. He would have to start all over again but the irate husband wasn't going to wait around. Charleston had lost its charm. Richard took Sidney's advice and caught the Greyhound bus for Miami.

It was a city which he knew from his visit many years before with Diana but it had changed drastically since then. He felt at a disadvantage not speaking Spanish as there seemed to be an ever-increasing influx of arrivals from Cuba and Central and South America. Latin American music was very much the rage and he incorporated it into his jazz playing. He got work as lead clarinet and soprano sax player with a large swing band. He even experimented on other players' alto and tenor saxes. He found that he could produce a passable version of Ben Webster's breathy tone. On one occasion, when the baritone sax player was too hung-over to perform, Richard took his chair but such an unwieldy instrument did not suit his itinerant lifestyle. While he was a good sight-reader, the Basie, Ellington and Miller charts were extremely complicated and he had to study them carefully. He also had to hire a tuxedo as they were playing in some very fancy venues. These included the extraordinary Villa Viscaya. It had been built in the nineteenth century by one of America's railway barons as a mini replica of Versailles with gardens to match, and he and his wife had scoured Europe to bring back antiques from all over. Strangely enough, it worked extremely well with its mixture of French, Spanish and Italian artefacts. On the one hand Richard felt very much at home in his white tuxedo playing smooth melodies for the high society of southern Florida but on the other he was beginning to become restless yet again. This was not the life of a jazz musician that he craved. He needed a greater challenge.

The Bechet dream returned: *Wild Man Blues* with Tommy Ladnier on trumpet and Sidney taking Richard aside while Tommy brayed his solo.

'We all spend time playing stuff we don't like that much. A cat's gotta eat. But don't let it take over your life. Time to move on.'

He resigned from the band the next day and set out by exceedingly slow boat for New Orleans.

CHAPTER TWENTY-ONE

DO YOU KNOW WHAT IT MEANS TO MISS NEW ORLEANS?

RICHARD. As our ship neared the quay, it was the smell rather than the sight of the place which overwhelmed me: a heady mixture of rotting vegetation, diesel oil, sewage and overall corruption. As I limped carefully down the slippery gangplank, I could have sworn I heard Sidney Bechet's voice: 'Welcome home, Dick. What took you so long?' Nobody else seemed to hear it but me. I made for the French Quarter. The boat had hardly been a luxury liner. I was one of very few passengers on board and we had stopped to unload and load cargo too many times on the journey. It was either a poor man's method of travel or suitable for one with a total lack of urgency in his life.

Although I had dawdled in the early stages of my pilgrimage to reach the Mecca of all true jazz musicians, I was now filled with excitement and eager to immerse myself in the life of New Orleans. I needed a little luxury after the voyage in my cramped and inadequate cabin. I checked into the Richlieu, formerly a grand house, but now a small private hotel at the high end of the market and a place of great elegance. The guests took breakfast in what had been the ballroom with its gilded panels and crystal chandeliers. I was served by a gnarled old Creole waiter who saw my soprano saxophone case and assured me that Sidney Bechet himself had played there in the old days many times at family dances. I never discovered if it was true or whether he was just hoping for a bigger tip. If the latter, I was sorry to have to disappoint him

I knew that my stay there would be short as I had to make sure that my funds did not run out before I found work. After a luxurious soaking in a deep bath using all the unguents and potions that this type of establishment always provides, I dressed lightly and casually. Even so, the sticky heat quickly got to me and the perspiration was making my shirt cling to my back. I set out to explore the Quarter. I took my clarinet and sax with me as I did not know what I might find.

I was drawn towards the riverfront. The traffic on the river was so busy and varied that I became completely absorbed. Not having remembered to bring a hat, I started to fry in the direct rays of the sun and sought the shelter of the nearby covered market called the Belvedere. Chairs were set out for a concert and a drum kit, microphones and amplifiers were already in place. I stood in the background and watched. At first, the audience arrived and then a sleepy looking group of musicians. They staggered up to the stage and took their places. They played my kind of music, starting with the old Louis Armstrong number 'Strutting With Some Barbecue'.

In the interval, I met them and was surprised that half of them were English. These were like-minded people drawn to the city like myself. New Orleans was the birthplace of jazz, even if better music was played later in Chicago and elsewhere. The clarinet player, Chris Burke from Nottingham, noticed what I was carrying and asked if I would like to sit in at the beginning of the second set. I was very nervous as I was so keen to do well. I played the first two tunes, 'Mahogany Hall Stomp' and 'Savoy Blues', including a rather intricate duet with Chris on the latter and then got up to leave as I did not want to outstay my welcome. However, Chris motioned for me to remain and I played with them to the end of the session. They asked me about my plans and I told them that I wanted to stay and work. They were happy for me to be a regular member of the band and so was I. The dream was beginning to come true.

***

CHARLIE GORDON. I was the cornet player in that band at the Belvedere when Dick Gregory first showed up. He was very modest and clearly a bit scared to begin with but we all realised as soon as he started to play just off the boat that he was already a better player than the rest of us. Being in New Orleans was some kind of touchstone for jazz musicians. If you listened and played, you could not fail to improve. If Dick was already as good as he was, there was no knowing how much of a star he could become. Listening to him on soprano sax, you could hear echoes of Sidney Bechet. Dick did not yet have Bechet's vibrato but there was already a quality about his playing all his own.

The local crowd was used to our band and many jazz buffs just strolled by, cocking half an ear as they passed. They reacted to the new sound of Dick's reeds and stopped listening closely. Suddenly, every seat was filled and there were crowds standing behind and on the fringes, at least twice as many as we normally attracted. The collection was almost double the amount of dollars that we usually took in. Is it any wonder that we were keen for Dick to become a full-time member of the band? The others asked me to find out what made him tick in order to persuade him to stay. Was it women, booze, gambling or drugs? Whichever it was, we were happy to provide it to keep him settled and playing with us. We knew a valuable asset when we heard one.

***

RICHARD. There was plenty of work for us. Apart from the daily lunchtime gig at the Belvedere, there were regular evening dates in certain clubs and pubs. New Orleans was alive with the sound of jazz. If we did not have an engagement that night, all of us or just a few of us would wander around listening to the other groups. Sometimes we would find a place where there was no live music that evening. There was always a piano and a drum kit in the corner. At a nod from the landlord, we would set up and start playing. The door was open and our music would attract thirsty customers so the landlord's welcome was not merely altruistic. If the others were not interested, I would explore on my own, instrument cases in hand. In the free and easy atmosphere that prevailed, I rarely failed to sit in for at least a couple of numbers. As I became known in that musical world, I was in demand for pick-up bands for various venues ranging from dances to concerts, picnics to riverboat shuffles, weddings to funerals. I even tried my hand at composing and found no difficulty in persuading the band to play the new tunes. There was talk of a recording contract but somehow it never materialised. I had entered my jazz heaven!

In the day, apart from catching up on sleep, I loved to explore the city. I soon learned about those parts that were off limits. I would pass from the shabby and dilapidated, which was fine, to the extremely shabby and dilapidated, when it was quickly time to turn back before trouble appeared round the corner. In spite of my education at an English, all-male public school where there was always an undercurrent of covert if not overt homosexuality, I found the gay quarter hard to handle. I think it was the sheer exhibitionism that I found too much. Coming from a country where homosexuality was at best tolerated providing that its practitioners kept a low profile, the peacock-strutting and open lovemaking were extremely foreign to me. Perhaps I was more petit bourgeois than I thought. I did contrast it all with the tragic end of poor Percy in London. Perhaps he should have emigrated to New Orleans!

I loved the architecture and especially the intricate iron balconies. Although it was called the French Quarter, the influences were far more Spanish. Bourbon Street, the centre of it all, was the synthesis, ranging from the smartest restaurants to the sleaziest strip clubs. When I was not playing, I liked to line up with the tourists for admission to Preservation Hall. You started at the back and as those seated in the front left, gradually moved forward until you were sitting so close to the stage that you could almost touch the musicians. They were all old and doddery, yet they played with such vigour and obvious enjoyment. It was a very basic and rudimentary style of jazz. They say that the best players went up the river to Chicago and only the dregs were left. I enjoyed the musical skills of the dregs, even if I sometimes felt that there should be a resuscitation unit on call as some of the players looked as if they were on their last legs and might speedily be in need of it. It was a sombre thought but I could imagine myself one distant day becoming like them.

I met Kitty at one lunchtime session at the Belvedere. She came up to me in the interval and asked me to play 'Indian Summer', a lesser known Bechet number. I was immediately taken by her auburn curls beneath her brown and shiny raffia hat. I was also glad that she waited until we finished the session. We went for a drink and she told me about herself. She was American, from a rich family in Montana. She had gone wild in college and married a heroin addict and dealer. She managed to kick the habit herself and her husband out at the same time, winning a place to study law at Michigan University. She had spent two years at King's College in London getting a masters degree in transport law and was now teaching law at Tulane University. The drink extended to more drinks and then to dinner. We went back to her apartment and I spent a happy night with her on her waterbed, an interesting new experience for me, making love and floating at the same time. I had moved into an unattractive and shabby room in a lodging house where a number of the band were living and I was more than happy a few days later to accept Kitty's invitation to move in with her.

***

KITTY. Richard was a wreck when I first met him. I heard this man playing his soprano sax like an angel as I was spending my lunchtime down by the Belvedere. Tulane was only a short streetcar ride away and I liked to come down between classes to hear what jazz was on offer. I knew the band well but Richard gave it a new dimension. 'Indian Summer' was not in their regular repertoire but when I asked Richard to play it he was completely assured and led the band through it with a beautiful solo directed very much at me. He was very pale and in poor physical condition. Not only was he obviously in pain from his crippled leg but he looked as if he had been starving himself. When we talked, we found that we had London in common. I very much enjoyed my two years there and it was a wrench to return to the United States.

I had no intention of going back to live in a small city like Billings, although there was a lot of pressure from the family to keep me there. I think they were scared that I was going to go off the rails again but, apart from drinking and smoking too much, there was no way I was going back to frying my brains with that terrible stuff, heroin. That was one habit that I was not returning to. Another habit which I far preferred was currently sadly neglected. I don't know what it was about New Orleans men but I seemed to frighten them off. Perhaps it was the enervating southern climate but none of them had the stamina to keep me satisfied.

Richard obviously fancied me as much as I fancied him and it was no surprise that we landed up on my waterbed. This was a new invention that my family's bank was financing. Mine was probably the only one in New Orleans. I had slept alone on it so far and it was a pleasure to 'christen' it with Richard, who was very inventive in the new environment. For the first time for a long time I was not left craving for more. I went to sleep totally satisfied. Next day he showed me his horrible tenement room and I did not have to wrestle with myself too much before inviting him to move in with me.

There was a deep sadness within Richard. One night, after some great lovemaking, it all came tumbling out. He missed his children so much. He produced dog-eared photos of Isabelle and William and I held him close to me as he sobbed quietly. He felt such a failure in relation to them but, as he told me the whole story, I comforted him that for the time being at least he could do no more. He also had had a tough time professionally in England which left him with a complete aversion to the law and lawyers. I nursed him back to health generally and I also reintroduced him to academic law. He had a fine brain and I hated seeing it going to waste. My students loved his British accent and his rather quirky exposition of comparative law. I also got him speaking to my MBA class where his experience of actually running a business gave a different dimension in contrast to all the academic stuff that came from the other lecturers, including me.

Where I changed Richard's life for the worse was in relation to drink. Until he met me, he was not a heavy drinker, but he suddenly found that it was more effective than the painkillers to mask the effects of his injuries. One problem was that when I drank too much, and I did far too often, my temper got out of control. This resulted in some very stormy scenes and I felt sorry for Richard who was by nature far more placid. Still, I did make it up to him and the sex following our reconciliations was super-satisfying for both of us.

***

RICHARD. Ours was a passionate but stormy relationship. She had a foul temper which was made worse by the amount she drank. I increased my own consumption to keep up with her and I have to say that it helped to reduce the increasing aches and pains of my injured body. We quarrelled violently and reconciled rapturously. She had a voracious appetite for sex which I found I was able to match. She used to say to me 'you're so easy!' when she found what little difficulty she had to get me to make love to her time after time.

I thought that I had finished with the law but Kitty persuaded me to give the occasional lecture on English law on a comparative basis to her students. I was very nervous on the first occasion but I soon got the hang of it. She also taught a weekly early evening class on business for an MBA programme to part-time students and she very quickly had me alternating the teaching with her. I found this a fascinating experience as the group was made up of all the races and nationalities under the sun. What they had in common was a passionate desire to integrate themselves as fully American and to improve themselves, being prepared to work all hours in the process. I found it very disconcerting the first time I stood before them that many were eating from brown paper bags as I lectured. Afterwards, I asked why this was and I was told that most of them came straight from their full-time jobs and had no other opportunity to eat. I compared myself to them in the opportunities I had had but so often wasted. It was a humbling comparison. Both Kitty and I had to stock a supply of extra strong mints to conceal the all too regular smell of alcohol on our breath.

I had another interesting brush with the law which showed the versatile and relaxed nature of New Orleans at its best. Kitty and I went to hear Harry Connick Senior sing at the Empress Club. Not only and unsurprisingly was he the father of the better known Harry Connick Junior, but his day job was district attorney for the city of New Orleans. He sang like a faded carbon copy of Frank Sinatra in front of a large orchestra, but that was not the point. Rather like Doctor Johnson's dog walking on its hind legs, it was not that he did it well but that he did it at all. I contrasted it with my own pathetic meeting with the civil servant in the Lord Chancellor's Department when my jazz playing was so roundly condemned. We British can appear as a pretty bloodless lot. My surprise was not complete as Harry was an old friend of Kitty and we went backstage after the show. Harry was extremely affable and relaxed. We ended up having a lot to drink, while we discussed the comparative merits of English and Louisiana criminal law.

Kitty was away visiting her parents in Montana. She had asked me to go and we had had a big row about it but I had an important series of gigs that week that I had no intention of missing. I also needed to stay and look after the cats. Kitty had had a hysterectomy some years before. The advantage was that we did not need to bother about birth control. The disadvantage was the proliferation of these child substitutes as she had never had any children herself. Under normal circumstances I have nothing against cats but she just had too many and they played much too important a part in our life. I was playing in an evening concert for charity at a huge open-air venue with some of the truly great jazz musicians. I was out of my league but they wanted to re-create the Bechet sound and it seemed that I was the best soprano sax player that they could hire. I viewed this as my big chance.

I always try to find one or two people in the audience on whom I can focus. It used to include a pretty girl but, since moving in with Kitty, I had become monogamous and had no need to look elsewhere. She was also extremely jealous and I feared her temper. I felt that she would skin me alive if she caught me gazing at another woman and I was still affected by these feelings, even though on this occasion she was many miles away.

My eyes settled on a very distinguished-looking gentleman, probably English, in the fifth row. He was dressed impeccably in an off-white suit topped with a panama hat. The lights were concentrated on the stage which had a dazzling effect so I could not see his features too well. When he removed his hat to mop his brow, I realised that it was Arthur. We met in the interval and I of course realised that his presence was no coincidence. The only person who knew that I was in New Orleans was my mother. However, I had enough experiences of his intelligence network not to be too surprised that he had tracked me down. He was on his way from London to Houston to chair a meeting of the board of a big oil company and had made a detour to New Orleans to see me. Over dinner at a corner table in Antoine's, where he seemed to be well known, he brought me up to date on family matters. He had no news of my mother who seemed to have become something of a recluse. He told me that he had tried to contact her before leaving on his trip as he guessed that I would want his take on her current state of health. Reynolds had done well in Australia. He was managing a large sheep farm in Queensland. Heather and he had two more children but there was no tension between his and mine. Isabelle and William were growing up nicely and doing well at school. He showed me photos to prove it. I was happy but at the same time sad that I was playing no part in their lives. That night when I arrived home to find the place empty, I needed much bourbon. The next morning, despite my hangover, Arthur and I had an enormous breakfast at Brennans including the best eggs Benedict that I have ever tasted before he flew off for his meeting.

***

ARTHUR. It was not difficult for me to keep track of Richard's progress in the United States and I was pleased with what I was hearing. He was making a very good name for himself in the best jazz circles in New Orleans and I resolved to meet him when my business travels allowed and my annual Houston trip was the ideal opportunity. I have to say that I was astonished at the improvement in his playing since I last heard him. I felt that he was now up there with the great players of jazz. To be part of a front line with Louis Armstrong, Jack Teagarden and Johnny Hodges from the Ellington Band, while in no way sounding inferior, was an absolute triumph. I could not help feeling proud at my own small part in setting him on the path to becoming a full-time jazz musician.

I could see that he was upset by my news about the family in Australia. Even though it was good news, Richard clearly felt that he was not playing the part in his children's lives that he would have liked. How could he when he was living the life of an itinerant jazz musician? I tried to console him but I do not think that I was very successful.

I would have liked to have met Kitty with whom he was living but she was off on some family visit and I could not change my itinerary to await her return. I wanted to talk to her about Richard's drinking. We had enjoyed a few too many brandies together in the old days but his drinking now was far more serious and compulsive. Frankly, I was worried.

**

RICHARD. Kitty returned in a foul mood. She had spent the whole week quarrelling with her mother. For some reason she seemed to blame me and took it out on me. I put that week as the start of the deterioration in our relationship. We were both hitting the bourbon to excess which only served to increase the violence of our rows. The previous passion of our reconciliations also seemed to be diminishing. We no longer found the same joy and release in each other's bodies. In fact, resentment was replacing love as the dominant force in our relationship. It was even beginning to affect my playing. I saw my colleagues exchanging exasperated glances as I fluffed my cues and hit wrong notes. I was no longer losing myself in the music but felt detached from it. It had become just another job which I had to do to earn my living. Kitty and I had started sleeping apart. I must stress that all this was a slow process over a number of months. I am not sure what finally triggered the eureka moment. Perhaps it was a particularly violent quarrel the night before coupled with a lethal mix of cheap brandy and even cheaper red wine. I realised that our time together was over. Kitty sadly but unsurprisingly agreed.

Ending our relationship was one thing but, put it down to my restless nature, I felt that my time in New Orleans was coming naturally to an end. I had arrived with such high hopes and now all I could see was a tawdry stage set overrun with an increasing horde of cheap tourists. But where was I to go? That night provided the answer. To the melody of *Blues in Thirds*, Sidney Bechet made his habitual and spectral appearance.

'Well, boy, don't you think it's time to move on? When things went bad for me in this town I hot footed it to France. Follow my example.'

The next day I booked an air ticket to Nice.

***

KITTY. I had always had this destructive element in me. I tried many times to overcome it but every time I seemed to ruin the good things in my life. Richard was definitely one of the good things but I had to watch like a helpless spectator as I inexorably drove him away from me. When he eventually announced that he could take no more, I could only agree that it was over. Would it have made any difference if he knew how long and deeply I wept after he had left? I do not think so.

CHAPTER TWENTY-TWO

DANS LES RUES D'ANTIBES

He deliberately avoided Paris. Its eternal damp and chill would not help his ever worsening aches and pains. He had been warned before he left hospital that this was likely to happen but ever the optimist he had hoped that the pain would diminish. The only ameliorating factors were a warm climate and alcohol. He could choose the former by settling in the South of France. He had no choice where the latter was concerned. The combined effects of Kitty's example and the increasing need to deaden the pain of his injuries added to his own addictive personality had turned him into an alcoholic. At least he recognised his addiction. He was determined to find out how to live with it. As the bus from the airport entered the outskirts of Nice, he noticed a tattered and faded poster on a wall advertising a Sidney Bechet concert. He now knew he was in the right place.

He found a cheap room near the station. Poor immigrants like himself were making this their *quartier*. He woke every morning to the pungent odours of Moroccan cooking. As ever, he needed to find work. Drink was gradually taking the edge off his playing. He was no longer as much in demand as he had been on arrival in New Orleans. Nice was full of clarinet players who were as good if not better than him. It was hard finding consistent work with it, so he sold it. This gave him a cushion towards paying the rent, as well as living and drinking expenses. He could take his time and spy out the land. He was lucky enough to find a small English automatic car with right-hand drive in a dilapidated condition, which he bought at a giveaway price from the garage where its previous owner had abandoned it. As part of the deal the garage carried out essential repairs including fitting a set of reconditioned tires which were less of an obvious danger on the road. He was now mobile and able to look for work along the coast.

It always surprised him how few musicians favoured the soprano saxophone. Emulating Sidney Bechet's vibrato was not for everyone. However, Bechet had left a great legacy of popular numbers so that anyone who could conjure them up was ensured regular work even if the standard of playing was not great. Richard located some like-minded musicians who played in a similar style. They called themselves 'Souvenirs De Bechet' and found themselves enough work between St Tropez and Menton to keep busy. The usual grouping consisted of Richard on soprano sax, a clarinet player who played in the style of Mezz Mezzrow and a rhythm section. They sometimes added trumpet and trombone if the gig was sufficiently prestigious and paid enough. Travelling together you get to know your fellow musicians. Was it a coincidence that they all had problems with either drink or drugs? He was not attracted to the latter. He had tried smoking marijuana on a few occasions but ended up feeling silly and talking pretentious rubbish. He was not stupid enough to try anything stronger. He felt safer with alcohol and especially wine, even if the resulting hangovers made the days after very difficult to manage. One necessity arising from their problems was a list of alternative musicians who could deputise at short notice for those too afflicted to turn up regularly.

Gradually, Richard was finding the atmosphere of Nice oppressive. The ever increasing number of pleasure-seeking tourists together with those whose job was to provide them with the services they needed at the maximum cost created a frenetic atmosphere. To escape whenever he could, he would drive his little car up into the hills or journey as far as Provence. He had taken up sketching. He did not think that he was particularly good but he was following in the footsteps of the masters before him. To test the market after one particularly well lubricated solo lunch in St Paul De Vence, he offered the proprietor of the small café one of his sketches in payment for the bill following the time-honoured method employed by impecunious artists the world over. The proprietor took a careful look at Richard's work, held it up to the light, turned it every way possible and then insisted peremptorily on payment in cash.

After Kitty, he wasn't keen to settle down with another woman. Several candidates presented themselves who wanted to save him from himself. He had no wish now for this kind of salvation. He had often read that alcohol blunts the sex drive but did not believe that it would ever apply to him. Eventually, he had to admit that it was true. If there was to be anything between them, the woman had to be as addicted to drink as he was. Although he was perfectly capable of drinking and getting drunk on his own, there was a certain pleasure in having a like-minded companion of the other sex. If sometimes their mutual endeavours resulted in drunken fumblings leading to sexual intercourse, so be it, but that was no longer the main object of the exercise. If all else failed and he did feel the need for sex, there were plenty of prostitutes available who demanded a cash rather than an emotional outlay, although he usually preferred to spend the money on drink. The only problem with the prostitutes was the risk of catching some nasty disease. A couple of visits to the doctor followed by weeks of unpleasant self-administered treatment made him less eager to follow that path in future.

His drinking was getting heavier and he was paying less attention to his appearance. To save the bother of shaving, he grew a beard and noticed in the mirror that there were many shades of grey in it. Until recently, it was other members of the band who called in sick. As the leader, he always made sure that he turned up. But now he was finding that on some days he was unable to drag himself out of bed. He found a good substitute, Hugo, a young man not long out of music school who revered Bechet and his work as well as showing great respect for Richard himself. When the axe eventually fell, Richard was taken by surprise. After what he thought was a particularly successful gig in Nice, he was drinking at the bar alone when the rest of the group gathered round him. Nobody could look him in the eye. Carl, the clarinet player, a much tattooed and burly ex US Marine bandsman, started the conversation.

'We have to make changes in the band.'

'You are right,' replied Richard. 'Didier is far too much a rock drummer and is giving us the wrong kind of backing and beat.'

'I'm not talking about Didier.' Carl paused and swallowed hard. 'I'm talking about you. You are sick and Hugo is now a much better player than you. We want him to replace you full time.'

All the other members of the band seemed to be looking at their feet but nodded in agreement with Carl.

'Of course, if we need a dep for Hugo,' continued Carl, himself a recovering alcoholic who was currently known for his huge consumption of orange juice, 'we will give you a call.'

Richard could only accept their verdict as they had long ago decided to proceed on a democratic basis, although he doubted whether there would ever be a call. Not surprisingly, they could not wait to get away but left him to finish his drink before limping back to his nearby room. He slept deeply that night. He awoke, as he thought, to the sounds of the New Orleans Feetwarmers playing *South*.

'Pull yourself together, man!' Sidney admonished him. 'A cat is judged by how he plays and you can do better than that.'

After that episode, work was becoming increasingly difficult to find. He was having to travel further for less pay and regular gigs seemed to be a thing of the past. Christmas was coming and he was not looking forward to it. He had not realised that winters in the South of France were nearly as cold and miserable as anywhere else. He was having to drink more to insulate himself against the chill and damp. Out of the blue, a huge hamper from Fortnum & Mason arrived. It contained Arthur's visiting card and plenty of exotic food and drink but no note. He exchanged most of the former for more of the latter but only rough local wine rather than the smooth offerings that Fortnums provided. He had not told Arthur where he was going after New Orleans but, once again, he was hardly surprised that Arthur had tracked him down. As Richard drank the fine cognac alone in his shabby room on Christmas day, he silently toasted Arthur, his guardian angel.

***

ARTHUR. I was worried about the news of Richard that trickled back to me. His drinking was clearly getting worse. There is only so much you can do to prevent a man destroying himself. I even thought of sending a squad to carry him off to some sanatorium to dry out but there was no guarantee that he would not smuggle in some hooch or otherwise relapse. I felt sadly that the cumulative reverses in Richard's life were on the way to breaking his spirit and destroying his will to live. I wished that I could find the antidote, as I felt it was such a waste of a talented life. I had been playing some of his tapes and realised just how good he was. The Fortnums hamper was the best or perhaps the least that I could do.

***

In his more introspective moments, Richard had guilty thoughts about his mother. He had not done nearly enough to keep in regular contact. True, their telephone conversations had become increasingly difficult and she was clearly becoming more confused but that was no excuse for the infrequency of his calls. He had tried calling her neighbours to get news of her but they objected to his reversing the charges. He was rarely sufficiently organised to supply himself with the correct change before making the call. Christmas Day was the obvious time to speak to her. Richard had no work that day and no excuse not to go downstairs to the insalubrious and draughty entrance hall and make a call on the communal pay telephone. He had some sort of premonition and he was dreading speaking to her. She sounded very far away and had a little difficulty at first in realising who he was. He was very worried and immediately called the neighbours. This time he had the correct coins ready. He was right. They too were concerned and urged him to come home as quickly as possible as they felt she was fading fast.

That night he slept badly. *Get Out of Here and Go On Home* was the prelude to Sidney Bechet's appearance.

'You don't look so good, man. Don't blame the booze. There's nothing wrong with drinking so long as you still play beautiful music on your horn. Get a grip. Go see your ma. She needs you.'

As soon as the shops opened the next morning, he went to the nearest pawnbrokers and handed over his soprano sax. This gave him enough for a bus to the airport, a one-way plane ticket, the train fare to Bridgnorth and a taxi to his mother's house. He doubted whether he would ever redeem his pledge although he retained the ticket just in case. His cherished saxophone was probably gone for good. Was this the end of his musical career? He left most of his paltry belongings so that his landlady would get some money for them to reduce his substantial rent arrears and set off on his long journey full of foreboding.

CHAPTER TWENTY-THREE

BUDDY, CAN YOU SPARE A DIME?

RICHARD. It was raining when I reached Heathrow, that typical, cold, fine rain which seems to permeate and penetrate everything. I had waited at Nice airport for a few hours for a London flight. This gave me far too much time to reflect on the progression of my life to this point. I had paid so much for my last-minute one-way economy class air ticket that I had to husband my remaining resources. This meant that I could not afford a drink which was not a bad thing in view of the likely ordeal to come, although it might have helped initially. I watched with envy the sleek, well groomed passengers taking their priority seats in business class and then slunk furtively to my own place at the back of the plane. I saw my immediate neighbour giving me the occasional alarmed glance. I had done my best to spruce myself up for the journey but I knew that my clothes were dirty and smelly. Furthermore, I had not been near a barber for several months. I heard my next door neighbour quietly asking the flight attendant if she could be relocated but she had to grin and bear it as the plane was full.

I took the underground to Paddington. I realised that I had been away far too long when I had to make a careful study of the tube map to ensure that I made the right connections. The journey by train to Bridgnorth seemed interminable. In addition to the scheduled changes, there were a couple of unexpected ones as well. I took a taxi from the station to my mother's house, using the last of my money in the process. It was still raining and I felt as cold, tired, hungry and depressed, as you would expect in the circumstances.

I had kept my front door key throughout my varied travels and experiences. I viewed it as a kind of talisman and potential means of escape. If all else in my life ended in failure, I could always go home to mother. At first, I thought the house was empty as there were no lights showing. I climbed the stairs to find her bedroom door open. There was a dim bedside lamp lit and a uniformed nurse sitting reading by its light. There was a strong smell of disinfectant in the air. My mother had oxygen tubes running across her face with a large cylinder behind the bed. She was having trouble breathing and seemed to be fitfully sleeping. The nurse almost jumped out of her skin when she saw me. I did not blame her as I had approached silently and I must have looked a fearsome sight with my bushy beard and shabby clothes.

'Oh my God, who the hell are you?' she shrieked.

I quickly introduced myself and set her mind at rest. She told me that my mother was moving towards her end. Her deterioration had been sudden and rapid. Her dementia was not the cause. She had been unable to fight an aggressive bowel cancer but there had been no time to transfer her to a hospice. She was therefore going to die at home. She was presently drifting in and out of consciousness but was unlikely to recognise me when she awoke. I told the nurse, who assured me that my mother felt little or no pain as she was now receiving strong doses of morphine, that I would relieve her for a while and sat by the bed holding my mother's hand. She did regain consciousness but, as the nurse predicted, looked at me with no recognition in her eyes. She died peacefully that night.

I had to deal with the formalities surrounding her death, including arranging the funeral service in the local church. It was almost like being a lawyer again. Fortunately, I found quite a lot of cash in her bedside drawer, so I had no immediate worries about payments or keeping myself fed. My mother had not been religious but I could think of no alternative to a church service followed by cremation. The funeral was a cold, sad affair. There was no point in lavish spending so I kept the costs to the minimum. Some of the neighbours and tradespeople turned up but I was the only relative. The vicar gave his obviously standard sermon for a dead person who was not known to him. I returned to a cold and empty house determined to sell it as soon as possible and try my luck again in London. Life in Bridgnorth was not for me.

The next day, I saw her bank manager and discovered that there was not much in the account. The house was still heavily mortgaged to the bank so I could not look forward to a life of luxury. I arranged an overdraft to cover any needed payments until the property was sold. I next visited her dreary local solicitor to find that I inherited everything under her will. I urged him to get probate as quickly as possible and offered extra fees if he could move fast. It worked and I was soon asking the local estate agents to sell the property. If I had been patient and waited for the spring, I would have got a better price, but I was keen to be out of there. The smell of death somehow pervaded the place and it felt damp and cold. It was impossible to heat the house adequately and I felt continually frozen. The contents were carted away by a local dealer. Those few items of value were counterbalanced by the majority which were worthless.

At last I could leave and was sitting on a train to London. I had money in my account which would last me a few months provided I could curb my drinking. I had avoided it in Bridgnorth. The place was too miserable for me to bother to drink. Then again, I felt my mother's disapproving presence hovering over me and abstained out of respect for her memory.

London was much changed after my years away, not necessarily for the better. I wanted to make a new start in life. Despite my many setbacks, I still felt that there were opportunities to employ my talents. I was open to what life might offer me. I just needed time to make the right connections.

I rented a small flat in Covent Garden and tried to find my old friends. The only ones left were the Cassidys. They too had fallen on hard times. Michael had served three years in prison for mortgage fraud and was now making a living dealing in second-hand cars, an occupation which particularly suited his talents and gift of the blarney. He was very good to me and introduced me to his circle of friends and acquaintances. I was able to supplement my funds by acting as informal legal adviser to them. I felt I was back in business again, although I had no practising certificate and the Law Society would have been down on me like a ton of bricks – but what they did not know would not hurt them. I was also conscious that I needed to keep a low profile, in case the ladies, the 'furies' as I called them, who had previously run me out of town learned of my return and were still feeling vindictive towards me. I comforted myself by the fact that we were not likely to meet as we were moving in very different social circles.

Then I rediscovered drinking and the money was fast running out. I could no longer afford the Covent Garden flat and I moved into a shabby room off Holloway Road which Michael Cassidy found for me.

'I know it's not the Ritz like in the old days in Paris,' he commented as he threw open the door, 'but you can still drink a bottle of good champagne here.' He duly produced the bottle and two glasses from a cupboard in the corner.

It was not much of a life. Still it was far better than what followed. I was spending my evenings in an unpleasant pub off Camden High Street where Michael and his cronies gathered. I had got into the habit of dispensing legal advice in return for drinks. The saloon bar had become my informal office. I sensed at the time that I was making a bad mistake when I countersigned that American cowboy's passport application. He was introduced by one of Michael's group. The form required me to have known him for at least two years. I had known him for little more than two minutes! He paid for my services with the usual drink. If I had known of the catastrophic consequences to follow, I would have asked for a lot more.

Six months later I was woken from my usual drunken sleep by a thunderous knocking on the door of my room. It opened to reveal two large uniformed policemen standing there with my small Irish landlady fluttering around and between them trying to make out what was going on. I knew it must be early in the morning but I had no idea how early. One of the policemen produced a photocopied form which he handed to me. I blearily made out that it was an application for a new passport but it still meant nothing to me until I saw my signature at the bottom. I then had blinding and total recall. I could not deny that the writing, the address and the signature were all mine. I was in trouble but I had no idea how much.

My luck was really out. The American turned out to be a double-dyed villain who had used the false passport to prove his identity in carrying out a massive fraud on a branch of Barclays Bank in the Midlands. The money had never been recovered but he had eventually been caught and was currently in jail awaiting trial. I needed a good lawyer but had no money to pay for one. I did make a call to John, my former partner, who had done well in the law after the disasters that hit our firm. He was cold, unhelpful and unfriendly. He could not get me off the line quickly enough. After that unpleasant experience I could not or would not approach any other of my former professional colleagues for help. In any event, crime was not their scene. I was too embarrassed to contact Arthur but I hoped that his renowned intelligence network might give him news of my plight and he would ride yet again to my rescue. But the phone remained silent. Either he did not know of my predicament or he had at last decided that I was beyond help.

I could not afford bail so I was stuck on remand in jail. The jobbing solicitor assigned to me on legal aid was a crass incompetent as was the barrister who defended me at the Assizes. I stood shoulder to shoulder in the dock with the cowboy. Out of the side of his mouth he uttered the words: 'You sure are the unlucky one.'

It was not much consolation. I was charged not only with unlawfully countersigning his passport application but also with conspiracy to defraud. The hanging judge gave the cowboy six years in jail and me one year.

He took the view that the American robbed the bank but I drove the getaway car. After all the bad things that I had done in my life, I felt like Al Capone ultimately imprisoned for mere tax fraud after a life of serious and habitual crime. I spent an extremely uncomfortable three months in prison, taking into account the time spent on remand. They took my stick away which made it hell to move around. There was plenty of cheap alcohol available when I could pay for it so that was no great problem.

I was then let out blinking into the sunlight of normal life. At first I pretended otherwise but life after prison was very different and far more difficult. Even more doors were closed than before. I could no longer make a living as a shady legal adviser and had to earn some money quickly. I had found a cheap room in Camden Road but the rent needed to be paid. The window of a pawn shop in Kentish Town provided the answer. For a few pounds, I bought a dilapidated clarinet. I made it more or less playable with the loving addition of some sticky tape and elastic bands. I thought of getting a busker's licence but, when I read the required forms, I realised that my brain was too addled to complete them. I thought ironically of the infinitely more complex paperwork that I had easily handled at the height of my legal career. Now I was mystified by a few simple questions. I could no longer deny to myself that I was not the man I once was. I resolved to risk it and play without a licence. I reckoned that if the police caught me the worst that they would do was caution me and move me on.

I was reasonably successful in my new career. I learned the hot spots to cultivate and the places to avoid. I found the importance of timing. Always play to the crowds before they have spent their money. I discovered that there was a code of conduct observed by my fellow buskers. If challenged by a competitor, I gave way, especially if he was younger and stronger than me, as most now were. My craving for drink meant that I never had any money for anything else. At last, my landlady lost patience with me and her husband threw me out bodily onto the street with my few remaining possessions. Fortunately, the weather was good and it was not too great a hardship to sleep rough on the slopes of Parliament Hill. The problem was keeping myself and my clothes relatively clean. I dreaded looking in a mirror. Wrapped tightly in my raincoat, I slept uneasily. The slow, haunting melody of 'Oh Didn't He Ramble' brought into view a New Orleans marching band with Sidney Bechet playing his gleaming soprano at the front and the unmistakeable head of the sousaphone rearing up cobra-like at the back.

'Don't give up, Dick,' urged Sidney. 'Many guys who played

like you hit the bottle so hard that they had to sleep rough. Let jazz inspire you to get your life together. You can still do it.'

The music slowly faded away and I woke up to the dawn and the seemingly deafening sound of the birds with just a little new hope in my heart.

That night, I knew that there was a gala performance at the Royal Opera House in Covent Garden so I resolved to busk the crowd after the event. People who could afford the opera always had money in their pockets so my normal rule did not apply. I had found an abandoned peaked cap in a rubbish tip which half covered my face and I was almost unrecognisable with my heavy beard and grimy countenance. This was all to the good as I thought it quite likely that I would come face to face with a former client or a judge I used to know.

I found a good pitch opposite the glass doors with an excellent view of the people inside as they came down the red-carpeted stairs. Musically, I was on autopilot and I was well into my medley of Sidney Bechet's greatest hits. This allowed me to keep a keen eye on the audience as it started to disperse.

The first few customers put banknotes in my tray. I must have been playing the right tunes. I was not too surprised to see Arthur, resplendent in white tie and tails with his decorations glittering in the bright lights. He was accompanied by Amelia who had aged and thickened since I last saw her. They were followed closely by a young and handsome pair, a girl and a boy. I realised with an almost paralysing shock that I was looking at my own children, Isabelle and William. The family resemblance was far too strong for there to be any mistake. They were joined by a similarly distinguished group and I watched them all in animated conversation. What was particularly noticeable was the chemistry between Isabelle and the young man in the other group, as well as that between William and several charming young women in that second group. At that moment, they made their farewells and Arthur shepherded his family out through the doors into the street.

I had just embarked on my rendition of *Petit Fleur*. I had time to see that Isabelle was even more beautiful than I had